CONTENTS

NEFARIOUS INTENTIONS

Another Case of Detective Lyle Odell

Paul John Hausleben

Cover design and concept by Paul John Hausleben
Cover art by Alana White
Beta-reads by Jasmine Pfingsten and Ms. Cali Rose
Final edit by One-eyed Cyclops Editing Services
The Detective Lyle Odell Logo, GBTKP LLC's logos
and the designs are by Paul John Hausleben
Cover photo of the author by Ms. Cali Rose
All other photographs by Paul John Hausleben

Published by God Bless the Keg Publishing LLC
Henrico, Virginia, U.S.A.

ISBN: 979-8-9894490-0-2

◆ ◆ ◆

DEDICATION

To Mr. Edward W. Hausleben

"Paulie. I love Detective Odell. I hope you bring him back in another adventure. You have so many great characters, but I have to say that, Odell is the best. He is so grimy, but he is somehow very likeable, too. What a great character!"

Quote from: Mr. Edward Westley Hausleben. October 2022.

R.I.P. Uncle Ed.

February 10, 1936 - May 12, 2023

United States Marine Corps

Korean War Veteran

Sergeant E-5

Semper Fi.

NEFARIOUS INTENTIONS

Another Case of Detective Lyle Odell

Paul John Hausleben

ACKNOWLEDGEMENTS

Thank you to our Beta-Readers; Jasmine Pfingsten and Ms. Cali Rose. Your efforts and contributions are very much appreciated! Thank you to the very talented Alana White for the amazing cover art! Thank you to all the folks that I met along the way that harbored nefarious intentions. There were a helluva lot of youse guys and gals out there! Congratulations! You inspired this novel. Good luck in the future. Be better. Be kinder. Know God. We are all in this together. Mend your ways. Make this world a better place to be. I assure you that it will be worth it in the end.

"Always remember, no matter what the circumstances are and despite any bombs dropping all around you . . . that exact facts and details are very important in investigations. And in our lives, too."

HOMICIDE DETECTIVE LYLE ODELL

November 2023

Nefarious:

It is an adjective: Meaning; evil, extremely wicked, and corrupt.

"The criminal had a dark plan of nefarious schemes."

Intentions:

It is a noun. Mostly used as in plural form: Meaning; a planned action and outcome with results.

"The manager of the baseball team had all intentions of playing the superstar on the next home stand."

PROLOGUE

The voice was powerful and confident. The voice was evil. Very evil. It echoed throughout the office and bounced off the walls.

"Now if only he had listened to me. If only he could have controlled the great power that he held over women. Over my woman. He made a mistake to show me those photos and to then to brag about what he shared with all those other lovely women and what he planned to do to my woman and what she felt for him. If only he realized what a commanding presence he was in her life, and in so many other lives, too. Perhaps he would not be sitting here in this office, in this chair, dead, in a lake of blood, with a slashed throat and with a ten-inch military-issued combat knife stuck into the top of his head."

The voice lost confidence and grew weaker in volume and softer in delivery.

The voice now crackled with pain.

Or was it with passion before continuing?

"He had his chance. I did, too. It did not turn out so well. For many reasons. Most of all, because he would not listen."

The voice then eerily shifted to addressing the victim personally.

"Oh no, oh no, you would not listen. Therefore, here we are. You are dead and I am not much better because I think that I am alive only in appearance. Sort of existing while I am walking around dead. If I cannot have her . . . then no one else can have her. That is just the way it is and will be. I will make sure of it. I assure you of that."

The blood from the victim's dead body still continually ran down the victim's head and it dripped on the floor. Giant drops of blood that hit the plush carpet, in the plush office, in the posh home as if they were waves crashing into a beach during a hurricane. Blood that dripped from a throat gash, and a few trickles from the knife stuck in the top of the victim's skull. The knife's edge protruded about three inches out of the skull, but about eight inches remained buried in the victim's brain.

There were no more voices. The door slammed closed in the office. Silence ensued.

CHAPTER ONE

Pizza, Beers, and Hockey

"Hand me those chips, will ya, Odell? Unless ya gonna eat 'em," Sergeant George Grundy said while he leaned in over from his folding chair to where his drinking buddy on this late Saturday afternoon sat and relaxed.

Homicide Detective Lyle Odell sat in his easy chair and kept his eyes glued on the television set sitting on an upturned cardboard box in front of the two men. Odell reached for the bag of potato chips on the floor in front of his chair. A television set with two rabbit ear antennas waving at the two men in the air of the room. Luckily, reception was solid on over-the-air signals here on the north side of Mohawk City, New York. The air in upstate New York in late November was clean and crisp and the transmitters in Albany were just to the south.

Without taking his eyes off the television screen, Odell plucked the bag up off the floor; he leaned over and handed the chips to George Grundy. Odell then leaned back in his chair and reached for his beer mug on the end table next to his chair and picked it up, brought it to his mouth, and took a long swig of the beer.

The two men sat in the living room of Lyle Odell's home. A living room that was very sparsely furnished. There were not even any pictures on the walls. The room contained the folding chair that Sergeant George Grundy sat upon, the television set, the easy chair, an end table with a lamp, and an old table radio, Odell's cellphone, and an ashtray full of spent cigarette butts filling it up sitting upon it and there was not much of anything else in the room. Unless you could count the bag of potato chips and the two beer mugs of the two drinking buddies as furnishings. Grundy plunged his hand inside the bag and eagerly gobbled up some potato chips. As Grundy massacred the chips, crumbs and remnants of spent chips tumbled upon Grundy's shirt and worked their way down to his belly. A very large belly that had captured a few chip and food remnants in its time.

Detective Odell took his eyes off the television screen, glanced over at George Grundy, and carefully studied him for a few seconds.

Odell then commented, "There are more chips in the left side cupboard next to the stove, George. The way you are tearing them up, I can calculate," Odell stopped speaking, glanced at his watch, and noted the time then his eyes went back to the bag of chips in Grundy's hand and Odell spoke again, "you will need more chips in about three minutes and fifteen seconds." Odell smiled and then reached for his beer, took another sip, and added, "Good timing. You can pick us up a two more beers on the way to the kitchen for a refill. The way Rumblehowser is stopping the puck this afternoon, the Rovers might just have a chance to win this game."

"Yes! I love it, Odell! Especially want to beat these damn Boston Bears! I can't stand any sports teams from Boston. In hockey, football, baseball, basketball, hell, maybe even the local high school teams and the beer drinking pickup horseshoe teams at the local bars. Nuthin' Boston. I had an aunt and uncle who moved there years ago. My uncle took a job there. They couldn't stand the dump. Moved back in six months. Said they could not even understand what the people said. They talk funny there. The fans are a bunch of sore sports and nut jobs live there. Nope, nuthin' Boston for me. Did I ever mention that to you before, Odell?"

"Ah yes, George. About five-thousand times."

Grundy nodded and continued to devour chips.

He swallowed, reached for his beer on the floor next to his easy chair and before taking a sip, said, "Okay, I gotcha, Odell.

Yup, Rumblehowser is usually a bum, but he is spot on today. We sure do need a win." Grundy pointed at the screen and said, "Sure do love these Saturday matinee hockey games. Especially on our off days, and when my wife decided to head down to see her cousin in Jersey. Perfect timing." Grundy grabbed a few more chips, crunched them down and asked, "Ya think we have a chance at the playoffs, Odell? Ya know everything. What do ya think our chances are? I know it is only November, but what ya feeling?"

Lyle Odell kept his eyes on the television screen and answered his friend.

"Difficult to tell at this point, George. We need more consistent scoring. We tend to come back strong in the third period if we are behind going in and then lose in overtime far too often. Better fore-checking from the centers, we need the defense to pinch more and take some damn shots from the point. Just like that! Yes! Score!"

Grundy and Odell both jumped up in unison as a defenseman on the Rovers blasted a slap shot from the point that slipped by the opposition goaltender.

"Damn, Odell. Ya called that one! Two minutes left in the first period. Not bad," Grundy said while he remained standing next to the folding chair. He crushed the now empty potato chip bag and looked over to Odell before saying, "I will grab us some beers. Should I call some pizzas in to Frank's West Pizza Shop or should I grab another bag of chips? End of the first period is coming up."

Odell glanced at his watch and mumbled, "Three minutes and twenty-two seconds. Not an error on my part. The goal scoring induced a delay in Grundy's chip consumption." Then, with a voice that had some increased volume, Lyle Odell said, "Call the pies in, George. Get one plain cheese for me and whatever you want. I know that ya love those all-meat pies. You know where the phone number is there, on the pad, right next to the phone. Please, George, I am cruising into the Irish now. Hold my beer. Please bring me the Irish whiskey and my glass. You know where they are. Thank you."

Grundy nodded, picked up his empty beer mug and made his way to the kitchen while yelling out in the direction of Odell, "They are just facing off. I have time to run off to the kitchen and make the call. Yell loud if anything happens!"

Grundy then turned to his friend and began to speak, but Odell held one finger up and cut his friend off before he could finish speaking.

"I have ya covered on the pizzas. I know that you are a little short this week. Still paying off those loans for your children's college educations. My wallet is in the top drawer next to the stove. Use the red and black striped credit card. That one is on file with Frank, and in theory, I am working on earning a free pie one of these days. After damn near a five-hundred pizzas, I must'b gettin' close to a free one by now. Any day, now."

Grundy smiled and shook his head at the uncanny abilities of Detective Lyle Odell. It seemed as if Lyle Odell was not only ten steps ahead of anyone else, but he was from another world, too.

Just as Grundy walked into the kitchen, the good sergeant's cellphone that sat next to the leg of the folding chair, rang. Odell leaned over and glanced at the number and then he quickly glanced at his cellphone on the end table and then shook his head in recognition of the situation.

"Better hold off on the Irish, the beers, and the pizza, George. Your cellphone is ringing, and it is the front desk at headquarters." Odell said while reaching over and picking up his phone, and staring in at the screen. "Most likely, they are calling for me. Must know that there is a Rovers hockey game on and we are together, killing beers, Irish whiskey, chips, and pizzas. Unlike your cellphone, which sits diligently on the charger, my phone is dead. I forgot to charge it."

Grundy stood with his hands on his hips and howled, "Damn! You've gotta be kiddin' me, Odell? You mean that is work callin' me, or maybe us?"

Odell leaned over to his end table, plucked his pack of cigarettes off the table, shook one free from the pack, and stuck it in his mouth. The cigarette danced on his lower lip as he spoke.

"Yuppers. Gonna be Sergeant Hawkins on the front desk at headquarters. I recognize the number and you will, too. He ain't gonna stop callin'. It just went to voicemail but he will call right back. He is following orders."

As Odell predicted and just as the good detective lit the cigarette, the cellphone rang once more. Grundy tugged at his pants to try to bring the waistline over his considerable girth and shook his head in disgust as he made his way to the cellphone.

The good sergeant complained the entire way.

"Orders, huh? What orders? A few days off on the weekend after twelve on. A home-at-home series with the New York Rovers versus the Boston Bears. Rovers ahead in the first game after one period, the wife is visiting her cousin in Jersey, endless beer, and pizza, and we gotta get a damn call. Correction, you have to go get a call. Not me. I am off for a few days. Now, even though I am just a patrol sergeant, you are gonna say that you need my help, even if you have it all figured out before I even know what the hell is going on and you will suck me into another one of your crazy homicide cases with your eccentric ass, and turn my life upside down. If it were not for those friggin' parent-student loans, I could be sitting on Mirror Lake in Lake Placid sucking down beers and enjoying life. But, no, I have to keep going. Thirty-seven damn years now."

"Don't forget the endless stashes of potato chips and my wallet offer, George," Odell quipped as Grundy angrily yanked the cellphone from the charging cord and picked up the call.

"Grundy here."

Odell calmly sat in his easy chair; he watched and listened while gently puffing on his cigarette and studying his friend's body language. Lyle Odell blew a long exhale of smoke into the air and it circled his head like a wreath of blue smoke as he closed his eyes and felt Grundy's words. Even if his friend was discontented at the interruption of their plans for a relaxing weekend of pizza, beers, and hockey, Odell relished the challenge. Not that he welcomed the homicidal madness. His heart truly pined and ached for the victims; instead, he had an endless thirst to defeat the seemingly unending waves of evil.

"Ya know, Hawkins, this really sucks. It is the first break we have had in forever. We are drinkin' beer and watching the hockey game. It is a home-at-home series this weekend. Today is the first game, and it is in Boston. Tomorrow is in New York. Huh? Yeah, Rovers ahead after one period. One zip and Rumblehowser is on his game for a change in the net. Yeah, I can't stand Boston, too. Sure, Odell is here. What?"

Odell waved his hand in the air in a tilting fashion as he anticipated the question.

Odell mumbled, "I am a little tuned up, but not drunk yet. I was just gonna get into the Irish. Sarge Hawkins and the murderers, or murderer, have good timing."

Grundy continued, oblivious to Odell's words and actions, "Nah, he ain't bombed yet. A little tuned up like me. Just beers for now. I was bunking in with Odell all weekend. Hockey, beer, pizza, and no wife. She is away visiting a cousin in Jersey. Okay, I am listening."

There was a long pause and Grundy shifted his weight and stood up taller. He dug his feet into the floor. Sergeant George Grundy complained, moaned, and groaned constantly about his work and position, even though he was spent from thirty-seven years of police work and seeing the ugly side of Mohawk City, but he was an excellent police officer. Sergeant Grundy took a deep breath before speaking again.

"Geez, a knife stuck in the top of his head! In his home office. Wow! That must have hurt. Oh, I guess not if he had his throat cut first. Doctor Rochester Gilding, huh? Nah, I heard the name but can't place it."

Odell mumbled, "Mohawk City High School, number one, is gonna need a new principal of the school and the school district is now in search of a new superintendent."

Grundy continued, as Odell snuffed out his cigarette, kicked in the footrest on his chair, and stood up.

Grundy listened as Odell spoke.

"I'll get dressed, George. Please ask Hawkins to send a patrol car for us. We had too many beers to drive."

Sergeant Grundy nodded and Odell disappeared up the stairs to his bedroom to change while Grundy obtained more details from Sergeant Hawkins.

When Lyle Odell returned to the living room, George Grundy stood in front of the television. He looked up at Odell, grunted and pointed at the television, while saying, "Rovers still ahead. Three minutes gone in the second."

George studied Odell some more and waved his hands in the detective's direction while commenting, "Geez, Odell, ya looked better before you cleaned up and changed. Do you ever press ya suits? That one has more wrinkles than my old ass has."

Odell's hair stuck up in all directions. His suit jacket had waves of creases and wrinkles and his necktie was, in theory, tied, but it was too short and the knot hung askew.

Odell seemed surprised at Grundy's observation. He looked down, glanced at his attire, and shrugged his shoulders while answering, "I did have this suit cleaned and pressed. A week or two ago, but I might have not hung it up properly. Lookie here, George. I am very glad that the Rovers are ahead but I am gonna. . .."

Sergeant George Gundry cut off Odell's speech; he held his hand in the air and said, "I know, I know. Save it, Lyle. I gotcha. I have it down pat by now. You need my help, my keen mind, my muscles, ya gonna thank me for saving ya ass on the serial killer case with Marlin, ya gonna tell me how ya gonna ask Cap Moore if I can tag alongside ya for this case. It is all good. I am in. Why? For the life of me, I dunno? But I guess someone has to keep ya somewhat sober, keep ya upright, and on track."

Odell smiled, reached up, mussed with his hair, and mumbled, "Thanks, George."

"Yeah sure. Ya gonna owe me big time, Odell. Endless damn grilled cheeses and beers at Gulliver's and hockey games up the kazoo."

George smiled and paused in his words while he shifted his

feet, tugged at his belt to pull it over his substantial girth and grew serious in his voice and demeanor.

Odell attempted to adjust his necktie and, realizing that it was rather hopeless he gave up and realized that Sergeant George Grundy was carefully watching him and studying his efforts.

Odell said, "George, I will also need you to try to stop me from my fumbling and my talking to myself to remind my own mind of where I put things. I need to be more . . . organized."

George shrugged his shoulders and said, "Okay. I will try. But why? I mean, it is part of your normal mode of operations and part of your shtick and it fools the bad guys and the good guys into thinking you are a clueless drunk and a washed-up fool."

Odell answered, "You know, George, you really are a genius."

"No, Lyle. You are. A genius that is. Not a clueless drunk and washed-up fool."

Odell smiled at his friend's clarification of his statement.

"Anyway, Sarge Hawkins said that ya should consider getting a landline if ya never gonna charge ya cellphone. Are ya gonna get one? He is sending a patrol car and a patrol officer for us. This doctor guy got whacked with a pretty gory method of death. Apparently, it is a very messy scene. Throat cut wide open, and the knife jammed right into the top of his head bone. Crump and his crime techie team are already on the scene and sniffing around. Fancy joint on the nice side of the city. The penthouse unit in those new fancy low-rise attached townhouses. Why people want to live that tightly together and climb all those damn stairs for four-hundred-grand is beyond me. Where they work in this dump of a city to earn that kind of dough to afford those dumps is also a mystery to me. They must owe more dough than I do with those stupid student loans. Doc Kent is on the way. So, this poor bastard with a cut throat and knife in his head . . . I guess a patient did not like his bill."

"No, George, he is not a medical practitioner type of doctor. He is an educator as in a PhD type of doc."

Odell closed his eyes and stood silent for a few seconds and George Grundy knew his friend and fellow police officer well enough to know that Detective Lyle Odell was tapping the seemingly unlimited resources in his brilliant mind. George remained silent, too.

Suddenly, Odell opened his eyes and spoke, "Doctor Rochester Gilding PhD. The current superintendent of Mohawk City School District and acting principal of the high school during a vacancy. A vacancy that might be of profound interest to us, George. I am going to guess that Gilding was in and around forty-two years of age. Educated at an Ivy League university. Majored in English Literature. He lived in that fancy new Fairview Townhouse Development on Fairview Drive. Number four, if I recall. I suspect that is where we are going, because it is indeed a beautiful home. Yes, Dr. Gilding lived in the exclusive end unit in that new development of very expensive attached townhouses. A very large and expansive unit for a single man. Gilding was divorced. No children. Handsome as a movie star, charismatic, charming, highly intelligent, highly social, and very well liked. The word was that he was flirting with a political career. He earned a whopping salary on the taxpayers here in Mohawk City, but he did not need the money. His father and grandfather were very successful, high-powered attorneys in a downstate law firm in New York City, and Rochester inherited a part of the family's fortune when his father and grandfather passed away. These super-wealthy types always divide fortunes up when the older ones begin to croak. Leave some piles of dough intact within the family members. Smart move. Especially so now that Doctor Rochester Gilding is dead."

Even though George Grundy, through the countless adventures and cases together with Detective Lyle Odell, had been a witness to his genius many times before, this testimony left George stunned. The good sergeant stumbled for his words and then found them.

"Geez, Odell. That was amazing. All you missed was his shoe size."

Odell was now fumbling with his cigarette pack, that he plucked off the end table. After removing a cigarette that bent over in two places and sticking it in his mouth, Odell then began tapping his suit jacket and pants pockets all over his body while searching for his lighter.

When he finally stopped his search and realized what Grundy said, Odell looked at George and said, "He was about six-feet, two inches or thereabouts, so chances are he wore a large size shoe, George. Maybe a twelve or thereabouts. By chance, have you seen my lighter?"

Grundy pointed at the floor next to his easy chair and observed, "There on the floor, Lyle. Ya must have sat on it along with those cigarettes. The lighter fell onto the floor when you stood up. So . . . this . . . dead guy. Ya think is it a botched robbery? I hear a lot of potentials in your voice and testimony, Odell. You already are working it over. Fancy unit in the brand-new expensive townhouses, big dough, and lots of wealth. Maybe robbers staked it out and whacked him during the robbery? I hear that a vacancy at the high school means a potentially unhappy ex-employee, handsome guy, divorced, so there could be lovers, and all the mess that brings. Then you add the historic and epic law firm and big education, too. Maybe a past coming back to haunt this guy? Lots of complex stuff going on here, Odell."

George Grundy gently shook his head when he stopped speaking because Lyle Odell was crawling around on all fours looking for his lighter that evaded him.

"Geezzzz, Odell, and ya never even got into the Irish!"

Grundy walked over, reached down, picked up the lighter, and handed it to Odell.

"Some detective. Are ya blind? It is gonna be a challenge to keep you organized and not have ya constantly reminding ya-self on where ya put stuff."

"See, that is why I need you, George. Yes!"

"What? To find ya lighter that was right in front of your eyes."

"No, no, no. I eventually would have stumbled upon it. Because you are right on in your perception of the details of this case. I am afraid that this is going to be a very messy and complex case, George. Very intricate. Not to mention that this townhouse community type of life opens up a world of possible suspects. Hundreds. He was very sexy, dashing, wealthy, and handsome. Within this community, there could be many people with many types of nefarious intentions out there, George. It could be a vast collection of potential suspects with spurned lovers, adultery, jealous boyfriends, and husbands. Not to mention all the school connections and female teachers that might have batted their eyes at the handsome Doctor Gilding. In hopes of a . . . promotion. This case has the potential to be a great challenge and perhaps one of the most complex of my investigations."

Grundy rolled his eyes and mumbled, "I knew you would say that. You always say that and then ya solve the case in a day or two. Say, Odell, tell me, why are these handsome and wealthy guys always divorced? Was this doctor guy a jerk? You just said he was well-liked."

Odell lit the cigarette dangling from his lips. Odell took a long drag and blew the smoke up in the air.

He dropped the lighter into his suit jacket pocket and mumbled, "Right side suit jacket pocket."

Odell's voice picked up in volume and he said, "Because the super-wealthy, movie star guys are usually horrible people. Very self-indulged and very conceited. Since I recently also heard that he was considering a political career, then I bet he had an ego the size of Texas. That would fit a political career rather well. Lookie there, George. The Boston Bears just scored. Game tied up now. It is a good time to leave now before you blow ya cork and go on a rant about how much that Boston sucks. Ah, George, it is best if you grab your service revolver. I have my badge here clipped to my belt . . . I think, ah, yes, here it is, but I did not load any ammo into my weapon. As you know, George, I seldom carry any weapons so early in a case, but you might want to change into your uniform and at least one of us will look like a police officer. I saw your gear on the floor of the spare bedroom upstairs. I figured you knew to be prepared when you decided to hang-out with me. Not that I think we have any gun-play on this crime scene. The bad guys, or gals, or guy or gal are long since gone from the scene. Best to be careful. Just in case. I do not want Captain Moore upset and reminding me of my messiness so soon into this investigation."

"Try not to remind ya-self of that location stuff, Lyle. Ya just mumbled 'bout the lighter. Just doin' my job. Lot of good it will do. Okay, give me a minute or two. I will get my gun and put my uniform on and make believe that I am a police officer. The car should be here any minute now. I would think that Cap Moore was used to your messiness by now, Lyle."

"Negative, on Cap Moore. As of late, I have been messier than usual. Thank you. Oh yes, and the orders . . . and no, George."

Grundy took a step up the staircase and paused when he heard Odell's words. He screwed his face up in puzzlement over what Odell meant.

George said, "Orders, and no?"

"Yes, you asked a while ago about the orders that I left. I told Sarge Hawkins to call your cellphone if anything came in because I never remember to charge mine, and no, I don't think I will get a landline. The only logical location to install it is on the old phone jack on the wall in my kitchen. I don't want any clutter on my end table here in my private space. That space is for my hockey, my baseball, pizza, listening to my music on the radio, smoking, and sipping my Irish. Therefore, chances are while rushing to answer the phone, that I would stumble and fall on my ass, because I had too much Irish whiskey on my way to answer it. Besides, things have changed so much. These days, you just can't get a landline, you have to bundle stuff all kinds of bullshit services and packages together. George, I would never use any of it."

Grundy nodded and shook his head and said, "Strange, but I actually followed all of that and understood it all. Gotcha. Be right back. I know that I am going to regret this. All I wanted to do was to enjoy beers, eat chips and pizza, and watch the hockey games."

CHAPTER TWO

Blood Everywhere

Sergeant George Grundy's breathing huffed and puffed quite a bit from the long climb up the townhouse stairs. These units were very expensive, very fancy, and stacked three to four stories above the ground as they spiraled to the heavens. The murder victim's unit was a fancy penthouse and an end unit; therefore, it sprawled out and over the other units in the center of the facility. The murder victim was located on the upper level, just under the roof patio—in his private office.

Grundy mumbled and grumbled between puffs and deep inhales of air, "I can't imagine why the hell anyone would pay four-hundred-thousand-bucks to climb up those damn. . . ."

When Sergeant George Grundy's eyes scanned the scene of the homicide, he stopped short in his words. Even for a seasoned veteran of police work, such as Grundy was, this was an upsetting and very disturbing crime scene.

There was blood everywhere.

"Geez . . . shit . . . that must've hurt like hell. No matter what this poor-son-of-a-bitch did, he did not deserve this," Sergeant George Grundy said as he stopped short in his words, his steps, and his breaths.

Grundy used his right pointy finger and the old patrol sergeant pointed at the scene in front of him.

His finger shook and quivered. It was as if the horror transcended his finger and spread to his soul and affected his emotions.

The murder victim sat in the office chair behind his desk. The blood emitting from the victim was everywhere; on the desk, on the floor, on the dead body of the man; the blood splattered and dripped from his slit throat; even if the actual murder occurred much earlier . . . and it ran all over on his shirt and was dripping all over the chair and onto the hardwood floors underneath the chair. The rather intense word of gruesome would not exactly properly classify the murder scene. The victim's throat was laid wide open from the blow of the murder weapon.

The wound was cavernous. The entire scene was horrifying. Beyond words.

A large knife protruded from the victim's skull, while sticking out at a two o'clock angle as the victim's head rested at an odd right-side angle on the back of the office chair above the blood-stained surface of the desk and some papers that sat upon the same desk.

The room where the murder victim's body was located was used as an office. It was located on the top floor of the townhouse unit. There were only two doors to the room. One was the entry door, which was located off the hallway from the floor below and there was another door leading out to a rooftop patio. A door that once you landed there, the entire patio was surrounded by a fence. The patio was a high point within the townhouse development, yet the fence blocked most of the views. Doctor Rochester Gilding's office was rather tastefully decorated and furnished. The room had several luxurious guest chairs, several glorious framed photographs on the walls of some sunsets and landscape settings, a small table with a vase of artificial flowers set upon it; and the desk and office chair where the victim's body remained. It was a tubular desk. The desk was very modern in design. It was a shiny black top to the desk, and the desk had bright chrome legs that twisted an interesting angle. On the desk there was, a laptop computer with the lid open, a clock, a cup with pens and pencils and some books and papers of which the blood from the victim's wounds immensely stained, and currently, swirled in pools of horror. Behind the desk, lining most of the wall, were solid oak bookcases; filled with books. Floor-to-ceiling. Books in a perfect order and organization.

The lead officer of the crime scene investigation squad for the Mohawk City, New York, Police Department, Sergeant Oliver Crump, stood behind the desk, on the right side—next to the victim. His team of crime scene technicians stood watching and waiting around the perimeter of the room. Doctor Patrick Kent from the Mohawk City Coroner's office stood close to Crump; the doctor held his medical bag in his right hand and his stethoscope was still hanging around his neck.

A uniformed police officer from the Mohawk City Police Department stood off to the far-right side of Doctor Kent. The officer was middle-aged, tall, and very stocky and powerfully built. He gave the appearance of being a weight-lifting gym rat.

Oliver Crump recently received a promotion to the rank of sergeant as a result of his contributions and heroism in the cracking of the now-famous Danny Clark serial killer case. Crump and his elite team were known for their keen insight and professionalism.

Everyone in the room, officers, and technicians, and the good doctor alike, all looked up and studied Sergeant George Grundy and Homicide Detective Lyle Odell as they entered the room. Sergeant Crump was now a seasoned officer . . . a veteran . . . and he was very used to working with the rather peculiar and systematic Homicide Detective Lyle Odell.

Doctor Kent, had also worked with Detective Odell for years now and he too, knew very well Odell's nuances, procedures, and his peculiar investigative actions.

Crump said, "Good late afternoon, George, and Lyle. Sorry to interrupt your hockey game and beer and pizza event. Welcome to another glimpse of Hell. Sergeant Grundy . . . you are right on in your words. You are not kidding. There is nothing about this bullshit and scene that is pretty. This poor son-of-a-bitch had a ton of blood. It is still a'drippin' out of him. I say this with all due respect because, us together, and us apart, we have seen a lot of ugly shit."

After Sergeant Crump spoke, all eyes turned their attention to Mohawk City Homicide, Detective Lyle Odell. The uniformed police officer with the muscles shifted his weight a little uneasily. It seemed as if he had never worked with Odell before; however, Crump and Doctor Kent most likely briefed the officer on the particular and peculiar ways and investigative methods of Homicide Detective Lyle Odell. The police officer stood silently and stoically, and his eyes darted around the room, shifting between the dead body and Grundy and Odell.

After Sergeant George Grundy stepped aside from the doorway, Odell took a few more steps into the room; he closed his eyes and held his hands out in front of his body.

No one spoke a word or moved a muscle. Every breath was taken with respect and only out of necessity.

Odell was following his usual methodology of his homicide investigations. He wanted to view the actual crime scene and the victim's dead body from a neutral standpoint. Detective Lyle Odell never wanted to have any preconceived notions of what he might see and cause an errant judgement in his mind. Sergeant Crump, the crime scene technicians, Sergeant Grundy, and Doctor Kent knew not to reveal any finding or details of the initial investigations until Odell asked for them to provide him with them. The good detective kept his eyes tightly shut for a few minutes and his hands remained outright, palms up from his body. He appeared to take some deep breaths and sniff the air as if he was sampling the air to detect an odor or a particular smell.

Suddenly, he opened his eyes and his eyes scanned the entire room, even the ceiling of the room, yet he averted his gaze when it came to viewing the dead body. He gently pointed in the direction of Oliver Crump and Doctor Kent, and then waved his arm as if to motion them to step away from the dead body.

It was very obvious that Detective Lyle Odell did not yet want to view the body.

Detective Lyle Odell said, "Hello, Crump. Hello, Doc Kent. Hello, C-S-I- team. Thank you for your jobs here. Good afternoon, to everyone. Please, no words . . . everyone knows the drill . . . my strange ways. Yes, welcome to another glimpse of Hell. Strange as it seems, right now, Hell might not be quite as bad as this. So much evil on this side of Hell. In this world. Damn shame. These murder scenes are always three dimensional. So much to study and take in."

Odell turned to Grundy and asked, "My cigarettes, George?"

Sergeant Grundy pointed at Odell's back pocket and George replied, "Right back pocket. Ya sat on 'em. They must'b all squished. I know that does not matter because ya just want to stick it in your mouth and taste it. Not light it."

"Correct. Just a taste. Thank you, Sarge Grundy."

Detective Odell, without even moving from the initial place that he stood, reached into his back pocket. He removed a very massacred pack of cigarettes and shook one twisted cigarette from the pack and stuck it in his mouth so that it dangled from his lower lip like an icicle would cling to a rain gutter in January. Odell stuck the pack back into his rear pocket and he looked at Grundy and smiled.

"I am not going to say the location, George. Doin' my best at breaking the habits and taking better mental notes of things."

Grundy nodded.

While the cigarette bobbed up and down with his speaking of the words, Odell then asked, "Doc Kent, it looks as he did, but please confirm for me . . . did he croak today? Time of death? To your knowledge and everyone else's knowledge . . . only, Doctor Kent answer, please, are you the only person out of our team to touch and approach the body?"

Doctor Kent reached into his suit jacket pocket, he removed a small notepad and, while still holding his medical bag with one hand, he flipped the notepad open and read from his notes.

"Hello, Detective Odell. Hello, George. A glimpse of Hell indeed. Yes. The victim died today. My estimated time of death is around 2:30 PM. However, that is estimated. I will need the body in the lab to verify the time. Yes . . . out of the team assembled here. I only touched the body with my hands to raise his tee shirt to listen for a heartbeat with my scope and with my thermometer to take a body temperature. I observed everything else in my notes from a distance and made notes. My examination efforts and death declaration seemed rather pointless. I mean, anyone could tell that this man is dead. But, but of course, it is standard procedure for me to declare the victim dead. My stethoscope touched his back. My thermometer went under his arm in the pit. The body is slumped at an ideal angle to slip the device into the armpit. I do not trust those new-fangled electronic thermometers where you shoot some dot of bullshit on the body and capture a temperature. Too unreliable. My fingers grazed the body to lift the shirt. Officer Miles Bradford here was the first responder to the scene out of our team. By his testimony, Officer Bradford did not come closer than three feet to the body. Honestly, as I just implied, it did not take my skills to see that Doctor Gilding was deceased."

Doctor Kent lifted his eyes up to Odell and he waited for his response. Kent did not want to offer more information unless Detective Odell asked for it. The fact that Doctor Kent used his notepad made Odell's genius mind whirl and engage. Odell knew the doctor had more notes of related information above what Odell requested on that pad to relay to him; the good doctor did not require notes to answer Odell's initial questions.

Homicide Detective Lyle Odell, because he was Odell, already had observed and knew of what the doctor was going to tell him from his notes.

"Excellent. Thank you for the careful notes and procedures. The amount of bleeding is bothering you, huh? Do you suspect anti-coagulants? Seems like he, until today that is, that he was in good health . . . not too old . . . I see he works out. Odell pointed at a set of resistance bands hanging on a door knob in the far corner of the office. I think that I know what the victim's health issues were. I highly doubt that it was some high cholesterol or genetic heart issues. How old was he, Doctor Kent? My original guess was in and around forty-two years of age. I know you have his actual birthdate on your page, but please do not tell me that right now. Just his exact age. Thank you."

Doctor Kent looked at his notepad and said, "Forty-three. The dead body is very muscular. I made note of extreme callouses on his fingers and centers of the palm. Consistent with working out with weights or the handles of those bands. Yes, I suspect blood thinners or some sort of herbal medication that interferes with blood-clotting. Maybe he had diabetes or sugar issues. I doubt he had heart issues; however, the autopsy will reveal more. It will be interesting to see the stomach contents and determine when he last ate a meal because. . ..."

Odell held up his hands to indicate to Doctor Kent to stop short in his words and theories.

Odell immediately piped up and said, "Oh, because you smell the maple syrup and want to see if his last meal was pancakes and syrup, or waffles and such? No, Patrick. I noticed the smell as soon as I entered the room. That maple odor is the cause of the lack of blood-clotting. I think you will find that Doctor Gilding was consuming an herbal supplement known as Fenugreek. Trigonella foenum-graecum. It is a plant with green leaves, grows about three feet tall and blooms with small white flowers and makes some seed pods that pack some golden-brown seeds. It is an ancient Chinese and Indian herb. Probably, the victim was a health nut, and he steered clear of normal medications with iffy chemical ingredients. Preferred the herbal stuff. Yes, it can be used for circulation issues or for sugar or diabetes, but in this case, I suspect that our victim here was taking large amounts of it to boost his testosterone levels and improve his erections. He was divorced, handsome, wealthy, and worked in a position of power, and as I mentioned to George when the call first came in and I heard the victim's name . . . most likely, he had many girlfriends and lovers on the side. Just the way it is gonna be these days. Women follow the money and the fact that he was a good-looking guy makes him even more of a chick-magnet. Just gonna complicate this case. Lovers by the wagonloads. Or maybe I should say by the bed loads."

Odell took the unlit cigarette out of his mouth and jammed it into his right-side suit jacket pocket without mumbling the location.

Sergeant George Grundy sniffed the air and said, "Talking about food always makes me hungry. I don't smell a damn thing and don't know anything about herbs. Twisted mess of a butt in your right suit jacket pocket. I gotcha covered, Odell. You left out all the potential jealous husbands, and boyfriends, and revenge seeking men wanting a piece of this guy for messing with their ladies. I know you have not looked at the body yet, and I ain't tellin' anythin' that I did not already tell ya, but a knife stuck in a skull takes some power and force. Some serious strength."

"Very true, George. That is all of our initial reactions. To suspect a man's strength is what forced the knife into the victim's skull. Yet, as I always say. . .."

To the surprise of everyone in the room, Sergeant George Grundy interrupted his partner and finished the statement for Odell.

"I know. Assumptions are the downfall of detectives and the dreams of criminals. Sometimes, we are just as far into the game as we are out of the game. That is what the bad guys count on. I remember and always keep that in mind on these cases. You keep me around for many reasons, Lyle. I know some stuff by now."

Odell smiled and nodded his head and said, "I do value your keen mind and your presence here, George. Thank you. You are invaluable to me and to us. I feel it is my duty to inform you that we don't keep you around though, for paying for beer and sandwiches and pizza."

Odell loosened his necktie and with too hard of a tug on it; what was let of the knot fell away and the necktie now hung around his neck in two sections.

"Oh, well. It was not exactly tied, anyway. Everyone is used to me being a mess. Why would I not be today? At least, I am not half-in-the-bag. I guess that qualifies as an improvement of sorts. Patrick, thank you for everything. Please hold your notes for now. George and I will visit you once you complete the autopsy."

In an unusual quest, Detective Lyle Odell tapped his suit jacket pockets. He stopped in mid-tap and shook his head. It was as if he changed his mind about searching for an item.

"Okay, time to get into this horror show a bit more. Crump, give me the scoop. Just these answers are all I need for now. Kind of, sort of, rapid fire. My apologies, Crump. My mind is whirling because I am not catching any vibes at all here. It seems very mysterious right now. But we do need to search this entire townhouse unit. Especially the victim's bedroom and the kitchen and those bookshelves behind the victim on that wall."

Crump nodded and widened his stance in anticipation of the questions. Oliver Crump was on his game; he felt confident that he could handle Homicide Detective Lyle Odell.

Even when faced head-on with Odell's genius.

"We did not touch anything. Yet. Other than Doc Kent's testimony so far . . . no one has moved anything or approached the body. We have all simply observed and noted various items, but we waited for you and Sarge Grundy to arrive before beginning any intense detections. Only one door into this room and that other door over there, which appears to lead to a rooftop patio of sorts. We are in the fanciest unit of them all, an exclusive unit here. Almost three-thousand square feet of potential clues and a mess to search and scour. We are at the top of the mountain, so-to-speak. I guess we are about thirty-five feet in the air. A difficult height to climb."

Detective Odell nodded and said, "Correct. Excellent point, Sergeant Crump. In my opinion, there is only one way in and out."

Sergeant Grundy asked, "How do they get away with that for the construction and the planning of these units, Odell? I mean, for a fire emergency. Only one way in and out. What if the fire is in the staircase? Seems dangerous to me."

Odell smiled and rubbed his hands together, and then tried to smooth out his messy hair. He gave up rather quickly.

"Great observation, George. Years ago, they built fire escapes on exterior walls in apartments and buildings such as this one is. Down the outside walls to the ground below to provide an emergency escape route. Now, with only one way of egress, they have wet fire sprinklers." Odell pointed at the ceiling, at the escutcheon ring around a wet sprinkler head. Odell said, "These buildings have full wet sprinkler fire protection," then he pointed at a smoke detector on the same ceiling and added, "and full heat and smoke detection. Lots of fireproof and fire-rated materials in these walls and frames, too."

"Gotcha, Odell. I see," Grundy said as his eyes scanned the ceiling devices.

"That allows the building inspector and fire officials to approve the single means of egress. For us, it means one way in and out for the killer. Unless they scale and climb exterior walls." Odell almost reached out and smoothed his hair out again, but he stopped in mid-reach and he smiled and said, "Once more . . . no assumptions. Crump, I noticed an alarm on the entry door. Have you had a chance to check the burglar alarm? How about the cameras at the doors?"

"Correct on the single means of egress. Yes, we gave the alarm a quick once over when we arrived on scene. We have not gotten into the cameras yet. No indications of any alarm trips. I suspect that no one set the alarm, or it is disabled. However, I am going to venture a guess by the large accumulation of leaves in the garage that the garage door was open and then closed. During my investigation, I will scan the alarm history for open-and-closed contacts and settings. That might be the reason that they did not set the alarm. The victim was waiting for someone he knew and did not set the alarm because the door was open. Sorry, assumptions. I know. Anyway, at this point, right now, we have nothing on the alarm. It is a key focus for my team to investigate and note for our crime scene investigation."

Detective Odell raised his hand to his face, rubbed the hints of stubble on his unshaven face, and pondered the moment.

He spoke after the pensive pondering, "No, no, no, Crump. You are fine. Right on the mark. Other than this room full of blood, this place is neat as pin and clean as a whistle. Excessive leaves in the garage indicate that the door was open for a period of time. It was windy today. Out of the west and the garage faces west. The housekeeper or the victim would sweep out and gather those dried up leaves at another time. This is not a botched robbery or an invasion of any sorts. The killer knew the victim and likewise. I know you have not dusted anything yet. Obviously, you still need to do it and follow through with all of you and your team's usual amazing proficiency. However, even though you and your team already know this . . . I must emphasize how you will find very little to nothing there, here, or anywhere. Even outside of the townhouse. The killer is not a professional, yet the killer was diligent. Highly intelligent, too. Please do check the master bedroom. I need the DNA and fingerprints of past and present lovers. The master bathroom off the master bedroom. It will contain many clues. Too many clues in that room."

Odell tapped his rear pants pocket and looked over at Sergeant George Grundy.

Grundy spoke up right away.

"No. Right-side suit jacket pocket, Lyle."

"Thanks, George."

Odell dug the twisted butt out of the suit jacket pocket and stuck it in his mouth.

"Crump, please confirm that the housekeeper found the body?" Odell pointed at a feather duster on the floor near to where he stood a few steps inside the door to the room.

"Correct."

"Time?"

The twisted cigarette butt danced on his lower lip with his words.

"Around three fifteen this afternoon."

"The housekeeper only speaks Spanish? Bradford here can speak Spanish because he is married to a Latina. Bradford took her testimony. I know the housekeeper is a woman because besides the maple syrup smell that pervades the air, I can smell some perfume in the air. The killer, if she is a woman, is too smart to wear perfume. Basically, the poor woman entered the room, saw this horror show, tossed her duster, and ran for her life. Headquarters received the call and Officer Bradford responded,"

"Correct to all."

"Thank you, Oliver. Please, you and your elite team . . . stand by. I will examine the body in a few minutes and then it is all yours. Please Oliver, I know you will do your best along with your team here, but please do not be discouraged by the fact that you will find very little in the way of clues. This case is going to be complex. Very intense and complex, with many, many suspects to choose from this time."

Upon hearing Odell's testimony of the complexity of the case, Sergeant George Grundy sighed rather deeply. He knew that the case would consume some of his valuable off time and potential relaxation time as he tagged along on Odell's investigation.

Odell continued to speak.

"It will be extremely helpful to know the exact vintage of the knife. Please have only Doc Kent remove it in the lab for the autopsy, but take extensive pictures of it right now. I need an exact angle of entry into the skull. How far away the killer stood and the arm span of the swing of the killer is of vital importance. The killer slit the victim's throat, stepped back, watched him die and gush blood, and relished in that fact. Because of some type of intense hatred. Evil never sleeps, and what motivates a person to harbor such hatred is my job to figure out. Then the killer plunged the knife into the victim's skull in a final nail into the coffin . . . so to speak. I suspect that the knife is a replica and not an original issue from the 1940s era of the Pacific Theater during World War 2. Just a knock-off. There is a flea market down the road, just a piece in Colonie, that sells knock-off military gear every weekend. Cheap stuff. Very affordable, too."

Officer Bradford's eyes had widened with Odell's statements about him, his vast knowledge, and his rambling words and testimony of the exact reenacting of the moves of the killer. Odell lifted his eyes to the police officer and removed the twisted butt from his mouth. He held it in his fingers.

"Hello, Officer Bradford. You look very strong and in great shape and you do present a perfect police officer's appearance.

Unlike me. I know you don't know me and we have never worked together before this case. I appreciate your cooperation in not speaking until now. It is my duty to tell you that I do know you. I make it a mission of mine to know all of the Mohawk Police Department officers, employees, and members and know as much as I can about them. Even if they own pets. You own a cat. Charlie is his name. Pardon the intrusion into your life. I mean no harm. It is just useful information that I might need down the road."

"Hello, Detective Odell. No harm. Correction, with all due respect. Everyone knows you, Detective Odell. I admire you and I know of your genius reputation."

"Ha! Genius. No way, Bradford. A drunken fool, yes, genius no. Regardless, thank you for the compliments. However, Sarge Grundy and I are only into a few beers right now. We had a hockey game, beers, and pizza on the agenda, but some deranged fool had other ideas for us. Although, right now, I am fairly sober. I promise you that will not be the case once George and I leave here and return to the remnants of our weekend. I will need some dabbles in the Irish to open my mind to some of what we find here."

Odell reached up and his hands ran through his thick, black hair. His thoughts were interrupted, and it was obvious that he was gathering them. When he did so and went to speak, his hair stuck up at odd angles. Odell was in his usual disarray.

"Officer Bradford, was the poor housekeeper shaking and rattling in her testimony? Did she just toss the duster aside and dash away screaming in horror? Because she speaks limited English, she called a family member who does speak English to call the crime into us?

Officer Bradford immediately answered.

"Correct. She called her teenage daughter. Her daughter called in the homicide to us."

"Did she tell you how long that she worked for Doctor Gilding?"

"Yes. Five years. It was a question that I asked her. I thought it was valuable information to have for the investigation."

Odell, uncharacteristically, became very enthusiastic and demonstrative. He almost jumped up and down with excitement into the air and he proclaimed his agreement with Officer Bradford's efforts.

"Yes! Excellent! For sure, it is valuable information. Great insight, Bradford! You have potential! The housekeeper can tell us of the coming and going of various people to this house. Five years in the workplace. That would put the housekeeper right in the mix. The community is about six years old. She might know of everyone around here and the comings and goings. Officer Bradford. Great work! Thank you. Ah, Bradford, your wife is of Dominican heritage. Where are the housekeeper's origins from?"

"The housekeeper is Dominican, Detective Odell. She is from the Dominican Republic."

Odell nodded, and then he waved his hands through his hair and attempted to smooth the errant hairs down.

Odell said, "Tight community . . . these days. Well, let's finally take a look at the dead body here."

Odell looked at Sarge Grundy and his eyes told the story as he began to pat his assorted pockets in search of something. Grundy knew what he was looking for; because Grundy all too well knew of the methods of investigation of Detective Lyle Odell.

Grundy pointed and waved his hands in the general direction of Odell and Grundy explained, "Your assorted gadgets and gizmos are in your inside suit jacket pockets. I think the right side has the flashlight. Who the hell knows where ya magnifying glass is, Lyle? Pat ya ass until ya find it. You are on your own for that one."

Odell nodded, reached into his inside suit jacket pockets, and pulled out a small flashlight, along with two spent and crinkled cigarette butts. The good detective looked around the room as if he was pondering whether to dispose of the butts in a trash can. After realizing that he did not want to taint any potential evidence, Odell simply jammed the cigarette butts back into the same pocket.

Sergeant Oliver Crump mumbled, "Geez, Odell. It must really suck to be your dry cleaners."

"It does. They charge me extra because they say that I am a mess. I agree and happily pay the extra fees."

Homicide Detective Lyle Odell then continued to pat down his body, he then reached into a back pocket, felt around and pulled out his magnifying glass.

Odell mumbled, "Tricky little thing that glass is. It hides."

Detective Odell with his magnifying glass now in hand, took a few more steps into the room and then focused his eyes on the dead body at the desk. Until now, his eyes purposely averted that scene.

Odell's investigative methods were peculiar, but calculated.

Detective Lyle Odell walked over to the front of the desk while no one moved or spoke. He tilted his head at various angles and peered into the work on the desk in front of the body; papers and a book now covered in rivers of blood. Odell then moved to the side of the desk while keeping his eyes trained on the body. His eyes then went to the bookcases behind the victim. Bookcases that lined the walls and contained hundreds, if not thousands, of books. Odell's eyes scanned the books. From the top of the shelves to the bottom and then right to left. He did not move or say a word. He then closed his eyes and stood motionless and silent for a minute or two. Odell opened his eyes.

He then removed his untied necktie and, without saying a word, he handed it to Doctor Kent. Odell then dropped to his knees, clicked on his flashlight, and placed the flashlight down on the hardwood floor. The detective then sprawled out and rested his body out in a prone position on the floor next to the light. The light illuminated the floor behind the desk and underneath the chair where the victim's dead body remained. He moved the flashlight around and scanned the floor as his eyes darted back and forth and he examined the floor under the light beam. He used his magnifying glass and peered in and around at the scene in front of him, and then he scanned the areas without the aid of his glass.

Odell said, "The housekeeper is excellent at her job. No dust, not too much here to find. I do need a measurement from the desk to that small blue piece of tape on the hardwood floor in front of the desk. We need to confirm with the housekeeper that Doctor Gilding instructed her to leave that tape there. It is a painter's masking tape. Easily removed without marking the surface. I suspect it was to pace off a photograph, and that is where the photographer is required to stand."

"Geez, Odell, I did not even see that. Damn, eagle eyes," Crump said as he peered over at the small piece of tape on the floor. "I bet no one else saw it, too."

"Ah, you would have eventually caught it, Crump. Just helping out. I was hoping for a little more to go on. There is an interesting fact here with a panic button mounted on the underside of the desk. It is most likely a single push to the alarm to send the police. The good doctor must have spent a great deal of time at this desk and he must have felt the need for a panic button. To guard his life, or his wealth. For protection. No doubt that Doctor Gilding was into some iffy shit. With some iffy people. A secret life behind the scenes. He expected that someday, he would be in a heap of trouble for bedding women or everything else iffy that this guy was into. Eventually jealous husbands and boyfriends and other people that you cross come calling. You make a deal with the Devil and eventually the Devil comes to collect ya ass and soul. This alarm button thingy is a key fact. I doubt Doctor Gilding had much of a chance to push that sucker with his throat cut like that. Crump, you might find that button would have been useless anyway because the alarm is disabled. I still feel as if the killer stood behind Gilding for a few minutes, enjoying his death. From behind the chair was the windup, the angle calculation, and the knife plunge. The killer is right-handed. I am sure of those details. Doctor Kent, I suspect that when you do the autopsy, you will find that the victim's last meal was breakfast. I see some crumbs . . . maybe a muffin or a pastry. Crump, please, have your superb crew of techs here, carefully gather those crumbs and analyze them for content and origins. I also need to know what the papers are on the desk there and what is on that laptop screen."

Odell pointed at some blood-soaked papers on the desk and continued to explain.

"Those papers and the files. It appears as even through the all that blood that those papers might contain some financial records. That could be interesting. As would be credit card statements. And the bedroom and bathroom. Not so much with the kitchen . . . other than the bag and empty container of coffee in the trashcan in the kitchen. That might be significant because I suspect that was where the muffin came from—hence, the crumbs. Perhaps his last meal was coffee and a muffin. Doc Kent will tell us that in his autopsy results. Crump, I know you and your team will leave nothing unobserved or untouched. That might be all we have to go on for now. Other than the odd-ball paperback book in the bookcase there."

When Odell mentioned the odd-ball book, everyone in the room turned their eyes to scan the bookcase. By their reactions, no one detected the aforementioned odd-ball book. Crump looked at Grundy and shrugged his shoulders. Grundy nodded to confirm that he, too, did not detect the book. Yet, they both knew not to interrupt Odell while he explains and does his thinking aloud. Odell continued with the details of his observations

"I do not think it was toast that they ate, I think it was a muffin or two. The killer sat in the left guest chair in front of the desk. The killer might have shared the same meal. There are some crumbs there, too."

Odell clicked the flashlight off. He groaned and wobbled a bit while he stood on his feet, and when he did so, Doctor Kent handed Odell his necktie.

Doctor Kent said, "Here is your necktie, Odell. So noted on the meal. I should have the autopsy done by two in the morning or three tomorrow. Sunday. That is, unless we have more victims or adventures."

"Thanks, Doc. Let's sure as hell hope not. Grundy is hungry," Odell said as he draped the tie over his neck and began to fumble with the necktie as if he was going to tie it and then he sighed and abandoned the effort and allowed the tie to loosely hang around his neck.

Sarge Grundy perked up at the prospect of wrapping this investigation segment up and with food on the horizon, he rubbed his belly a bit, groaned a little, and carefully observed Detective Odell for his next move.

Sergeant Grundy waited and when Odell looked at him, George said, "Odell, I am hungry and damn curious if the Rovers won that hockey game."

Since George Grundy knew of Odell's ways and his habit of mentioning random items or comments to revisit later down the road, Grundy sighed and spoke with some reluctance.

"I know this is going to lead into a maze of investigative Odell madness, but I must ask. What book?"

Odell smiled as he replaced the flashlight in his suit jacket pocket and mumbled, "Right-side inside suit jacket pocket."

He still held his small magnifying glass in his hand as he walked over to the bookcase and tilted his head as he studied a book on the second shelf of the bookcase. A book in the dead center of the collection on the shelf.

"This book, George. Great question! I am sorry to prolong your meal, but this might be the most important clue we have. It might be the only clue. See how this one book is sticking out a bit more than the others are? All these thousands of books and this one sticks out a bit. The good doctor was systematic and organized and that may or may not be to our advantage here. Perhaps even a touch of a little obsessive-compulsive disorder, too. I suspect the victim did not place this book in the case and in this position. He would have made sure it was properly placed and not sticking out."

Odell walked closer to the book, took his magnifying lens, and peered in and carefully examined every aspect of the book and the area of the wooden shelf around the book.

As he observed, Odell said, "Of course, Doctor Gilding would have so many books. His doctorate and education are in English Literature. Crump, please have your C-S-I tech-photographer aim that camera around his neck and stand on the left corner of the desk as you face the desk. I need shots from that angle. Wide-angle shots. Crump, how tall are you?"

"Five-eleven. Why?"

Odell did not answer him, instead he whirled around and took an inventory of the persons in the room.

"Doc Kent. . . you are five-nine or so. George is the tallest. Six-three. Bradford is about six feet. I am six-one."

Odell turned to Doctor Kent and said, "Doc Kent, please stand here behind the victim and place your feet right here while facing the victim."

Odell reached down and pointed to an exact spot on the floor and demonstrated how he wanted the doctor to stand. Odell then scurried out and stood in front of the desk and excitedly observed the scene. He reached up and nervously smoothed his hair out with one hand. Realizing that he still held the magnifying glass in his other hand; Odell simply handed the lens off to Sarge Grundy, who now stood next to Odell. Grundy stuffed the lens in his pocket.

Doctor Kent moved into the location and so did the C-S-I photography tech.

Odell conducted the orchestra.

"Doc, as the tech snaps away . . . I want you to move your feet right to left, then pivot and reach for the book. Don't touch it! Just pivot and reach as he snaps the photos."

Doctor Kent nodded and did as Odell instructed as the photographer clicked off shots. Odell folded his arms and watched. He waved his hands as if to repeat the sequence several times.

"Good. Thank you, Doc. Now. George, please you are the tallest. Please move in place of Doc Kent and do the same motion. Crump, please, as George moves . . . please have a tape measure ready and measure the distance from the skull of the victim to the book. Record the distance in your notes, but do not tell me what the measurement is. Thank you."

The officers did exactly as Odell requested, while the photographer took the photos. After about five repeated moves by Sergeant Grundy—Odell was satisfied.

Homicide Detective Lyle Odell mumbled, "The killer is tall."

He then waved his hands in the air to stop the process and then turned to Sergeant Oliver Crump and said, "Oliver, please have your C-S-I photography tech take close-up shots of the book and then use your gloved hands to remove the book and we will place it on this table over here on a crime scene plastic sheet. Please move quickly! I feel my focus fading!"

Sergeant Crump nodded and waved to his techs to follow the orders, and Crump and his team quickly moved into action. Crump was one of Odell's most trusted associates and Odell stood and watched and admired Crump and his professionalism. After removing the book, Odell watched as Crump placed the book on the table on the special plastic set there by his crew. Odell folded his arms, and rubbed his head, and then his chin, as he carefully observed the book.

"Most unusual. Most of the books in the cases are hardbacks. Elegant books. Expected because of the victim's education, standards, and reputation. This book is a paperback. Paperbacks have memories. They reveal where the book was last opened to. This is most fortunate for us. The Adventures of Sherlock Holmes. A classic. Most ironic. Please, Crump some gloves."

Crump handed Odell some gloves and the officer and Doctor Kent all stood in wonder as to what it was that Odell was dissecting here. Even for these seasoned Odell veterans; this was a most unusual process.

Odell put the gloves on his hands. He then carefully studied the book. He leaned in and then gently moved to the book and placed his finger on a page and flipped open the pages. The book flipped open and Odell leaned in and smiled when he saw where the book opened to within the pages.

"A Study in Scarlet. Interesting. An excellent case and one of the few cases of Sherlock Holmes that deal in murder. Death. Ruthless killers. A stabbing with a knife was a key aspect of that story. A person could learn quite a bit about detective work from the author. Fiction or not. It is a remarkable story. Very complex. The storyline and settings changes scenes and locations quite often. A person would need to be very intelligent or a borderline scholar to appreciate the true genius of the story."

Odell then flipped the book closed and turned it over in his hands, and first studied the back cover and then the front cover. He placed it back down on the sheet, yet he kept his gloved hands on the cover of the book as if he was absorbing energy and details from it.

Or perhaps, secrets.

Detective Odell lifted his eyes and gazed over at Doctor Kent.

He asked Doctor Kent a question.

"Doc . . . did you know that the genius author of these multitudes of stories of Holmes . . . Sir Arthur Conan Doyle was a medical doctor before and during his time as an author? He began writing for income when his medical practice became slow and non-productive."

Although a seasoned veteran of working with Detective Lyle Odell and his varied and eccentric ways, Doctor Kent seemed to be caught off-guard by the question.

After a few seconds of what appeared to be confusion mixed with pensive pondering, Doctor Patrick Kent shook his head and, in a voice just above a whisper, said, "No, Lyle, I was not aware of that. Thank you for sharing that fact."

"You are welcome. That fact, as are many facts in life, remains vital to the success of his stories. Doctor Watson being a medical doctor too, and such. With, of course, Watson being the primary narrator of the stories."

After speaking those words, Odell seemed to drift off. To where, no one will ever know. He was lost in a mysterious world of Odell investigations and clandestine clues and such.

Odell took a deep breath, and he closed his eyes for a few seconds while he took his hands off the book. With his eyes now open, Odell plucked the gloves off his hands and he handed them off to Sergeant Oliver Crump.

Odell then said, "We are done here. Crump, the book is official evidence. Please do your usual amazing job. Please do not be discouraged by the lack of evidence. Of another interesting note . . . please find where the victim stashed his condoms. Hopefully, they are still in the box and we can count how many of them remain there. Then we need to find store receipts or credit card information to find the store and a date when he purchased them. Very important. Thank you. Doc Kent, you can take the body once Crump is done."

Odell then turned to face Officer Bradford.

He asked, "Have you arranged for additional uniforms in front of this joint? I imagine the press is out there and all these neighbors are gathering like a bunch of pain-in-the-ass laundry ladies. A mess of potential suspects and busybodies are out there now. Why the hell anyone wants to live in and amongst all these people and pay this kind of dough for a dump like this is beyond me? And they are building more and more of them. That new construction right across the street from this one. And they're breaking ground on another set of units over on the west end of the property when the new one is not even finished for the day. I guess some people like this style of living, but it is not for me."

"Not my style, either. Too tight and too many people for my taste. Yes, Detective Odell. I called in for extra police officers just when Sergeant Grundy and you both arrived. The officer . . . Officer Kane, who drove you here, is fronting that mission up now while he waits for you to finish. He will drive Sarge Grundy and you back to your home. We should have a solid crowd control patrol out there right now."

"Good job, Bradford. Thank you. George and I will leave now. You can sign off on the release of the body to Doc Kent. But first, I will need you to assist in the crowd control observations and media control. You seem to be on top of your game. In fact," Odell's eyes went around the room and then he said, "I need most everyone here to come outside with George and me. Crump, leave one or two of your techs inside here to guard things. Bradford, give me uniforms at the doors. I even need Doc Kent outside. Especially, Doc Kent because you are a medical doctor trained to perform autopsies. Attention to every detail is your bag."

Doctor Kent nodded and said, "Of course, Lyle. Glad to assist in any way."

Odell continued to explain.

"Thanks, Patrick. As I mentioned, there will be a large crowd of neighbors out there. All them are curious and all of them are gathered around and the press and media will be there, too. I need everyone to observe every person, every detail, and every movement of every person. Crump's photographer will snap away at the entire crowd. Feel free to take photos with your cellphone gizmos if you can. The more the merrier. This is a maximum team effort because of the number of potential suspects we have here. This is a tight-knit community of very intrusive and nosey people. No boundaries with these clowns. The victim was involved with many things; not the least of which was having sexual relations with many of the residents here. The killer might be here right now . . . or maybe not. Perhaps, watching from afar. Perhaps, from a window in this complex. Regardless, this is a vital step in this case. Please . . . I will need everyone to do their best. George will use his big body to plow the road and his booming voice to keep the media off me. I do not want to speak with them but if any of the on-looking neighbors catch my eyes, I might speak with one or two of them. Thank you."

Sergeant Grundy looked at his friend, then he placed his massive hand on Odell's shoulder and said, "Glad to be part of the team, Lyle. Even if I miss out on pizza, beer, and hockey. Of course, I will plow the road for you. Anytime. Whatever this Doc Gilding guy did to get whacked like this, deserved, or underserved, it took one mean son-of-a-bitch or sons-of-bitches, to kill him like that. I am ready."

"Thanks, George. I know you will be ready."

"Ya gonna call Cap Moore now? This Doctor Gilding guy was an important guy . . . kind of famous here in Mohawk City. Chances are the local news, both radio and television are live and, on the air, right now. Reporting live and on the scene type of bullshit. Cap is gonna be watching it, too."

"Nah. I will wait until we get in the patrol car. I will need to use your cellphone. I did not even bring mine. In fact, I am not even sure where it is."

"It's on your end table next to your radio, Odell. Not worth a shit . . . because it ain't even charged. As usual."

Oliver Crump spoke up, and he said, "Odell. Maximum team effort. Sounds familiar. We are a team. Damn good, too. Thank you, Odell. For being . . . Odell."

Odell smiled and nodded.

He then turned and waved to his partner and said, "George. It is almost pizza, Irish whiskey, and beer time. Maybe we can find another hockey game to tune into tonight. C'mon."

"Thank goodness. I am starving."

"George, where is it? Can I have it, or will you keep it?"

George Grundy knew his friend all too well and knew exactly what he was asking for, even if it hit Odell's genius mind so long after Detective Lyle Odell initially thought of it. There were many thoughts colliding in Odell's mind right now. Grundy did not immediately answer, but he just plowed ahead to the steps and the exit.

Eventually, Sergeant George Grundy waved in the air and said, "Lyle, I got ya magnifying lens. Ya not gonna need it for now. I don't want ya poking around at dust on the steps and prolonging this bullshit. I am keeping the lens. Ya can have it back when I take that first sip of cold beer and swallow a bite of delicious pizza. Not a second sooner."

"Okay, George. Cigarettes?"

"Back rear pocket of ya pants. Right side. Not that it means anything to ya, but ya squished them. Again."

CHAPTER THREE

Suspects Everywhere

Sergeant George Grundy waved his arms and stomped his big body, as he indeed, plowed the road in front of Homicide Detective Odell.

"Nothing to see here! Go back to your homes! For the media and the press, Detective Odell has no statements or comments at this time! This is an active crime scene, folks, back away! Police orders. Don't make me tell everyone more than once!"

George Grundy's booming voice echoed throughout the community.

Odell's prediction was correct. There was not only a large crowd of media representatives and the press gathered around on the edges of the crime scene tape wrapped around the entire townhouse end unit, but there had to be at least one-hundred more onlookers standing around the perimeter. Along with Officer Taylor Kane, at least ten uniformed Mohawk City police officers stood watch just outside the crime scene tape, preventing any intrusions beyond the barriers.

As soon as the media and press spotted Homicide Detective Lyle Odell emerge from the doorway of the town house and fall in line behind Sergeant George Grundy, they erupted in shouts of questions hurled toward Odell.

Odell was very well known.

As Officer Bradford said, "He is a legend."

"Detective Odell! Detective Odell! Can you confirm that Doctor Rochester Gilding is dead? Is it a homicide in his own home? Was it a robbery?"

The local beat reporter for the largest television station in the city shouted at the police entourage as they made their way up the front sidewalk leading from the door and porch of Doctor Gilding's townhouse unit.

Another reporter tried to lean in over the crime scene tape as a nearby Mohawk City police officer gently warned him to honor the perimeter.

The reporter shouted, "Detective Odell! C'mon! Give us something! If you are here, then it must be a homicide!"

Sergeant George Grundy grew frustrated with the media and the reporters and the crowd's actions.

He threw his arms up in the air and shouted, "People! Did ya not hear what I just said? Do I have to get ugly here? Calm the hell down!"

Reporters and onlookers nodded and slow silence enveloped the crowd. Grundy commanded a presence. He was that kind of man. Commanding.

The microphones were all turned on, and the cameras rolled to capture the scene. Odell remained stoic and focused, with his head down as he continued to follow Grundy's large footsteps up the path.

While remaining oblivious to the shouts and requests from the media and reporters, and the commands of the good Sergeant Grundy, Homicide Detective Lyle Odell stopped in his tracks. He gently tugged on the arm of George Grundy to signal that he wanted to stop and, much as a combat officer walking point on patrol would do; Odell lifted his hand in the air to signal to the rest of the team to stop. Every member of the team knew what Odell wanted to do; his previous words and requests hit home. Loud and clear.

Detective Lyle Odell looked past the crowd of the media, the press, the lights, and the cameras, and the vans equipped with antennas and communication devices to beam the news back to the studios. His keen eyes focused on the crowd of onlookers gathered in the distance and, if ever a pair of eyes captured details, then the eyes of Detective Lyle Odell did so. His eyes relayed the captured vision to his brain and his eyes narrowed as he calculated, assessed, and analyzed his observations of each person in the crowd.

The rest of the elite team did the same. The C-S-I photographer aimed his camera, zoomed in, and panned out, and he snapped away. Frame after frame. Shot after shot. The clicking sound of the shutter of his camera signaled the frenzy of photographic action. Even Doctor Kent stood and scanned the crowd. At one point, he removed his cellphone from his white doctor's jacket and began to snap away with photos of the crowd, too. The team was on point.

Sergeant George Grundy now stood with his feet spread evenly and squarely on the edge of the sidewalk where the crime scene tape met the edges of the roadway in front of the townhouse units and the entrance to the community. Grundy held his pose with his hands on his hips, as his massive frame blocked the sidewalk and his eyes studied the crowd.

After a few minutes of study, Detective Lyle Odell reached out to Grundy, he pointed to a specific direction with the masses of the crowd, and he spoke in a low voice, "George this way. Please, lead the way."

He had spotted something or someone.

In the haze of his visions and investigations and scanning the crowd for clues, Odell remembered Grundy's assistance with the previous location of his cigarettes; he spoke the words, then found his squished cigarettes in his rear pants pocket, plucked the pack out of his pocket, shook a cigarette loose and stuck it in his mouth.

"Top shirt pocket," Odell said as he pulled his cigarette lighter from his shirt and flicked it to light the cigarette off. After a few heavenly drags, Odell sighed and blew the smoke into the sky. George Grundy smiled as he observed that Odell recalled without his assistance the locations of his cigarettes and his lighter, too.

"You are getting focused now, Lyle. Soon you will not need me."

"Bullshit. I will always need you, George. Let's go this way.

That woman standing on the edge of the grass on the other side of the road. Next to the stop sign. I want to ask her a few questions. The woman . . . who is sobbing her eyes out."

"Oh, yeah, okay, show me, I will keep 'em away from you."

Odell turned and waved to the team and he said, "Doc, Kent. Sarge Crump. Please come with George and me. Bradford and Taylor and the remaining C-S-I techs . . . please stay here and keep observing. Everything."

As the media continued their frenzy and spinning and snapping cameras, and despite the momentarily calm enacted by Sergeant Grundy's threats, they resumed with shouting out ignored and unanswered questions, Detective Lyle Odell led the way through the crowd. Grundy waved the media and onlookers back and warned them to keep their distance. Doctor Kent, Detective Odell, Sergeant Grundy, and Sergeant Crump stood on the edge of the roadway and in front of a young woman who was indeed, as Odell had observed, sobbing her eyes out. She wiped her eyes and nose with a tissue, stood up straighter, and attempted to compose herself as the team stood in front of her. Odell took a long drag on his cigarette and blew the smoke off on the side away from where any persons could encounter it. He then tossed the butt on the ground, snuffed it out under his shoe and picked up the spent butt and stuffed it in his suit jacket pocket. The young woman stood silently while carefully observing Detective Lyle Odell. Her dark eyes studied him and then her eyes traveled to the rest of the men standing there along with Odell.

Her eyes were narrow and black. A very deep black. She was fair-skinned, yet had some features that were obviously Latino in nature. She was short, she wore a heavy overcoat, black jeans, black canvas sneakers and even through the overcoat, a person could see that she had a shapely and attractive female figure. Her face was long, her nose was narrow and nicely shaped and her mouth was pouty; and it was not because of her crying. Her lips were full, well-rounded, and attractive. The young woman was quite attractive and her long black hair shimmered with brown dyed highlights in the late afternoon November sun.

"Hi there. I am sorry for your loss," Detective Lyle Odell said to the young woman.

She nodded and then studied Odell again, as if to ask with her eyes who he exactly was.

"I am Mohawk City Homicide Detective Lyle Odell. This is Sergeant Grundy, Doctor Patrick Kent, and Sergeant Oliver Crump. You are upset and cold. Perhaps you should go home." Odell turned and pointed at the door to the unit right next to Doctor Gilding's unit, and he then turned back to the young woman.

Detective Lyle Odell said, "You live right next door to Doctor Gilding. Nice joint. Not as fancy as Doctor Gilding's joint—but his was the fanciest unit of them all."

She seemed very startled by the fact that Odell knew where she lived!

The young woman touched her neck with her fingers and rubbed it a little and then crossed her ankles as she stood in one place and balanced her weight on her feet. She seemed to ponder the situation for a few seconds before she spoke. The young woman had now regained her composure. Perhaps the shock of Odell's words and knowing where she lived and who she was, helping her to regain her emotions. When she spoke, her words almost came out as a shout.

"Ah! Woah! How did you know that?"

"Well, it was very easy. You are, Ms. Christina Fuentes. Are you not?"

Her black eyes widened, and she shifted her feet and leaned forward just a little. The young woman was assertive. Strong in personality and yet, there was something melancholic about her and fragile, too.

"I am," she said.

The wind blew stronger, and Odell reached up to smooth his hair out a bit. It was an exercise in futility, as his hair was messy and unkept. Odell needed a shave and a haircut; his hair was currently out of the standards for police regulations.

"I am sorry, not at my best today. Or any day, to be honest. The last occupation that a person would think that I worked at was a police detective. In my defense, Grundy and I were hanging out for the weekend together. Watching hockey and drinking beer and whiskey when the call came in about your friend. He was your . . . friend. Was he not? I mean, you were sobbing your eyes out."

Christina blinked and wiped at her eyes with her fingers and answered Odell.

"He was. Rock was a good man and friend."

"Ah, yes. Rock. Cute little nickname. For a . . . friend. So back to how I knew your name and where you lived. Ah, there is a book that we found in the bookcase there in Doctor Gilding's office. A Sherlock Holmes book . . . and this book, as opposed to most of the doctor's books, is a paperback and it stuck out a little in a massive array of magnificent books. Someone did not stick it into the masses properly. It has a sticker on the rear cover with your name and address. Of course, I recognized the address as being the unit next door to his. I scanned the crowd, saw you crying, recognized your features as being Latino and here we are. I am a detective. As was Holmes. The difference is, Holmes is fiction and I am unfortunately non-fiction. Are you Mexican-American in your heritage?"

Christina nodded and said, "I am. I see that you are real and a very impressive detective in your skills." She waved her hands over Odell and said, "Not so much in appearance. You are very sloppy. Yes. I bought that book so Doctor Gilding could teach me about great literature. After all, he is an educator and literary expert."

The wind blew strong, and the temperature dropped. Christina studied Lyle Odell and her eyes went to the rest of the team. She settled back on Odell as she pulled her coat around her tightly and hugged herself.

"Ah, Ms. Fuentes . . . correction . . . he *was* an educator and literary expert. He is dead. As in very dead."

"How did he die, Detective Odell? Was he murdered?"

"I am not the doctor here. Doctor Kent is, but I think Doc Kent would agree that he bled too much. I will leave it at that."

The media erupted as they overheard the words from Detective Odell, and in defiance of a red-faced Sergeant George Grundy, they shouted out questions as the crowd of onlookers sighed in a unified horror. Crump now assisted Grundy, and they both attempted to keep the media quiet and the crowd at bay.

"Thank you for your time and our condolences on the loss of your friend. I gotta ask. Why did you not take your husband's last name? What does the mailbox name state?"

Odell went to turn around and studied the mailbox in front of the units to capture the name, but Christina answered before Odell could speak any words.

"Colombo. I like to keep my family identity. My family is successful in business. Both here and in Mexico. I always want to be my own person. He is Italian and I am not. His family is very wealthy in Italy and his family name carries prestige. Despite my husband's prodding, I remain a Fuentes. I am not into prestige."

"Colombo, huh? Nice name. I like it. Sounds like a solid name for a detective to have."

Odell patted his right-side rear pants pocket. He pulled the squished cigarettes out and shook a single cigarette from the pack and stuck it in his mouth. He offered the pack out in front of Ms. Fuentes and she almost laughed as she waved her hand and negated the offer.

"I do not smoke . . . cigarettes. Even if I did, I would not want one of those. They look like you sat on them."

"Okay. I see. No cigarettes. Maybe some other stuff. Well, you are correct. Thank you for the correct observation. I have sat on them many times. I am going to light this once I walk away. I would not want to blow any smoke up anyone's . . . well, let's just leave it at that. Good day, Ms. Fuentes."

Odell turned on his heels and made his way to the patrol car parked on the side of the unit. He waved to Officer Taylor to indicate that they were ready to leave.

Odell spoke to the group as they walked to where the patrol

cars and official vehicles were parked.

"Please only give me your observations on Ms. Fuentes. We can meet tomorrow for more testimony and to study the photographs of the crowd. For instance, the bulky weightlifter guy with the two bull terriers standing about ten feet away from where Ms. Fuentes stood is rather intriguing. He has the look of a good guy posing as a bad guy. But he is a bad-ass tough guy with keen observations skills. Look at how he has narrowed his eyes and pulled up his face to concentrate on the surrounding persons and the situation. His dogs are the same as he is. Observant. On guard."

As he puffed on his now lit cigarette and the group of police officers and Doctor Kent gathered around the side of the patrol car, Sergeant Crump offered up his first observations.

"Ms. Fuentes is very attractive and does not like her husband too much."

Odell nodded and took another drag as he looked at Doctor Kent.

"Her hands are very small. In my opinion, too tiny to wrap around the handle of that large knife. I agree with Crump in that she is very attractive. Exotic appearance. Difficult to tell, but using my medical skills, I would say she has a full and shapely female figure, not sure about her strength to plunge that knife so deep into a skull bone. I would need to see her arms and muscle tone. It is conceivable. I doubt it, though. Plus, if I understand what the exercise was all about in the office, with the reaching for the book of those of us of various heights and Crump's measurements, then Ms. Fuentes is too short."

Odell exhaled, and the smoke gathered around his head and then drifted off in the wind. He nodded and looked over at Grundy.

"It was difficult for me to concentrate with all this media hounds and crazy nosey-ass people, who I imagine are neighbors. And I am hungry as hell. But I would say that she was romantically involved with the whacked guy in there. I think they had something going. I think she was doin' more than studying great literary classics with old dead Doc Gilding in there. There might have been some study goin' on in there, but it might not have been too much about Holmes tracking down bad guys. All that crying and shit-face of tears. Fuentes shut the emotions down rather quickly when ya began grillin' her. Seems awful intense for the loss of a friend. Don't you agree, Odell?"

Odell took another long drag on the cigarette and then tossed it on the ground, snuffed it out with his shoes and, once more, stuffed it in that same desperate suit jacket pocket.

After he checked his fingers for soot and cigarette ashes and wiped the remains on his pants, Odell went on with an explanation.

"I tend to agree, George, that there was more to it than just book study. Not sure if it reached the physical point yet. Emotional affair for sure. There are many types of affairs, George. Affairs of the heart, affairs of the body, and worse of all, affairs of the soul. She is highly intelligent and likes to use her beauty to her advantage. She plays men like a fine violin. That, my fellow males, as well as law enforcement types and a medical doctor . . . is a dangerous and treacherous woman. Therein lies the source of her unhappiness. Those types of women never are happy because every male is seen as another potential conquest to boost her ego and verify her appeal. I guarantee in her younger years, as a child or a teenager, her father was unsteady and left the family. Anyway, let's get together tomorrow. By then, we can have some autopsy results. My mind will be full of influences from all the Irish whiskey that I am about to indulge in and we can pow-wow. Taylor, please drive Sarge Grundy and me back to my joint. But we will need to stop at the liquor store on the way home. I need some more cancer sticks and some Irish whiskey and beer. George, let's call Captain Moore on the ride back and give him the scoop. Thank you for all you do."

George Grundy huffed a little and then said, "I don't like two things about what you just said, Odell. The fact that you seemed to include me in calling Captain Moore, and two, you never mentioned the pizza we were about to order when the call came in."

◆ ◆ ◆

"Damn disappointed that the Rovers blew that game in overtime. Just like you said, Odell. Why am I not surprised? They came charging back in the third period after giving up the early lead and then blew it in overtime. I am beginning to think that you are some kind of fortuneteller as well as a genius. Honestly, I am more disappointed that we missed it. At least we get another shot tonight. Praying for no calls! This case is enough, Odell. So . . . what is the next move, Odell? What are you thinking? Or should I not ask because you ain't been in the Irish too much yet."

George Grundy asked as he picked up a slice of pizza, stuck it in his mouth and chomped it down. He followed it with a long swig of beer from a frosty mug.

Lyle Odell and George Grundy sat at the table in Odell's dining room and enjoyed their pizza, beers, and Irish whiskey. It was the only table suitable for dining on in the entire house and the only two chairs (they were folding chairs) that Odell owned other than his faithful reclining easy chair that sat next to his favorite spot in the home. His recliner sat next to his end table with his old table radio and the overflowing ashtray of cigarette butts. Odell was freshly showered and shaved and he wore a Mohawk City Police Department collared polo shirt with the police department logo emblazoned on the left side of the shirt near the shoulder. His longish hair was combed and slicked back. Odell actually looked fresh and presentable. That was usually not the case.

"Well, George. That is the beauty of a home-at-home series in hockey. Revenge can be readily available. You should be happy we missed it. Your stomach would be all churned up and you would not be able to eat so much pizza."

"Oh bullshit, Lyle. On that fact, ya wrong-o! Nothing gets

in the way of food for me. Especially pizza. Certainly not our crummy hockey club. I was speaking of the game but also meant about the murder. Or maybe you don't want to share. Yet."

Odell nodded, grabbed the whiskey glass next to his plate that was full of about three fingers of Irish whiskey, lifted it to his lips, and took a gentle sip. After swallowing and placing the glass back on the table, Odell leaned back in his chair and closed his eyes for a few seconds and then opened them as Grundy downed the last bite of his pizza slice and grabbed another one out of the box.

"It's fine, George. I am feeling it a little. A touch of the Irish and a touch of the details of earlier this afternoon. Not too much to go on . . . of course, we will meet tomorrow. I suspect Crump and his team are just wrapping up their C-S-I investigation right now. All the details off to the lab. If I know Crump, and I think that I do know him very well, his dedication will keep him up most of the night writing a preliminary report. I gave Cap Moore some details, and he was satisfied. Captain Moore authorized you to work with me on this case and shelve your patrol sergeant duties for a bit."

"Shit. Of course, he did. Any doubts that he would have? I hope he moves Sarge Hawkins off his ass and off that desk and out on the road. That way, Hawkins will stop buggin' us."

"No. Sergeant O'Malley will ride lead patrol. Any doubts on Cap Moore authorizing you in your assisting me? None. Whatso-ever. Cap Moore is very smart—he knows how valuable you are to the homicide team. He will meet us tomorrow to be part of the team, too. I am now convinced that Ms. Fuentes is the key. The focal point of the case. Not the killer, but the focal point. She was very upset but also very nervous. If you noticed how she touched her neck with her fingers when she first spoke to us and then crossed her ankles and stood straight up as she balanced. Classic signs of a nervous woman. She is not nervous because she is the killer. Instead, she is nervous because she does not want her husband to find out their level of involvement together. Ms. Fuentes is nervous and perhaps filled with some deep regret about what she might have caused and who that she knows is involved in the gruesome homicide."

George swallowed the first bite of his pizza slice and waved his hand in the air and said, "Ha! That is Odell's stuff to notice. I don't know much 'bout that body language stuff. She is a little hottie, though. You still think they were not having sex? Just reading classic books and sipping tea and wine together in innocent meetings on quiet afternoons as he was teaching her 'bout them classic books, and they were being friendly and such?"

"I do. The tea is debatable. The wine is not. Crump can tell us more. That is why I wanted him to give the kitchen a careful check. It was an affair, for sure. Just emotional at the point of his death. Her husband allowed them to be friends and suspected it was on the edge of more. She did not want to elevate it yet. Doctor Gilding did. Ms. Fuentes would have eventually caved in . . . but now it is irrelevant."

Grundy took a long sip of beer and emptied his mug. while Odell studied his friend for a reaction. Odell wanted to hear Grundy's response.

It was obvious that although Sergeant George Grundy pretended to be reluctant to be pulled into Odell cases, he enjoyed it immensely. Grundy was an important member of the team, very intelligent, and street-savvy from his years of police experience, and was not only a trusted friend to Lyle Odell, but a brave and dedicated police officer. Perhaps the most important parts of Sergeant George Grundy's contributions to the homicide team were in his brains combined with his muscle, too. A lethal and effective combination. George might have packed on a few pounds, but he was not a man that a criminal would want to confront physically without weapons in hand. Sergeant Grundy was immense, in size and power.

"I need another beer, Lyle. Ya sticking with the Irish, or do ya want me to grab ya a beer, too?"

Grundy slid out from his chair, picked up his mug, and stood up.

It was glorious beer refill time.

"Sticking with the Irish, George. Thanks."

"So, Fuentes' husband, this Colombo guy, becomes the main suspect. He whacked Doctor Gilding before his wife could jump in bed with the doctor that teaches more than just books. Is that what ya are thinking?"

Odell smiled and leaned into more Irish. The glass was now nearly empty and Odell pleaded with George with his eyes.

"Yeah, I will get the bottle of Irish from the kitchen when I grab my beer."

The two friends were intuitive.

"Thanks, George. It is a remote option. Not a primary one or likely one, though."

Grundy stopped in his tracks—mug in hand. He seemed stunned by Odell's testimony.

"No? Why not? The guy was moving in on his wife!"

"Gilding was and had deep nefarious intentions to sleep with another man's wife. Chances are he had achieved success with countless wives in that community and Fuentes could be another conquest. The husband knew that and as I said, for some reason, allowed the relationship to continue. Regardless, I believe the husband has a solid alibi."

"Now, how the hell do you know that, Odell? Or maybe I should say, oh, okay, and stand here knowing you are right because you are Odell."

Odell downed the remainder of the Irish in the glass.

He set the glass down and said, "The firefighter sticker on the car in the driveway of the Colombo home. The car also has professional firefighter license plates. I believe that car is the car that Ms. Fuentes drives because the license plate has a number two dash on the end. The number two indicates that there is another car with an identical license plate number. Therefore, the number one car is driven by her husband. The number two car is driven by Fuentes. I will need to run it and check it, but I do believe there is a firefighter on the Mohawk City Fire Department with the last name of Colombo. He was not out there with his wife, in the wind, in the cold, with all the multitudes of other busy-body neighbors. So . . . I think he was working on his shift. I suspect they both come from wealthy families. Therefore, they could afford that nice new townhouse unit. He wants to serve and while the firefighters do fairly well on pay and benefits, as we know all too well from our own careers in public service—never gonna be rich. He serves out of honor not for the dough."

Grundy stood and nodded. He seemed a little sad and then spoke.

"Hell, no. Never rich. Damn. Poor guy. A firefighter. The brave and fearless. Risking his ass like we do and his wife is bored, out flirting with this doctor guy. Damn shame. He allowed his wife to flirt and mess around?"

"Yes, George. Ms. Fuentes is the classic femme fetale. Attractive and dangerous. There was a famous song by that rock band a few years ago. The song wailed away with something about an evil woman. She enjoys it. Knows of it and plays it up. Colombo knows it and accepts it because he loves her, he feels he is lucky to have snagged her and married her, and gets to have sex with her when he wants to do so, but knows he can never have her completely because she is never happy nor satisfied. Every man that Fuentes sees or engages with is a potential lover in her eyes and in her heart. It is more than lust. It is a way of life. A game of treacherous conquest to fulfill what she perceives that she missed when she was a child. Every man who falls for her allure ends up sad, hurt, in despair, shaken, worse for the wear, or. . . ."

"In this case . . . dead," Sergeant Grundy said as he finished the sentence for his friend and associate. "If not the husband, then where do we go now, Lyle?"

"George, the suspects are limitless. You saw how many people were out there. Doctor Gilding was not only chasing after Fuentes, because he was a panting dog, a player, a dangerous man, too, in his lust. Let's not put this all on Fuentes. Two can tango. Not to mention his workplace, teeming with female teachers full of attractiveness and potentials."

Odell bowed his head, and he ran his hands through his hair before speaking again. This time, his hair remained steady.

When Odell looked up, he said, "This case is very complex. Too many suspects. Revenge is not just for the home-at-home series in hockey, George. Anyway, let's enjoy our evening. Time slips away. Now, please, the last slice of pizza is yours. I will refill the Irish and you can finish the pizza and enjoy your beers. I will retreat to my chair and tune in my radio. You can slide the folding chair over and join me as we listen together. Great concert on the radio tonight. Irony is a funny thing, my dear friend. Symphony out of Philadelphia and a very talented bunch, they are. Paganini in the 24 caprices. It is op-piece number one, number two section played in B Minor. The piece is based on revenge. So ironic. Composer is Niccolo Paganini. Talented guy."

Grundy just looked at Odell and then he waved at the kitchen.

"I will get the whiskey and the beer. Odell, thanks, but no thanks. Good ole, classic rock and roll is my gig. That classical music bullshit is out of my league. I am going to finish the pizza, suck down a few more beers, call my wife, and hit the hay upstairs. I will leave my cellphone on because I know yours ain't worth a hill of beans. It has been a helluva day."

Odell only nodded and smiled at his friend's words.

Grundy took two steps towards the kitchen, and he stopped and turned.

George said, "I know you will stay in your chair and suck down the rest of the Irish and maybe not solve the case, but by morning, you will get us pointed in the right direction. Good luck, Lyle."

"Yeah, thank you, George. Maybe. Maybe not. Right now, I need the music, the Irish and a cancer stick."

CHAPTER FOUR

Direction

"Odell! Odell! C'mon! Wake the hell up! You called this meeting for nine at police headquarters. It is eight fifteen and I know you have been in the Irish, but you need to get your ass up now!"

Sergeant George Grundy rather desperately shook the shoulders of Detective Lyle Odell for the third time as Odell sat in his chair in the living room of his home. Odell sat amongst an interesting array of a mess at his feet with an empty bottle of Irish whiskey, and two stacks of papers, and a few crinkled-up papers, all randomly tossed on the floor and scattered about at his feet. An overflowing ashtray of spent cigarette butts sat mournfully on the end table next to his chair. The old radio on the end table softly played some classical music. Odell opened his eyes, and he looked around, as if to find his bearings and location. After doing so, he painfully reached over and turned the radio off. The music faded away. Slowly.

Odell spoke almost in a whisper, "I hated to cut that piece off right smack in the middle. But I did so. Wolfgang Amadeus Mozart. Requiem. Irony. It is all so profound. Good morning, George. Coffee? Geez, George, I need coffee. This is a painful morning."

"I have the coffee ready."

"Thank you. Did you sleep well, George?"

"I did. Did you come to any conclusions while floating off on a raft upon a sea of Irish whiskey?"

"Not a damn thing, George. Anxious to hear of the results of Crump's investigation and the autopsy and everyone's observations from yesterday. I cannot put anything into slots until I have more details from them. Otherwise, what came to me last night is conjecture and bullshit. Is your wife having a good time?"

"Yes. Better than I am right now. Trying to get your messy ass up and rolling so we do not have our boss on our ass for being late. For a damn meeting that you called for. Now, get your hungover ass up. Get dressed, get less messy, have coffee, and let's get this day going. We gotta be back for the face-off of the hockey game at seven tonight."

Mohawk City Police Department boasted many qualified and outstanding police officers. Professional officers; dedicated, honest, and hardworking. None surpassed Captain Connor Moore. The captain maintained a squared up, perfect appearance. He was in his mid-forties, his dark skin and perfect complexion as a stalwart and handsome black man did him proud. He was tall, standing well over six feet, and his build revealed his dedication to physical fitness. He had dark brown eyes, and a close-cropped perfect haircut, that kept his preferred hairstyle from his years in the United States Army Reserve. Captain Moore served for over twenty years as a military police officer, reaching the rank of major, and his hairstyle gave him away as being a military man. Captain Connor Moore was a picture-perfect police officer.

Currently, on early Sunday morning at around fifteen minutes after nine o'clock in the morning, Captain Moore paced the floor of the conference room in the police headquarters of the Mohawk City Police Department. He paced several times, then glanced at his watch. Seated in the conference room while Captain Moore paced was Sergeant Oliver Crump and Doctor Patrick Kent from the Mohawk City Coroner's Office.

Captain Moore turned to the men seated at the table and said, "My apologies that Odell is late. I know this is a Sunday morning and you both have better things to do today on your day off. Thank you. Especially your efforts and presence, Doctor Kent. I know you had a long night performing the autopsy on a rushed basis. You are probably very tired."

"It is okay, Captain Moore. I am running on a little empty but I am used to working uneven hours. I am honored that Lyle asked me to be such an integral part of the investigation team. I must admit that even for a detective of Lyle Odell's extraordinary capabilities, this case seems to be very complex."

Captain Connor Moore sighed, and he pulled out the chair at the head of the conference room table and he sunk down into the chair.

"That is what I reported to my chain of command after Odell called me late yesterday afternoon. Of course, they want instant results and clarity and an arrest. Doctor Gilding was a popular man in the city, and this case is very high profile. Now it is on the national news outlets. He comes from a wealthy family of aristocrats that yield tons of political powers and the pressure on our elected officials for a quick arrest and a quieting of the media is immense."

Sergeant Oliver Crump cleared his throat and said, "Cap, as of late, don't all these murder victims seem to be cut from the same mold? Maybe it is the money and influence that gets them whacked. They get into shit that they should avoid."

"True, Sergeant Crump. True. If anyone can solve the case quickly . . . we know that Detective Lyle Odell can. If he ever gets here, that is. He is a genius, the best of the best . . . it is just that he brings some drama and extra rather interesting baggage along with him, too."

Crump laughed and waved his hands in the air and said, "Ya think?"

The door to the conference room opened and the immense frame of Sergeant George Grundy appeared and he plowed through the open door.

As he thumbed with his right hand and right thumb over his head and behind him, George said, "Apologies for being late, sir.

It is all on Odell. I could not get his ass going this morning. He is a hungover mess."

Homicide Detective Lyle Odell wandered in slowly, a few steps behind Sergeant Grundy, who had already made his way to an open seat at the conference room table, pulled the chair out, and landed in the seat with a resounding thud. Everyone turned and looked at Odell, who had stopped a few steps into the room and, as he looked all around the room, Odell leaned back and slowly closed the door. Odell's hair stuck out from his head in many directions. His suit jacket was full of layers of wrinkles. It was the same suit that Odell wore yesterday for the initial investigation at the crime scene. Around Odell's neck hung a wrinkled necktie with the necktie cloth behind his neck hanging stuck over the collar of his shirt, rather than under the collar; the necktie knot was not actually a knot; it was more as if it was a crisscross of the cloth and his necktie hung askew. It was either too short or too long; since everything about Odell seemed to be mired in an unruly untidiness, it was difficult to tell. He held a cup of coffee in his hand and he wore no police badge that was visible. Perhaps it was on his belt somewhere, but even with a careful examination of Odell, a person could not see it or detect it. Odell's eyes continued to wander around the room, and then he studied each person sitting around the table. For some reason, Lyle Odell was capturing details of the room.

He then closed his eyes.

For a minute.

Or maybe it was three minutes, or five minutes or more. Not a single person in the room said a word.

Not a single person even moved a muscle. Or a finger. Or even dared to take a breath.

Odell finally opened his eyes, and he spoke.

"Please do not take Officer Miles Bradford's lack of an invitation to this party as being in any way, or any form, under any conditions that I think he has some nefarious intentions or involvement in this case. Given my past history . . . in other cases . . . that could easily be a conclusion that this team of my fellow officers and associates might jump to. Quite the opposite. I need his observations later. Not sooner. He already has been of great assistance to me, and to us, and to this case. George, please note . . . I think he is a fine police officer to have on your patrol corps."

Sergeant Grundy nodded but did not comment.

Odell closed his eyes once again; this time, only for a few seconds and then he opened them again and said, "All of this madness for the love and attention of a woman. Death, deceit, murder, dishonesty. We miss leisure time off. We work on Sundays, take time from our lives. Time away from our families and friends and the few simple pleasures we have left in this life. Pain. Suffering. Blood and brutality. All because of the dynamics between a woman and man. A woman. An opportune and lust-filled and ego-driven man. It is all so interesting. Repercussions for her actions. Or his? Are there any? Most likely not. Maybe for his? Whom am I to judge that? I guess he now knows the ultimate judgement. Yet, I guess this madness and evil keep us employed. And, so, it goes."

Odell closed his eyes quickly, and then he opened them and blinked a few times before he spoke again.

"Yes, my apologies for the lateness. George is correct on two of the three things he mentioned. Yes, I am the cause of us being late, and I am a mess. He is wrong in that I am not hungover. I actually feel rather well after such an intense study with the assistance of copious amounts of Irish whiskey consumption last night. Rather well."

Captain Moore pointed at Odell and said, "Apology accepted Odell. I am happy to hear that you are feeling rather well this morning. Late as hell, but well. Because we actually are police officers and professionals such as Doctor Kent is . . . let's do a shakedown and checkup from the neck up and down. Do you have your badge on your belt or on your suit, or even with you?"

Odell stopped studying the details of the room and the persons therein and made his way to the open chair next to where Sergeant Grundy sat.

As he walked, Odell he answered, "No, sir and no . . . I do not have my service weapon, either. George has his. I seldom carry my weapon until I must do so. Most of the time, the bad guys give up before I need to do so."

Odell placed his coffee cup on the table. He nodded to Crump and Doctor Kent pulled the chair out and sat in it.

"Not always. But most of the time."

Captain Moore shook his head and commented as Odell tried in vain to smooth out his unruly hair.

"Your hair is not meeting regulations."

"Correct, Captain Moore. Honestly, not too much about me is regulation. I had a haircut on my weekend to-do list. Right now, that list is kind of pushed off to the side because, well, we had this big shot guy with this giant cut in his throat. It interrupted my plans."

Captain Moore persisted in a futile effort to bring Lyle Odell to some type of awareness of what regulations meant to a police detective.

"Your suit is a wrinkled mess and you are a general mess. No one in the world would take you to be a top-notch, world-renowned homicide detective."

"Yes, I agree. Not too sure about the accolades, though. I am a mess and often a drunkard. Most of the time, I am a mess. Sherlock Holmes, though he was fictional, had his influences in order to dig into the case. Cocaine was common in those days. The opium was a rumor and cover for him in the stories. Influences helped him focus. Odell is guilty of the same. I have my Irish whiskey, my music, my sports, my cancer sticks, pizza, and the occasional beer. And I do read quite a bit, too. Regardless, focus is the key here. Me. Lyle Odell, a drunkard, well, only at times. When needed. In my defense, George and I had this weekend off."

Captain Moore twisted his mouth up like a corkscrew and eventually after unraveling his mouth he spoke.

"True. Well, with that noted and out of the way, let's get to it, Lyle. What did your forays into the whiskey tell you last night about his case?"

"As I told Grundy when he asked me the same thing early this morning, not a damn thing, Cap. I mean, I have many parts and pieces, but right now, it is conjecture and bullshit."

"Oh great, Odell. What the hell does that exactly mean?"

"It means that I need many, many details from Crump and Doc Kent and George and you, too."

Captain Moore seemed slightly relieved at the clarification provided by Lyle Odell.

He nodded and said, "Ok. Where do you want to begin, Odell?"

Immediately, Odell stood up and began to pat his suit pockets and his pants pockets as Grundy sighed at his friend's confusion and reactions.

"With my black-covered notebook. I just need to find it."

"I am quite sure that ya left it on the end table next to your old table radio. I was not sure that ya wanted the black one. Otherwise, I would have said something. Yesterday, you were using the blue-covered notebook." Odell scratched the top of his head as he slowly sat back down in the chair.

He tilted his head and said, "Correct, George. The blue-covered notebook is here in my suit jacket pocket. Left side inside pocket. That one is for the crime scene notes. My pensive wandering black-covered notebook is for today. Yet, I am quite sure it does not matter. We can roll without it. I think I have most of what we need in my head. In my memories. When is the funeral, Doctor Kent?"

Doctor Kent answered.

"This upcoming Wednesday."

"Did Doctor Gilding's younger brother come in from Vermont to identify and claim the body? His mother did not come in to view the body, but she was there. Poor woman—she must be close to ninety years old. His father is dead."

"That is correct, Lyle. His brother. . . ."

Odell cut off Doctor Kent and said, "Harold Gilding Junior. Three years younger than Rochester Gilding. His primary mission is in operating the fancy hotel and ski resort outside of

Burlington, Vermont and running and operating various craft breweries in New England. The Gilding family made a fortune in hotels. Thank you, Doctor Kent. Sorry to interrupt you, Patrick. It is just that my thoughts are wandering a bit here."

Doctor Patrick Kent smiled, waved, and said, "It is okay, Odell. Does your mind ever stop wandering?"

"Usually not, Doc. Usually not."

Odell directed his attention to the stacks of folders on the table and the notebooks in front of Doctor Kent and Sergeant Oliver Crump.

Detective Odell waved to them and said, "Crump, thanks for working through the night with your team and gathering everything up and sending what little that you had to send off to the lab. Please do not be discouraged because you feel as if there is almost nothing to go on in this case. Let me guess here, no fingerprints on the murder weapon or the book. Wiped clean. The murder weapon is not an official military issue, but it is a knock-off. An effective, and damn sharp knock-off, but nothing we can trace. Tons of prints throughout the apartment. The housekeeper, the murder victim, assorted other prints, looking as if they are women's fingerprints. And hair. Long hair, medium hair, short hair; however, his housekeeper was very efficient. She would have captured some of that evidence except that her work yesterday hit a drastic interruption of sorts. Many different women and a few men left fingerprints and hair. Very few men, though. You found the condoms and they are in a large box. Maybe half-full. This guy had a lot of action. He used up condoms like I empty whiskey bottles. You did not find any store receipts, but the box has a store price tag on it that we could potentially trace to a local store. You took the bedsheets off his bed and are having them checked for clues, and maybe some DNA blobs. Your team found used condoms in the trash cans. I am guessing it to be two condoms. My idea to search the kitchen came up a bit short—nothing but some breakfast dishes and perhaps some lip marks to be determined as to their origins. Maybe some saliva blobs on a fork or a spoon. Doctor Kent can tell us about his last meal, which I suspect he shared with an early morning lover, or if you choose to do so and label that lover a late-night guest, then please do. The security system, both on the intrusion alarms, the desk alarm button, and on the cameras, were all disabled. Most likely by a professional technician. A technician that knew what he was doing. Not just cut wires and stuff that a clunk-head like I am could do. They trashed the memory and the controller. Drilled holes through the memory chips or something like that. Nothing there. Allegedly, based upon what was on the screen of the laptop, it appeared as if the murder victim was studying a general ledger of financial records on his desk when he was brutally murdered. The blood-soaked papers on his desk are also financial records. Your crime scene experts have the laptop and need more time to go through it. Based upon the measurements and our re-staging of the murderous act, and our use of stand-in models, your study and calculations agree as it appears as if we were correct in that the killer is tall—at least, six-feet-three inches or more and is right-handed, too."

Detective Lyle Odell had his reputation, but so did Sergeant Oliver Crump. Crump was known to be one of the best of the best in the art and professions of crime scene investigation through the State of New York and beyond. After Odell finished speaking, all eyes at the table turned to the crime scene expert. The good Sergeant Oliver Crump's eyes were wide and his mouth was slightly open. His jaw hung down a bit. It seemed as if even though Crump was a seasoned veteran of working with and witnessing the genius of Homicide Detective Lyle Odell, that he was still amazed by his testimony and what appeared to be dead-on insight.

Odell paused in his long comment and he patted his shirt pocket and held his finger up in the air, and quickly darted his eyes over to his friend. It was as if to signal that he knew exactly what he was looking for and did not require Grundy's assistance in discovering the location of what he sought.

Lyle Odell plucked a pack of cigarettes out of his pocket,

he shook one cigarette loose and stuck it in his mouth while mumbling his well-worn words of, "Ain't gonna light it . . . just need to taste it."

Captain Moore shook his head but did not comment. Doctor Kent chuckled and Grundy ignored it. Crump remained wide-eyed.

Odell asked, "Crump, tell me, did I miss anything? Please."

To everyone's amazement, Crump answered, "Yes." Then, as everyone paused and waited, Crump quickly added, "Only two things. Everything else, of course, was spot-on the mark. We found urine in the master bedroom toilet. Whoever used it last forgot to flush. It had some toilet tissue in there, too. Therefore, without jumping to detective conclusions and overstepping our bounds, we guessed it to be a female that last used the toilet. We pulled a sample. It was stone cold. Not fresh, but we pulled a sample, anyway. We also found hair in the shower. Not long hair but medium-length brown hair. The shower was wet in spots. Doctor Gilding had dark black hair, and it was cut very short. I am not jumping to conclusions or making assumptions, Odell, but the hair in combination with the toilet tissue and unflushed urine makes me think a female took an early morning shower there."

The cigarette butt danced on Odell's lower lip as he spoke. "Nice work, Crump. Many thanks to you and your team. I appreciate the all-nighter. I know it was not too much fun. It surprised you because the hair in the shower was medium-length to short and not long hair like Ms. Fuentes' has. Assumptions . . . yes. Tricky business, this is. It is so easy to become sidetracked. Please keep me posted as the results trickle in over the next few days. I hope to nail the killer and have an arrest in hand within four days. Today is day one. So, the timing is critical."

Captain Connor Moore's facial expression changed from gloom to a glow of optimism. Moore excitedly piped into the conversation.

"Odell! That is wonderful news! Only four days! I thought

you said this was a very complex case with a huge number of witnesses?"

"I did, Cap. I did. It is very complex."

Captain Moore had worked with Detective Odell on one previous convoluted homicide case before this, but in the world of Detective Lyle Odell, he was still a bit of a novice to his eccentric ways. His predecessor, the now retired Captain Tucker, was used to Odell, and he had done his best job to prepare Captain Moore as to what he faced with Odell, but Moore still needed to find his way.

While leaving Captain Moore rather speechless and in a mode of deep pondering, the good detective turned his attention to Doctor Kent and asked, "Doc . . . Patrick . . . can we pull DNA from urine?"

Doctor Kent immediately answered.

"Lyle, honestly, it could be difficult. It deteriorates rather quickly. I guess it depends on the timing. Not impossible, but difficult."

The doctor was a superior professional. Approaching sixty years of age now, his hair remained dark black with very little in the way of any visible grey hairs, and the doctor was very handsome, with chiseled features and keen eyes. Just like Detective Lyle Odell—Doctor Kent did not even wear eyeglasses. Both men were in and about the same age. Doctor Kent was as sharp as a tack.

"The hair is, of course, a slam dunk and very easy to extract the DNA from."

Doctor Kent studied Detective Odell for a reaction, but Odell sat silently while staring off over the shoulder of Doctor Kent. He glued his eyes to the windows of the conference room that faced the parking lot. It appeared as if he lost focus or was daydreaming. Suddenly, Odell returned to reality.

He pointed at the booklet sitting on the table in front of Doctor Kent and asked, "Is that the draft of the autopsy report? I know you have had a long night, too. Thank you, Doc. Please, if you can give me the highlights of what you found in the autopsy.

I know we all have put in long hours and I rather not prolong this meeting any longer than necessary."

George Grundy chimed in with a low mumble of, "Amen to that. I am getting hungry. Thinking we might have time to stop at Gulliver's and grab some beers and grilled cheese sandwiches before we head back for the hockey game. Gonna make Odell pay, too. For all this talking bullshit, we must sit through."

Doctor Kent smiled and said, "George. I might just join you for one of those blessed grilled cheese sandwiches. We all deserve to unwind a little after these last fifteen hours or so." Doctor Kent placed his hand on the cover of a booklet sitting on the table in front of him and said, "This is the draft of the autopsy, Detective Odell. I should have the final lab results and the final reports and such by this coming Tuesday."

Odell lifted his right pointy finger and said, "Sorry to interrupt, Doc. Did Harry O'Shea assist you in the procedure?"

"Yes, he did, Lyle. We began the autopsy around eight o'clock last evening. We finished up around three in the morning. Today. I called Harry when we left Doctor Gilding's unit and he met me at the coroner's office."

"Great man. A Saturday evening. Very loyal. Thank you, Patrick. Please continue. Just the main points, please."

Odell, still with the unlit cigarette stuck on his lower lip, closed his eyes and he then slid his backside out on the chair. Continuing in his eccentric methods of study, and concentration, Homicide Detective Lyle Odell then slumped in the chair while clasping his hands and fingers together as if he was praying. He then began drumming his fingers together as he listened to Doctor Kent's testimony.

Doctor Kent opened the book in front of him to the first page but he did not look down to read any of the material or to reference any words as he began to speak of the results of the autopsy.

"Well, your non-medical assessment of Doctor Gilding's manner of death to Ms. Fuentes yesterday was entirely accurate. He bled to death from the very deep throat cut. He died a gruesome death as he bled out rapidly until his heart stopped from a lack of blood. Death was in a matter of minutes. Maybe three minutes at the most. The knife plunged in his skull was merely symbolic—it was not a death blow. The victim did not fight back. It appeared as if he was totally surprised by the attack. The cut throat and the knife in his skull were the only wounds. They were certainly enough. The knife extracted from his head was the knife used to cut his throat, and Odell was correct. It is not an official military-issued knife of fame; however, the knife did a rather efficient job of murdering the victim rather quickly and very painfully. Time of death was around three in the afternoon. Doctor Gilding was in very good health. He was physically fit and very well-built. Very muscular and his cardio-vascular systems were in excellent condition for a man of his age and size. No issues other than some minor arthritis in his fingers. Seemed to be sports related. Perhaps, he broke his fingers playing sports, but his right ring finger knuckle was the worst—it was rather swollen. Odell, you were correct about the herbal supplement. What blood in his body that remained did smell like maple syrup. I need the lab results to confirm the presence . . . of Fenugreek."

Until now, Doctor Kent had not used the draft copy of the autopsy report for reference. He flipped some pages in the report and stuck his finger on a page and said, "Trigonella foenum-graecum. I researched the herb. Primarily, it is used for new mothers to increase breast milk flow. However, it is also used by men to increase blood flow to the male organ for increased sexual activity and enhancement. His last meal was a blueberry muffin and some coffee. Black coffee. That is about it for the highlight and lowlights. Tuesday will provide us with the complete lab results and I will publish my final report then."

Doctor Kent stopped speaking and looked at Odell. The good detective remained in the same position with his eyes closed. If it were not for his fingers drumming together, then you might think he was asleep.

Grundy spoke, as Odell had no reaction.

"How the hell did ya know about that odd-ball stuff, Odell? Although, you are Odell and fifty bajillion other people on this crazy planet are not—so—I might have just asked a stupid question. I mean, we are drinking buds, so I can ask this. Do you use the stuff? This fenny-whatever?"

Odell kept his eyes closed. The unlit cigarette danced upon his lower lip as Odell answered, "Research, George. General research. It is my job and in the best interest of the Mohawk City Police Department for me to know a little bit about many things. No, I do not use it. I have no need for it."

George laughed and said, "Ha! I bet! With a gal like Marlin Santini as ya gal, ya would not need it! She could cure any male sex problem by walking down the street. Ah, sorry . . . for the interruption and bringing up sore spots, Lyle."

Odell smiled widely and nodded his head, but did not open his eyes as George referenced Lyle Odell's former lover and girlfriend. Usually referencing Detective Marlin Santini was a sore point with Odell because they were still very much in love, just star-crossed. If it was any person other than his best friend, Sergeant George Grundy, then Odell might have simply ignored the remark. Instead, Odell shifted gears and his attention back to Doctor Kent.

"Patrick, were you able to detect any recent sexual activity by Doctor Gilding?"

"Once more, I require lab reports, but yes. I think there were remnants of semen on his male organs and in his undergarments. I think he did have sexual relations earlier in that day and had yet to take a shower and wash off."

Odell's eyes lurched open, and they opened wide.

With his eyes now wide open, Odell said, "Not very hygienic, huh? I guess Doctor Gilding had all kinds of action yesterday. Both good and very bad, too. Highs and lows, for sure. Sucks for him."

He plucked the cigarette from his mouth and set it upon the surface of the conference room table.

Captain Moore lifted his eyes and pointed at the cigarette and said, "Not there, Detective Odell. Please. This is New York and smoking is akin to dropping wayward nuclear weapons."

It was obvious that Odell did not want any distractions, so he nodded and plucked the cigarette off the table, and when he did not know where to place it, he handed it off to George Grundy. Grundy shrugged his shoulders, leaned over, and tossed it in a wastebasket behind his chair.

Odell excitedly jumped up in his chair.

"This is wonderful! Fantastic report, Doctor Kent. Please, thank Harry for his dedication. And thank you, Patrick! Very vital information! What a wonderful team we have!"

"I will thank, Harry. We have worked together for many, many years, and yes, I agree that he is very dedicated and capable. You are welcome."

Odell then turned to Sergeant Crump and asked, "Pictures of the crowd gathered in front of the townhouse units, Oliver? The nosey neighbors. Suspects. Countless suspects. Are those in the folder there in front of you?"

Crump answered, "Yes. They are in here. Doc . . . I need your pictures . . . if you took any. Whenever you can send them to me. I know it has been hell the last few hours."

"I took some, Oliver. I will share them to the police cloud tomorrow. In the afternoon. After I sleep. As long as no one else is murdered in our wonderful city of peace and bliss."

"Thanks, Doc."

Crump slid the folder over the surface of the table to Lyle Odell. Odell grabbed them and held his hand over the cover of the folder. As anxious as he was a few moments ago, he now paused before opening the folder. While he closed his eyes with his hand on the folder, Homicide Detective Lyle Odell spoke.

"George. Could I please have that cigarette back?"

"Sure, Odell."

Without any hesitation, Grundy leaned over, plucked the cigarette from the wastebasket, and handed it off to Odell. The good detective opened his eyes. He stuck it in his mouth and hung it on his lower lip.

Captain Connor Moore only shook his head, but he did not say a word.

Odell, now equipped with his trusty cigarette, opened the folder, and poured into the photographic prints of the crowd provided by Sergeant Oliver Crump and his elite C-S-I team. He patted his pockets as he sat in the chair, but lifted a finger in the direction of Sergeant Grundy to indicate that he did not require any assistance to find what it was that he sought.

"Left side inside suit jacket pocket."

Odell produced his folding magnifying glass. He unfolded it, leaned in, and poured over the photographs. For at least fifteen minutes or more, no one in the room said a word while Odell studied one photograph, then a second, then a third, and then a fourth photograph, and then a fifth. Odell then retrieved the third photograph from the folder, and he set the third photograph aside and lifted his eyes to Captain Moore.

"This is such vital information. Thank you, Crump. Vital. Cap. Do we have any markers here? I need a red color. Yellow color. A black color and a blue one?"

"I will see what I can do, Detective Odell."

Knowing the eccentric intricacies of Detective Lyle Odell, Captain Moore rose from his chair and asked, "Are those colors specific? I mean, we are not exactly an office supply house."

Odell removed the cigarette butt from his mouth and held it in his hand, and said, "Yes. Except that purple or pink will work for blue."

Captain Moore disappeared for a few minutes and, while he was absent, Detective Odell continued to pour over the photographs in front of him with his magnifying glass. Captain Moore returned to the room, he walked over to Odell and dropped a handful of markers on the table in front of Lyle Odell and said, "Pink is blue."

Odell grabbed the markers. He nodded, and feverishly went to work. His intensity was amazing, and he scoured each detail of the photos for at least twenty minutes, both with his magnifying glass and without. All the time while he studied the photos, the group remained silent and mesmerized by the detective's actions. Odell messed his hair with his free hand and it stuck out in all directions. He twirled the unlit cigarette hanging on his lips with his fingers. Suddenly, after leaning back in his chair for a few seconds and closing his eyes for the duration, Odell opened his eyes. He took the photographs and the individual markers and madly worked over them, while circling objects and persons within the photographs. After about fifteen minutes, he slid them over to Captain Moore, who had re-assumed his chair at the head of the conference room table, and Odell looked at his commanding officer with the cigarette still dangling precariously from his lower lip. Odell plucked the cigarette from his lips and stuffed it in his shirt pocket without identifying a location.

He turned his head to Captain Moore and said, "Captain Moore . . . sir, I need your assistance. We need the identities and complete information of the people that I circled in the photographs. Black is a low priority. Red is medium. Yellow is high and pink is imperative. For the woman in pink . . . after I speak with her, there is a chance, if she is uncooperative, that I will need a search warrant for her residence. Hopefully, after some questions and discussion, she will be cooperative and helpful. I also might need one for the man in red—with the camera around his neck. Unless he is willing to provide us with the photographs that he took. My apologies, but I also need permission to visit Mohawk City High School Number One tomorrow. I will need to interview the head of maintenance for the school. The facility manager. The person in charge of the operations and maintenance of the school. However, they might choose to title the position. The facility guy or gal knows everything."

"I will see what I can do, Odell."

"Thank you, Captain Moore. Thank you to everyone here. I cannot thank you enough for the extra effort and professional direction you have given to me today and now. It is amazing that within just a few hours, we have a direction. Let's go to Gulliver's

Bar and Grille on the corner of Fifth Street and Main Street in downtown Mohawk City, New York, for some exceptional grilled cheese sandwiches and some assorted libations."

Detective Odell rose from the table, he straightened out his necktie, rather futilely attempted to smooth his hair out and said, "Did anyone else notice it here today? I have been studying it since I arrived and it has bothered me to the point of distraction to where I had to close my eyes to shut it out. Any of us that were in the office yesterday at the scene of the crime with the dead body of Doctor Gilding. The sunlight."

Oliver Crump stood up from the table and he nodded and said, "I did notice. The office in the townhouse faces the west. It was late afternoon. A windy but sunny day. Around five or so in the afternoon when we were all on the site. The victim's time of death was around three in the afternoon. The sun was so strong and bright, yet the laptop screen was facing into the sun."

Odell clapped his hand together and exclaimed, "Exactly! I think the laptop was moved from another location on the desk or even within the townhouse, perhaps, the kitchen countertop, and then staged there by the killer as the victim bled to death. How would Doctor Gilding be able to see the screen in that sun? He would have moved it to the other side of the desk. Why was this done? I do not know. The laptop was open to spreadsheets full of financial files. And the papers on the desk were financial records, too. I need to see what was on that screen at the time of his death and I need to study the papers, too. Did you record the screen shot, Sergeant Crump? Can I view the papers?"

"We did, Detective Odell. The laptop is full of blood, but the crime lab techs can clean it up, and it is, as far as I know, still operational. We can get into the hard drive even if files are deleted. You can view the papers. They are messy, too but viewable."

"Excellent. I am sure we need to wait and see what state that Doctor Gilding's finances are and what was on that screen and on those papers. A mystery for sure. But just for now. Anyway, wonderful observation, Crump. Let's be off to Gulliver's. It will help us all to relax."

Odell took a few steps out of the conference room and he stopped in the hallway as the group all gathered up their folders, the photographs, the papers and reports and supplies.

The good detective stopped in the hallway and then turned and said, "Oh, Cap. Three. I gotta get outside and light and suck on this cancer stick before my head explodes."

With those words, Odell then turned and began to walk down the hallway to the side exit door of police headquarters. Captain Moore shrugged his shoulders and looked at the members of the group, who also shrugged to acknowledge that they too had no idea what Odell meant.

Suddenly, Captain Connor Moore thought hat he had successfully connected the dots in the conversation and yelled out to Odell just before the detective exited the door to smoke his cigarette.

"Oh wow! Three days instead of four, Odell! That is even better news."

Odell stopped and turned, with the cigarette hanging from his lips, and answered his commanding officer.

"Negative. It is still four days. You said before in the conference room that we have a huge number of suspects. We have three suspects, Cap. Three."

CHAPTER FIVE

Suspects Narrowed

Annie, the old, yet, very reliable and efficient bartender at Gulliver's Bar and Grille since forever, dropped fresh beers in front of the Mohawk City Police Department team members and a two-finger-pour of Irish whiskey of his favorite brand sat in an elegant Glen Cairn glass in front of where Detective Lyle Odell sat at the bar. Odell was rather brooding; almost melancholic at this gathering. It did not have the same sweet flavor nor the same celebration demeanor as previous gatherings with this group. Odell sat rather slumped on his barstool with his right hand in his right pocket, as he slowly sipped his whiskey. His sandwich sat on the plate in front of him with only one bite out of it. Sergeant Grundy was already into his second sandwich.

Detective Odell's spirit was far away from the grilled cheese sandwiches and pints of beer and pours of Irish whiskey.

All of the team tip-toed around Odell's pensive behavior. Of course, it was his friend, Sergeant George Grundy, that finally broke the ice with Odell.

"Odell, c'mon man, it is time to relax. Leave the investigation alone for a few hours. Enjoy your sandwich and the drinks and then we will get to watch the hockey game tonight. Ya gotta leave it. Sometimes."

Odell nodded, took his hand out of his pocket, and took a bite of his sandwich.

After he chewed and swallowed, Odell commented, "I am fine, George, just thinking about one particular angle."

"What's that?"

"Which of those persons that I circled with markers will the killer want to try to murder next?"

Sergeant George Grundy almost spit his recent sip of beer out as he quickly swallowed and loudly asked, "What? Are you kidding us?"

Detective Lyle Odell narrowed his eyes and said, "George, I wish that I was. The trouble with humankind is that there is a tiny percentage of humans that harbor nefarious intentions. Unfortunately, and sadly, for us, that percentage keeps us employed."

◆ ◆ ◆

"Captain Moore called me while I was out. He has the persons identified that you circled in those photos. You were deep in thought last night, both during the game and afterwards. I did not want to bug ya ass too much. I am curious. There were four people that ya circled in those photos, but ya told us there were only three suspects. Are those not all suspects?"

"Correct. They are not all suspects, but they are all involved in some way. I can tell by their facial expressions, their body languages and where they stood in relation to Ms. Fuentes."

"Shit. Ya, something else. Must be damn near fifty people in those photos, and ya pick out four."

"Yes, four, George. Including, Fuentes."

"Right. Including, Fuentes. Here, I went down to the corner store for coffee."

George Grundy handed his friend a piping hot container of fresh coffee.

"Thanks, George.

"I guess a split on the home-at-home was better than expected. Boston has the best record in the league. Have to admit that I did not expect to find you up and at 'em and dressed and ready so early. You fell asleep in your chair right after the hockey game and were still asleep when I left for the coffee run. Say, Odell, I am a little short on dough. Those damn student-parent loans. Do you have some dough for the coffee and the honey buns?"

"Yes. Of course. You know where it is. My coffee and beer money. I keep it in the metal coffee can. You remember, right? The can that is in the cupboard in the kitchen. The right side, directly above the coffeemaker and to the left of the stove."

"Oh yeah, I gotcha. Okay, thanks," Grundy said. He then began to dig around in the paper bag from the corner store and pulled out a large honey bun. He took a bite of it and pointed at the bag, which he now placed on the end table next to Odell's chair, and said, "There is one in there for you, too. Ya have not eaten much as of late. Only a few bites of the grilled cheese and one slice of pizza last night. This case has you in knots. Ya did not get bombed last night. What's up with that, Lyle?"

Lyle Odell took a sip of the coffee and set it down on the end table next to the paper bag.

"Maybe—I need to change my ways. Not getting any younger. Captain Moore is right. I need a haircut. Friday. I will get a haircut on Friday. George, I have my badge, but I am not going to wear my weapon. Please make sure you are armed and ready."

"I am, Lyle. Are you expecting action?"

"Ya never know. Not likely . . . but ya never know. We need to stop at headquarters and pick up the information and Officer Bradford. Cap Moore allowed me to steal him from your patrol corps. I would have asked you, but you would just tell me to go to Captain Moore because you do not want to do the paperwork." Grundy shrugged and took the last bite of his honey bun and a sip of coffee.

"Yup. Correct on that one, Odell. Damn paperwork sucks. It is all okay, by me. He seems like a solid guy. Never gives me any bullshit or adventures. Ya gonna eat that bun or can I, have it?"

"It's got your name all over it, Sarge Grundy."

"Bradford, you met your wife in college, huh?"

Officer Miles Bradford was driving the patrol car with Sergeant George Grundy in the front seat and Homicide Detective Lyle Odell sat in the back seat of the police vehicle.

Bradford lifted his eyes to look at Odell in the rear-view mirror and answered.

"Yes. How the hell did you know that, Detective Odell?"

"Pfffttt!" Grundy snarled from the front seat. "Bradford, I know this is your first roll with Odell, but ya got to know that he knows everything. He probably knows ya waist size." Grundy spoke the words and then he spun his head around and pointed at Odell in the back seat and said, "Don't mention mine or the next pizza and beers and grilled cheese sandwiches are all on your tab, Lyle!"

"Before or after those two honey buns? By the way, I paid for everything all weekend, George. Remember your student loans for parents? Still paying them suckers off, George. Otherwise, you would be retired and not having this much fun."

"Damn parent-student loans. Fun? Huh?" Grundy mumbled.

"Bradford, honestly, I did not know. It was purely a guess based on the university's ring that you wear. That school is in Newark, New Jersey. Highest population of Dominican Republic folks in all of the American cities. Newark, Jersey City, Paterson. Dominican havens."

"Correct. We met in senior year. We married three years later and moved here to Sin City to be close to her parents. Her dad was sick at the time. He is better now. We would have stayed in Jersey, but it worked out okay. Mohawk City kind of sucks, but it is okay. For now. I nailed this job out of college, no military, just a criminal justice degree, and here we are. Next up is kids. We are running out of time. We are both thirty-seven years old now."

"You have time, Bradford. Just stay safe. Glad your wife's father is better. Sorry you got stuck in this horrible old city. However, it does have job security for police officers. What are your thoughts on the persons that I picked out of the crowd from yesterday? I respect your thoughts and observations and wanted to ask you separate from the rest of the team."

Officer Miles Bradford was very animated in his mannerisms and speech and he began a long explanation without much pause.

"Thank you. First off. I really and truly appreciate the opportunity to ride with you guys on this case. It is an opportunity to learn about detective work. I always was interested in being a detective. Just being honest because I am not sure I have the aptitude for it. We are going to see and interview Mr. Larry Hicks. The blockhead, muscle-bound dude with the aggressive bull terriers. The defiant guy standing with his arms folded across his mighty chest while holding the two leashes while standing behind Ms. Fuentes and next to the very pretty woman with the medium-length brown hair. Fuentes is marked in yellow and the small Asian guy is circled in red. Curious that you circled this muscleman in black and the woman in pink."

Bradford paused for a few moments and once more, lifted his eyes to check on Odell in the rear-view mirror. When Odell did not comment or react and neither did Grundy, Officer Bradford continued his thoughts.

"Mr. Hicks is a low priority, and she is a high priority. This guy looks like he hates everything and everyone. Everyone else is freezing to death and wearing coats and hats, and this guy is wearing a muscle shirt. I mean, why the hell do you have to bring your two killer dogs out there, too? Just to snarl at people and show how tough you are? The guy strikes me as a big-time idiot and he is my number one suspect. No offense, Odell. Obviously, I am not the detective here and have a lot to learn. He certainly had the strength to plunge that knife into the skull of Doctor Gilding, and he is tall, if your theory on the windup and pitch and plunge from behind is correct. And we now know that he is an ex-police officer. Kicked off some small-town police force on Long Island for being too insubordinate and too many verified instances of angry outbursts and some brutality. Now, he manages the late shift at a weightlifting gym downtown where he can display his muscles and be a general jerk."

Odell was obviously anxious and excited at the observations and long explanation of Officer Miles Bradford. He answered directly and immediately.

"Excellent assessment, Miles. Impressive. However, not everything is what it appears on the surface. Be careful about making pre-judgements. The muscle-bound guy might not be as he seems. At least on the surface. We need to investigate everything very thoroughly. Be cautious but investigative. The woman with the medium-length hair, Ms. Maguire, was supposed to be blue. Cap Moore only had pink markers. No blue. I suspect that Ms. Kathleen Maguire is the muscleman's love interest. They are on and off lovers. She is in pink because Doctor Gilding was also Ms. Maguire's lover and her primary sexual partner on multiple trysts. In fact, I am sure they were together and having sex all night and in the early morning on the day of his death Additionally, I believe they were deeply involved in other iffy business laced with nefarious intentions of a different order. Time will tell. That is an investigation for down the road. Her DNA will match the hair in the shower that Crump's team found and, if it is possible, to confirm, it is her urine in the toilet. Perhaps the condom will yield some interesting DNA, but, again, time will tell. Detective work requires patience."

Mohawk City Homicide Detective Lyle Odell's eyes glanced out the window of the police patrol car and they widened just before he spoke once again.

"Here we are. Men, please keep your nerves steady and weapons holstered but at the ready. Be cautious. In theory, and based upon our initial observations, Mr. Hicks is an angry man and between him and his dogs, it would be a handful to control him. He is an unlit fuse of explosives that just needs a match. If it turns violent, then please, I will bring him down on my own. I know he is a former police officer and professionally trained. However, muscle-bound guys always succumb to throat blows. I do not have my weapon with me and I would rather not kill him, but it is a possibility if he attacks and is uncontrollable. Yet, please, keep in mind . . . not everything is as it appears during the initial observations. Mr. Hicks could actually be a good guy. Sometimes, you need to make calculated moves based upon observations. Not based upon assumptions. Let's find out."

Officer Bradford looked at Sergeant Grundy, who nodded in acknowledgement of Detective Odell's request.

The massive and imposing police sergeant mumbled, "Well, just in case he is a bad guy then I will say, just light that fuse, big guy, and you will see what happens."

Grundy then waved and motioned for the team to move out of the car. While Grundy opened the door of the patrol car, he stood up and unclipped the leather latch on his holster holding his service weapon. Officer Bradford did the same as his sergeant did, and the two police officers scanned the driveway and the property, which was about five doors away from Doctor Gilding's end unit. They were on full alert. Detective Odell opened the door and stumbled out of the vehicle. His suit was the same suit that he wore for the last three days, and his shirt fell out of his waistline. His hair was messy, and he stuck a twisted cigarette in his mouth as he exited the car.

"Just got to taste it," Odell mumbled as the team made their way up the walkway to the front door of the Townhouse unit. "Let me walk the point, men. Chances are he is watching out the windows and would have shot already if he had nefarious intentions. Of which I think he does not. I have been wrong before, though."

When the team was about halfway up the walkway, with Detective Odell in front leading the way and Grundy on his right wing and Officer Bradford on Odell's left, the front door to the townhouse unit violently swung open and Mr. Larry Hicks appeared in the doorway. He was a large and powerful man; his hair was shaved high and tight, his face shaved perfectly clean, he wore a tee shirt cut off at the shoulders to display his bulging muscles, a pair of black side zip military boots, black jeans, and most of all, he had a scowl on his face. A mile wide scowl. Mr.

Hicks crossed his arms in a letter X across his mighty chest as an indication that he was unarmed. Men such as Mr. Larry Hicks are, do not put their arms and hands up; they cross their mighty chests.

Officer Bradford and Sergeant Grundy both abruptly paused in their walk and poised with their hands on their weapons as they quickly and professionally assessed the posture and intentions of Mr. Hicks. Odell plowed onward, with the cigarette stuck on his lower lip and his eyes intent upon the man in the doorway.

"Relax, Sarge Grundy, and officer, whoever the hell you are. I don't have any weapons. I mean, I do, but they are locked up. My dogs are locked up, too. Otherwise, they would tear your asses out."

"I highly doubt that, Mr. Hicks. Dogs generally like me," Detective Odell said as he now stood about five feet in front of Hicks as the large man loomed in the doorway.

Hicks was large and aggressive in nature, but when his eyes wandered over Sergeant Grundy, it was obvious that Mr. Hicks respected the size and power displayed by Grundy. Officer Miles Bradford was tall, and muscular but was somehow, less imposing, yet he displayed a quiet confidence.

Hicks growled, "Well, I don't like you, Detective Odell."

"Stand in line, Mr. Hicks. Dogs like me, but most people don't like me. Some of those people are dead and pushing up daisies because they were evil, some are in jail, because they are evil and captured, and some are alive and very pleasant and good persons; who just don't like me. I am not in the business of having people like me—I am in the business of justice."

"You are everything that I despise in a police officer. Especially for a homicide detective. Look at you. You look like a drunken bum who just crawled out of a garbage can."

Odell nodded and said, "I cannot disagree with your statement. That is a very fair assessment of my appearance, Mr. Hicks. Quite fair, indeed."

As everyone watched, Odell plucked the unlit cigarette out of his mouth and stuffed it in his suit jacket pocket while mumbling, "Right side suit jacket pocket."

Larry Hicks growled out some more words.

"Sure . . . you are a legend in homicide detective circles, but you represent everything I despise about sloppy and unprofessional police officers. I was picture-perfect. Always regulation, my uniform was always perfect, boots polished, squared up and professional. I captured the bad guys and made them all pay the price for their crimes. Those stupid ass politicians posing as police officers still canned my ass. In the end, I was proven right, and they were wrong. They had to pay my ass with tons of dough when I won the wrongful discharge lawsuit."

Grundy waved in the air and said, "Beating the hell out of bad and good guys usually is frowned upon, Hicks. We read your record. You have some major anger issues. Look at how you are acting now."

Hicks waved the air and dismissed Grundy's statement. "Sarge, the record ain't all accurate . . . most it is bullshit, but whatever. A stacked deck against me because one or two of the bad guys got out of line and I laid a little lick on their asses. Internal affairs got it all wrong. It was self-defense and the jury agreed with me. Come on in and ask me what you need to ask me and then get the hell out of my house and life. I know Odell here picked me out of the crowd. He is a genius and reads body language and how I stood and acted. I was a cop and worked with detectives before. I know how it works. C'mon in. As you can see, I am doing quite well for myself since I left police work. That dough they paid out worked in my favor."

The townhouse unit was a middle unit, in another section from the affluent and sprawling end unit that Doctor Gilding lived in, yet it was furnished nicely and very comfortable and in Mr. Hick's mind and many other's minds, it was expensive and the equivalent of living the high life.

A beer mug filled with an overflowing dose of beer sat on an end table in the living room and Mr. Hicks pointed at it, smiled, and said, "I would offer you a beer, but you are all on duty.

Although, with Odell here, that does not much matter. I heard all the stories about you. The great drunken detective and he brings along his muscles to handle a potential uprising of the big and mean ex-cop Larry Hicks."

Odell ran his fingers through his messy hair and smiled back.

With the smile still lingering on his face, Odell said, "And most of those stories are true. If it was a glass of Irish whiskey, I might just take you up on that offer." Odell turned to Officer Bradford and said, "Please, Bradford . . . take some notes. Thank you." He then turned back to Mr. Hicks and said, "Lookie, here Hicks, I would love to stand here and trade insults with you for a few more minutes while you expel your bitterness with police work and your failures and bad deals and dealings with clueless idiots in a past career, but let's get to it here. Please tell us what you know about Doctor Gilding. Did you cross paths with him at all in the complex?"

"Ha! I can tell you that I did not kill him. I sure would have liked to kill him, but I didn't. Love to shake the hand of the person who did so . . . but I did not kill him."

"Interesting," Odell said, as he patted his right suit jacket pocket and extracted the now bent cigarette butt and stuck it back on his lower lip. "Ain't gonna smoke it, Hicks. Just need to taste it. So, suddenly you want to reward the bad guys and gals that you just previously said you enjoyed beating the hell out and locking up? What was it you said, make them pay the prices for their crimes? Now, you want to shake hands with a killer or killers? Quite the flip-flop, Mr. Hicks."

Hicks laughed again and this time, he ran his hand over the top of his shaved head, took a few steps over to the end table and picked up his beer mug and took a long sip. He set the mug back down on the end table and smacked his lips. "Love a good beer buzz in the morning. Except that I worked all night, so this is actually afternoon. You played on my words, Odell. You are a tricky one. I fell into that, but as I said, I did not kill him and honestly, I have nothing to hide. What I mean is that I am happy that son-of-a-bitch is dead and ended up with a knife stuck in his skull and a cut throat. He was a smug, wealthy, money bully whose main objection was to bed and have sex with every woman he crossed paths with. He was an evil sexual predator and if I was still in police work, then I would make it my God-honest mission to lock his ass up on some charge so he could not harm another woman. Emotionally or physically. From what I know, he damn nearly was successful, in bedding every woman he knew, too. Including my own gal. I am sure he had a romp or two or three or more with her. Although, she denies it."

"Ya married, Hicks? I don't see any wedding ring, or looking around here, signs of a womanly touch. It seems very manly in décor," Sergeant George Grundy said as he pointed at the room and then focused upon the sports logos of professional sports teams on the walls, and photographs of gym rats and muscle builders and weight rooms.

"Nice observations, Sarge Grundy. Nope, I am a typical angry cop. Divorced. Ten years ago. She hated me being a cop. But I have a chick that I am dating heavily."

He spoke and intuitively because his past life as a police officer, looked at Officer Bradford, who looked up from his notes and asked, "Her name?"

Mr. Hicks had correctly identified Officer Bradford as the detailer of events during the investigation.

"Sure. You are gonna find out, anyway. Kathleen Maguire. She lives in the far outskirts of the complex, but not in the high rent district. Per se. We have been heavy for two years and suddenly, doctor-screw-a-lot moved in and she became all fluttery, as all the women here do when he waltzed in, all charming and handsome and shit. I don't like sharing my woman. And a man can tell when their woman is throwing her love around and it is not a good feeling."

Hicks took another sip of his beer, and, with the mug in his hand, he waved in the direction of Detective Odell and said, "You have your work cut out for you on this one, Odell. Ain't a man living in here that liked that guy and some women, too. I suspect some gals here bat from both sides of the plate, if you know what I mean. Especially, the husbands and the boyfriends hated Doctor Gilding. That one gal. The pretty Mexican chick. Fuentes. Married to the firefighter guy. She flirted with every man around, and especially with Doctor Gilding. Big time, you-know-what teaser, she is. Flashing her smile and her curvy body. Always over there, with his so-called reading circle of friends. Bet her husband will tell you the same thing that I just did. Glad he is dead. Could not happen to a more deserving son-of-a-bitch. Honest."

Hicks held the near empty beer mug in his hand and studied Detective Lyle Odell. Odell took the cigarette out of his mouth and held it for a few seconds, then he stuck it back on his lip.

"On the surface, I see nothing wrong with a reading circle. After all, the guy was an educator. His doctorate was in literary works. Education and culture are wonderful things. On the surface. We met Ms. Fuentes, and she is a charmer. For sure. Tell me about that reading circle, Hicks. Did your gal attend?"

"Hell no! She never reads. Unless reading the labels of wine bottles counts as reading. The reading group met a couple of times per week. Not exactly sure on what days. The reading circle was made up of mostly women from the complex. Of course, women to meet, impress with his amazing education and knowledge and then charm them into his bed. Fuentes was always there, a few young guys, maybe from the high school where he worked, or the local college and some teachers from the school. One teacher is a knockout, Odell. Tall, redhead, magnificent chest, tight skirts. Doctor bed-a-lot must have drooled over her. Oh yeah, you're gonna want to check out the high school. That was another potential resource of women for the good doc to bed down with. Ha! Oh yeah, Odell, good luck with all of this. You are gonna strike out on this one. Too many suspects for even the great Odell to sort out."

"Thank you for the vote of confidence, Hicks. Tell me, other than Ms. Fuentes and the redheaded teacher, would you be able to identify any of the members of the reading circle?"

"I can tell you that my neighbor here, Charlie Aki, was always over there. Aki lives two doors down from me. He is Japanese and always has a camera around his neck. Nosey guy. A big busybody in everyone's business. Kind of a nerd, but I hear he takes great photos. As far as the other persons go . . . maybe. From photos, yes. Not without."

"How tall are you? How tall is your gal? Ms. Kathleen Maguire."

"I am six feet three inches. Kathy is 'bout five-eight or so. She has a lot of curves and great breasts."

"Gotcha. A little too much information there, but thank you. Congratulations on having a gal with curves and great breasts. Speaking of curves and breasts, did Fuentes flirt with you, Hicks?"

"Hell, yeah! Never took her up on anything. I don't mess with married women. And even if she was not married—I would steer clear of her. Trouble in the end. She is all about disappointment and heartbreak. She flirts and plays every man. She is a player and a tease. Fuentes even hangs out with some of the young guys from the reading circle. I think they are college guys. Immature punks and dopey young college guys and they drool over Fuentes, while playing with their skateboards, and making believe that they enjoy books. One day, one of the punks had something to say when I was speaking to Fuentes when I was walking my dogs and ran into her as he pulled up with another guy in front of her unit. He was in the passenger seat and he wanted to jump out of the car and try to beat my ass. Ha! He was out of his mind with rage. Guy has it bad for Fuentes and the punk is out of his mind. Angry guy. Very violent. I set him straight really quick. Young punk—told him I would clean his clock so quick he would never know what the hell hit him. She is exhausting to watch as she works them and plays them like a fine violin. If I was her man, I would set her ass straight. You are either in or out, baby. Your choice. Her poor man works all the time. He is a firefighter. A good guy working the shifts. You guys know the drill. He is out there risking his ass and she is out playing the games. Not cool. At all."

Odell nodded and asked, "Do you set your gal straight? I mean, are you two exclusively dating each other?"

"Nah, not exclusive. I mean, I try to control her and get really serious because I do care 'bout her, but she don't want to commit."

"Gotcha, Hicks. Thank you."

Odell pointed at Hick's beer mug and said, "It is almost empty. Time for a refill. One last question and with you being an ex-cop, you know what it is, Hicks."

Mr. Larry Hicks nodded and took the last sip of beer and set the mug down on the end table.

"Yup. Alibi. Where was I when Doctor Bed-A-Lot got whacked? I know the drill. I was here the entire time until I went to work for the late shift and left around eleven-forty-five or so. I usually work two weeks on nights. Two weeks on days. I am on nights for another week. I was here alone, so I have a shitty alibi, Odell. The only time I left was for a beer and cigar run to the big beer and wine and cigar warehouse out on Broad Street. Left around two or so, back here by three or so. I have a receipt with the date and time if you wanna see it. Generally, keep all my store receipts. They pack and stack the joint with cameras, and I am, obviously because of my appearance, very recognizable. The manager knows me and he waved to me. He will vouch for me. Like I said, I got nothing to hide, Odell. Not sure of the exact time that Doctor Diddler got whacked, but that is all I got. Other than that, I was here. Drinking beer. Smoking cigars, hanging with my dogs, and watching the mindless boob tube. Kathleen was working, so she was not around. We only get to see each other when I work days."

Odell nodded, and he extended his hand out to Larry Hicks and said, "Thanks, Hicks. We will let you go now. You have been very helpful. We will be in touch. Go get a refill there and let your doggies out of lockdown before they eat your curtains and furniture in that back room. We can let ourselves out."

Odell waved to his team; Officer Bradford nodded in the direction of Mr. Hicks, as did Sergeant Grundy. Odell took a few steps to the door and stopped and turned and faced Mr. Larry

Hicks. Odell took the cigarette out of mouth and held it in his hand while he spoke.

"Say there, Hicks. Ya ought to consider losing the anger and getting back to police work. Admit ya a little angry and uptight, but I can tell that you were a good cop. A very good cop. They played you. You won your case and proved them wrong. Water under the bridge so to speak. We could use you here in Mohawk City. By the way, I didn't need it."

Hicks narrowed his eyes as if he did not follow the conversation. After some thought, he said, "Thanks, Odell. I think that I was an excellent cop. So did a few others. Circumstances sometimes suck. I will consider your suggestion. But what the hell do you mean you didn't need it?"

"The muscle. I don't need the muscle. I could handle you on my own."

Hicks smiled and said, "Ya sure 'bout that, Odell?"

"Positive. Ya big, strong, and tough, but never underestimate an old Coast Guard man. We fool you. Our basic training makes the Marine Corps basic training look like a walk in the park on a bright spring day. Be seeing ya around, Hicks. Head up. Powder dry. The killer, who, by the way, is not you, might strike again. Now . . . I gotta light this cancer stick up."

Hicks nodded, waved, and smiled as he said, "Thanks, Odell. For the warnings and for the advice."

The three police officers left.

Odell stood on the stoop and patted every pocket on his person, then looked at Grundy for advice.

"Top shirt pocket, Odell."

Lyle Odell nodded and plucked the lighter from the confines of the shirt pocket, struck off the light and leaned into the flame while he sucked on his cigarette. He exhaled the glorious smoke into the air and leaned back as he handed the lighter off to George Grundy.

"Here, George. Please hold this for a bit."

Odell closed his eyes while he smoked the cigarette and stood on the stoop of the townhouse owned by Mr. Larry Hicks.

After a few puffs and exhales, he opened his eyes and asked, "Bradford, did you get all of that down? Do you have the address for where Kathleen Maguire works?"

Officer Bradford first looked at his notepad, which he still held in his hand, and he tapped the cover of it and said, "Check and check. Is that where we are going, Detective Odell? To her workplace?"

Odell took one last drag on the cigarette and he exhaled the smoke and then tossed it on the concrete path. He snuffed it out with his shoe, then reached down and picked up the butt and placed it in his suit jacket pocket.

"Go right in here with the rest of your buddies," Odell mumbled.

"Negative on Maguire. For now. But I do have some missions for you. First, I need to know the miles from Maguire's workplace to this complex, Bradford. Second, I need you to contact Sergeant Crump and ask him to work on checking out that local store where Doctor Gilding shopped for the condoms. See if the manager will pull the video for that day and time. I need to confirm something. Can you have that information and do that for me? I also need to interview the housekeeper. Not today, maybe tomorrow. So, I need your translation skills."

"I am on it, Detective Odell."

"George, can you check with Cap Moore and see if we are clear to land right now at the high school to speak with the facility guy?"

"Ya got it, Lyle. Ya wanna check out the tall redhead, huh?"

"Yes, and a few other things. Hicks is innocent of murder, but he is a wealth of information and mountains of courage within his soul. He is very valuable to this mission and future missions, too. He is a good guy. Once a cop always a cop—for the most part. We just narrowed our suspects down. Considerably."

The three men made their way to the patrol car as Grundy made a phone call on his cell phone.

On the way down the pathway, Officer Bradford asked Detective Odell, "Detective, you were in the Coast Guard?"

"Yes, I was. Almost twenty years. I was a warrant officer. A charlie, whiskey, oscar figure four."

"What did you do?"

"Investigations, Bradford. Investigations."

CHAPTER SIX

Always Interesting

"Nice to meet you, Detective Odell, and your fellow police officers. Heard a lot 'bout you, Odell. Everyone here has. You are a legend in this crummy old city. A legend. Let's go out on the back loading dock and speak. Fewer ears. Fewer eyes. Although, for strategic reasons, I have the security camera shut down over the dock. For now. I like to steal a puff or two on a cigar out here or in the boiler room without having people freak out and keel over from fears of secondhand smoke. Damn, if they ever knew what was lurking within the ductwork here in this joint, they would faint. Feel free to smoke if ya have 'em. I will turn the security camera back on when we are done here. I figure the school, teachers, and students, are safe with three police officers and my old tough ass here."

Mr. Chester Winslow walked with a decided limp and an arched back. He was the lead maintenance person for the Mohawk City High School Number One. He had just a wisp of white hair left on his head, gentle blue eyes, and a bit of sorrow on his face. His hands were gnarled and bent from a lifetime of mopping and waxing floors and wrestling with boilers and plumbing and electrical troubles.

"Please, pull up a few milk crates here. Best I have to offer. They are rather comfortable to sit on. Your ass eventually conforms and accepts the plastic edges and grates. The dairy guy leaves 'em here for the milk deliveries. I often sit here and catch some air and steal a smoke or two. Love the cold. Hope it does not bother you guys."

All of the police team joined Mr. Winslow and pulled up milk crates to sit on.

After sitting, Detective Odell spoke first.

"We are good, Mr. Winslow. The cold makes me whole. Sergeant George Grundy has lots of padding and he is generally impervious to most outside influences, and Officer Bradford has his vest on. Appreciate the time and the milk crates. Nice spot you have here. How long have you been maintaining the school here?"

"Small talk. Impressive tactic. Look, I know why you are here. Doctor Gilding got murdered with a knife in his head and the maintenance guy knows everything. Very true. We do know all the secrets and you are a very smart guy to recognize that. I will help you any way that I can do so. To answer your question. Thirty-two years next month. Started right before Christmas. Thirty-two years ago. Seems like a blur in time. In between, I got very old, my wife died, and I managed to get prostate cancer. I am gonna make it. Gonna work until I am dead or they push my old ass out. What the hell else is there to do for you when you get old? When you lose your purpose in life then you lose your will to live. I have to work. I love what I do. That is a guarantee that I will make it, Detective Odell. A guarantee. For sure."

Odell nodded.

Lyle Odell plucked a pack of crushed cigarettes from his pocket (without any location assistance from Grundy) and shook one smoke loose from the pack, stuck it in his mouth, and looked over to Mr. Winslow for permission to light the cigarette up.

"Go ahead, Detective Odell. As I said, the security camera is shut off."

"Thank you," Odell said.

Grundy plucked the lighter from his shirt and lit the cigarette for Odell.

Odell drew a long drag on the smoke.

The good detective said, "I am sorry about your situation and the loss of your wife. I agree that you will persevere. Your first name in Latin means fortress . . . a walled town. You are a tough guy."

Mr. Winslow said, "Don't know shit about Latin, but I will take your word for it. Look here, Detective Odell. Please don't be concerned. When you are very lucky in life and you live to my age, you look back and realize that you have been working on dying for a very long time."

Homicide Detective Lyle Odell nodded, and he almost smiled, but the smile never arrived at his lips. It was obvious that Odell enjoyed the meeting with Mr. Chester Winslow and he admired the man's genuine toughness and intelligence.

While the small group remained in silence, Odell took about five drags on the cigarette in his mouth. After the last drag, Odell pursed his lips and exhaled a cloud of smoke. After the smoke dissipated, Odell studied the cigarette in his hand. He tossed it on the concrete surface of the loading dock, and he ground it out underneath the scuffed shoe on his foot. Odell reached down and picked up the expired butt, and stuffed it in his suit jacket pocket. Right-hand side.

That butt, in unheralded glory, joined the rather dubious collection already living in the same pocket.

Odell looked up at Chester Winslow, and mumbled, "Haven't we all?"

"Yes, we have."

"Mr. Winslow. . . ."

"Call mc, Chester. Please."

Odell paused, smiled, and said, "Officer Bradford. Notes, please." Then he turned his attention back to Mr. Winslow and said, "Chester. What did you think of Doctor Rochester Gilding?"

Without any hesitation, Chester Winslow answered the question.

"He was a rich-boy-pompous-entitled jerk. All he thought about was smiling and seeing which female teacher he could have sex with next. If ever there was a man who was not gay . . . then it was Doctor Gilding. Next to chasing women, all he thought about was how he could run for some damn political office and achieve power and more fame. He was handsome and very intelligent, and all the women found him to be sexy, charismatic, and charming. All that being said, he was a pretty good boss. He left me the hell alone and allowed me to do my job and run the joint from a facility's point of view as I saw fit to do so. Smart guy. He knew shit about boilers, HVAC systems, and what polish-wax to use on the gym floor so the kids did not slip on their asses, and the guy did not pretend to know that he did. I respect a man who keeps it between the lines and knows his own knowledge and boundaries. On the flip-flop, I know shit about classic novels and literature. Unless *Jim Jumps* counts. We were on an even keel. He used his assets to his best advantage, and I used mine."

Odell nodded and looked over at George Grundy, who also nodded at the profound honesty displayed by Mr. Winslow. The two friends agreed. Odell lifted his eyes toward Officer Bradford, who met eyes with Odell and took a pause from his mission of notes to acknowledge his gaze.

Detective Odell nodded to Officer Bradford and then he turned his attention back to the conversation with Chester Winslow.

"Chester," Odell spoke, "you mentioned Doctor Gilding's affinity for female teachers. Do you know of an attractive, tall, redhaired teacher? Great figure. Tight dresses and skirts. Maybe who has an interest in English literature?"

Chester Winslow sighed, and he rolled his eyes before answering.

He did answer.

"Ah yes, Mrs. Amanda Sheffield. Outward beauty is beauty, but inside and outside beauty is a beauty that is beyond words. Maybe one word, and that is immaculate. Mrs. Sheffield is beyond beautiful. She teaches English here. A wartime widow. She lost her husband, a brave Marine, in combat in the Middle East. The first Gulf War. Amazing woman, but always there is an understandable sadness that follows her every step. Yet, she is strong. Powerful. Great figure. Deep redhaired beauty. That woman . . . can melt paint off the walls where she walks because she is too hot. She is at the gym every day. Takes care of herself.

Fit as a fiddle. Gilding was always hanging around her classroom and sitting with her at lunch and on coffee breaks in the teacher's lounge. I am quite sure that Doctor Gilding was locked and loaded on her. In many ways. Perfect prey for the predator."

"Chester . . . do you believe, in your heart, that Doctor Gilding was a predator of women?"

The question seemed to affect Mr. Chester Winslow in a very profound way. He almost fell off the milk crate that he sat upon. Not that it was a steady perch by any means. He gripped the edges and then his body and emotions grew steady.

After a period of steadiness, Mr. Winslow motioned to Detective Odell for him to hand off a smoke to him.

"Please, Detective Odell, do you have an extra cigarette?"

Remarkably, from the seemingly endless confines of Odell's complex world, the detective produced a cigarette rather quickly without any mumbling or direction as to a potential or actual location.

Grundy provided a light.

Mr. Winslow took a few drags on the cigarette and did not speak. The group watched in silence.

Finally, Mr. Winslow spoke.

"I do not pretend to be anything other than a maintenance man, taking care of this facility for many, many years. Just a high school education. Served in the army for four years. Did my time. With all due respect, Detective Odell, but I too, have seen a ton of shit and I am a keen observer of people. You are, too. I get it. Yet, have you any idea of the amount of people that I have seen pass through the hallways of this school in over thirty years? Both good and bad. Happy and sad. Students and staff. So many people. You tend to get a feel for who is good and who is bad. A sort of tingling. It is a by-product of this business that I am in. I take care of buildings, but the people that dwell within overwhelm the spirit and occupy the energy, too."

Chester Winslow puffed away until the smoke was gone. He snuffed it out and after a short pause to ponder what to do with the expired butt, he tossed it aside.

Out into the abyss of the loading dock.

It seemed as if for a few minutes that he harbored a deep disdain for the property that he cared for so deeply for a very long time.

Mr. Winslow spoke again.

"I guess that over the years, maybe because of those same observations, I have become a misanthrope. I have a deep distrust of humankind. Regardless, I hate to see anyone die and to speak poorly of a dead person. Especially how I heard he died. But I have to call it as I see it. Yes, he was a predator."

Odell stood up from the milk crate that he sat upon, as did Sergeant Grundy and Officer Bradford.

"I understand. Other than a few people on Earth—I, too, am a misanthrope. My theories in detective work and in life are that most everything and almost everyone is corrupt and almost everyone and everything has evil and nefarious intentions in their hearts and in their purpose. No one does anything these days unless it is of a benefit to them, or they are crazy, or just plain evil. I might be tainted by all these years of dealing with criminals and homicides. Maybe. Anyway, with that being said, that is my baseline. I then work in from there and if a person, place, or thing, prove me wrong and are good and honest in their words, actions, and intentions, then honestly, I am shocked to all hell."

Odell took a deep breath. He collected his thoughts and continued to speak.

"I must get back to the investigation. Thank you for the philosophical interlude and sharing of theories. I need to ask, did Doctor Gilding often leave the school? Maybe at lunch hour or leave early for the day before the business office closed?"

"You are welcome. Most enjoyable, Detective Odell. I can see that you are a man of high intellect and very deep thoughts. To answer your question . . . oh yes. If he was not prowling around Mrs. Sheffield, then he left for lunch. Usually, he went to lunch around one or so."

"Can we meet with Mrs. Sheffield? Is that something you can

arrange, or do we have to go to the assistant principal to arrange a meeting? Are there any other teachers or staff that Doctor Gilding could have had a relationship with?"

Chester looked down at his watch and smiled.

"Perfect timing. I had a drill instructor in basic training in the Army tell me that timing was everything in life. I had walked into the head to take a leak. When I did so, the drill instructor handed me a toothbrush and told me to scrub the urinals. I must'a done something to deserve that mission. Not exactly sure what—but I guess I deserved it. That lesson stuck with me forever. I think nowadays, more of us need lessons like that. Yes, indeed. Anyway, Mrs. Sheffield has a coffee break coming up. That man was constantly in pursuit of her. For sure. I know she was part of his so-called reading circle where he shared his literary genius with everyone. I think that gig was more about luring the prey into his lair. Anyway, no need to go to the management. Maintenance guys have it all under control. We know everything. Leave that to me, Detective Odell. Be glad to help. In any way that I can. Gilding was a pretender and an awful person, but as I said, no one deserves to die like that. Let's go."

◆ ◆ ◆

Detective Lyle Odell could not help to think that Mr. Chester Winslow's description of Mrs. Amanda Sheffield was entirely accurate. Spot on! She could melt the paint off the walls where she walked because she is too hot.

Her beauty was intense. It penetrated a person's soul and their mind and their body. Yet, one could not help but sense her eternal and irrevocable sadness. Her sadness hung in the air like a dark and ominous cloud does just before a storm arrives. Even her beauty could not eliminate the cloud.

She spoke in a voice just above a whisper.

"I wish that I could help you, Detective Odell. So many people could have wanted him dead. Including me. I did not kill him. I might have had my reasons to do so, but I did not. Honestly . . . he was a scoundrel. Doctor Gilding was captivating and charming and handsome and intelligent and sexy. He sucked you into his world like no other man I ever met. His loss is profound, yet soothing."

"I understand, Mrs. Sheffield. If I might ask you, and impose on you, were you a part of the reading circle with Doctor Gilding?"

"Regrettably, I was. I thought it was all about reading and sharing with the great Doctor Gilding's knowledge of classic works of literature."

"Was it not about classic works of literature?"

Mrs. Amanda Sheffield threw her head back and closed her eyes, and then she answered Detective Odell's question.

"Ha! It was, and it was not, part of sharing great works of literature. Most of all, it was about identifying and seducing women that Doctor Gilding could have sex with. That was the main purpose. Oh yes, we discussed literature and read and he taught but the men there were props. It was really about luring the women."

Detective Odell blinked a few times and then he nodded his head and said, "I see. Thanks for the honest assessment, Mrs. Sheffield. If Officer Bradford provided you with his notepad, could you list the persons by name who usually attended the reading circle sessions?"

"Yes. From my memory, I can provide the names of the people that I am aware of. Please, Officer Bradford, a pad and pen or pencil."

Odell nodded in the direction of Officer Miles Bradford and Miles nodded in return of the requested orders. He hustled over and provided Mrs. Sheffield with the pad and writing utensil, and she anxiously jotted down the notes. After she completed the recording of the information, Mrs. Sheffield handed off the notepad to Officer Bradford. Detective Odell waved to Officer Bradford for him to give him the notepad and when Odell received it, he quickly scanned the names.

Odell looked up at Mrs. Sheffield and said, "These three men's names, Alan Hudson, Robinson Thorpe, and Connor Escott . . . are they all young men? Maybe college-age? Skateboard enthusiasts and kind of immature and irresponsible?"

"They are Detective Odell. I think they came out of a class that Doctor Gilding taught as an adjunct at Mohawk University. I believe they all are seniors. Although, I think that Alan Hudson is much older than the others. I guess he started college later in his life than the others did."

Odell nodded and ran his hand rather violently through his hair and then he closed his eyes and with his eyes closed, he handed the notepad off to Office Bradford. Odell's hair was now an official mess.

When Odell opened his eyes, he asked, "Did Christina Fuentes flirt with the young men in the class and with Doctor Gilding?"

Mrs. Sheffield reacted with zeal.

She emphatically nodded her head and exclaimed, "Oh yes! Christina flirts with every man and she especially took those young men for a ride with her flirting and seduction. She is very nice and fun and charming, but she loves the attention, and for a married woman, she behaves rather inappropriately with men."

"I see. Thank you. Do you think she was sleeping with Doctor Gilding or one of the college guys? Or was it just teasing?"

Amanda Sheffield thought about the questions for a few minutes and then she answered.

"I don't think with Doctor Gilding, but there was some mounting sexual tension there for sure. Doctor Gilding wanted her for sure . . . but he wanted to have sex with most every woman that he met. The young men—difficult to tell. Maybe, but if I had to guess, she just teased them and played with. . . ." Her voice quivered, and she stopped and started again to finish her thoughts, "Played with their emotions."

After answering the questions, Mrs. Sheffield then covered her face in her hands and began to sob. They had been standing in the corner of the teacher's breakroom, and now, Mrs. Sheffield staggered over to the dining table, pulled out a chair and sat down.

All three police officers stood by and patiently watched, and hoped for her recovery. Mrs. Sheffield removed a tissue from her purse and dabbed her eyes, and tried to capture her composure. She wiped her nose and then stood up, walked over to the corner of the room, and disposed of the spent tissue in a nearby wastebasket.

After a few minutes, Mrs. Sheffield spoke.

"My apologies, for the loss of composure."

Sergeant George Grundy spoke first.

"It's all right, Mrs. Sheffield. Please take your time."

Amanda Sheffiled nodded her head and spoke. Her voice was soft but her emptions were now in check.

"I will confess that I gave Doctor Gilding my body in a moment of weakness. He was that sort of man. Very powerful and seductive. We went to dinner one night. I had too much wine, and it just happened. I am not ashamed—just honest. And regretful of my actions and my weakness. It is a great regret in my life, because he was just a scoundrel. Yet, loneliness plays with your mind and it eats away at your soul and makes you do regrettable things. Honestly, so does too much wine. It was willing, consensual, nothing as if he forced himself on me or something like that. I was tipsy but not staggering drunk. I was aware of what was happening. After he conquered me . . . he tossed me aside like a used dishcloth. He would hardly even speak to me since he achieved his goal of bedding another woman!"

Once more, she lost her composure. The tears ran out of her eyes and down her cheeks like a river. Officer Miles Bradford looked around and he spotted a box of tissues on the counter. He grabbed a few and handed them off to Mrs. Sheffield. She thanked him and dabbed at her emotions once more.

After regaining her voice and emotions, she spoke again.

"I feel as if I have voided my love for husband by sharing my body with that man. Did I, Detective Odell? Tell me please, did I? My husband was a hero! He died in combat with a damn bullet through his head. My lover, my husband, my life. Dead. With a bullet that split his skull into ten pieces. Dead! How did that happen? I am and always was a good Christian woman. What is with all of this? I was weak and became his prey! Why does evil like this exist? Please tell me, Detective Odell."

Detective Lyle Odell bowed his head and folded his hands in front of his body. Some tears welled in the corners of the eyes of Detective Lyle Odell. You could see the emotions in the eyes and in the faces of Sergeant George Grundy and Officer Bradford.

Odell spoke.

"If there is one thing that I will never be mistaken for, Mrs. Sheffield, then it is a clergyman. I do attend Catholic mass once a year. Never go to confession. My best action as far as religion goes is to let God sort it all out and be the final judge of things. But I can tell you as a detective who pokes around some really dark corners of life and deals with unsavory and evil people, no, Mrs. Sheffield. You did not void any love. Sometimes all one needs is a knowledge of all souls. But what do I really know? Nothing. I am just a homicide detective. Full of faults. I am seeking justice in an unjust world and all of us, here, Sergeant Grundy, Officer Bradford, and Detective Lyle Odell, and many other good, brave, and powerful men and women, make it their missions to snuff out evil and bring justice to those who choose evil ways. Take consolation in the fact that Jesus heals us. He forgives our faults and missteps. A sacred head wounded. For us. Please . . . we all thank you for your time. Thank you for you, and yes, your husband is a hero. Our country thanks him, this world thanks him, and both Heaven and God welcome him. With open arms. We will leave you alone now. My heart bleeds for your loss and I will pray for God to send you healing blessings."

After speaking, Lyle Odell gently touched Mrs. Sheffield on her shoulder and gripped it in a show of support and caring. She smiled at the healing gesture and concern.

He then turned and said, "Officer Bradford, today is done. I need to think and to be alone. Please drive us to my house. George's car is there. In my driveway."

◆ ◆ ◆

Detective Lyle Odell sat solemnly and sulking in the back seat of the patrol car.

Odell finally spoke.

"Bradford, how many miles from the workplace of Ms. Maguire to the complex?"

"Eight miles. No traffic. Eight minutes."

"Thank you, Bradford. Nice work. You are on your game. It is always interesting. This world is full of evil. Full of twists and turns. Even the good guys are bad guys, and the victims, in some cases, are somewhat deserving of the punishment that they receive. It is so difficult to accept and to understand. Is Sergeant Crump making headway on that store mission?"

"He is. I think he has some details on the security cameras video to share."

"Great. Crump is the best of the best. George. Is your wife home safe and sound?"

"She is. Anxious for me to be home."

"That sounds wonderful. You need to greet her at home, George. She is a glorious companion and a beautiful woman. I will retreat to my chair, there are some leftover pizza slices, and my Irish and my smokes and some music. After today, I need a pick me up. Tonight, is a glorious concert out of Boston. The big symphony with a performance of Mozart's Sonata No. 17 in C. Wonderful. A refreshing pick me up!"

"Do you have enough Irish and smokes, or do we need to stop and pick some up for you?"

"I am good, George. Thank you. Bradford, please make a connection with Sergeant Crump and see if he can join us tomorrow. We will meet at the police headquarters. Ask him to bring the enhanced photographs of the crowd, his findings at the store, and his summary of evidence file. Also, please pick up the final autopsy report and let Captain Moore know we are meeting, and if he is free, please ask him to join us. I might need that search warrant."

"Will do, Detective Odell. I am on it."

"Thank you, Bradford. You are doing a fine job here. You are very observant and efficient."

"I appreciate that, sir. It has been a learning experience. I would not have guessed that you were so religious. You do not wear it on your sleeve."

"Okay, Bradford, please call me Lyle or Odell, or detective, but never call me, sir. Bad vibes and memories. Be careful of assumptions and note your observations, Bradford. Not everyone wears things on their sleeves."

Officer Bradford turned the patrol car onto the street where Odell lived and as he spun the steering wheel, he lifted his eyes to the rearview mirror and said, "Gotcha. Odell."

Odell sat up straighter in the back seat and prepared to arrive at his home.

He said, "George, I enjoyed our time watching the hockey games and hanging out. Next time, we must plan to do this when there are no homicides. Let's book another hockey weekend. Maybe right before Christmas if your wife goes out of town on visits. Before the hockey teams go on the holiday break. Anyway, please pick me up tomorrow at eight in the morning. Bring coffee. I will be ready. Tomorrow, we will speak with Mrs. Perez, who is the housekeeper and I suspect she will bring her daughter with her. We will sit down with Ms. Fuentes and Ms. Maguire and Mr. Aki. Please arrange all of those appointments, Officer Bradford."

"I am on it, Detective Odell."

"Thank you. After that, I would think that we should be right on the cusp and edge of the killer. I think."

Sergeant George Grundy said, "Thanks for the nice words about the wife. She is the best. Ok. Got it. A busy day coming up. Yeah, Lyle. The weekend was fun. Great pizza. At least we won one game. It was a good time—minus the dead guy and all that blood and evil. Next time . . . no murders. Eight it is, Lyle."

CHAPTER SEVEN

A Killer on the Edge

"Here is your coffee. Looking good, Odell. Ya up, dressed in a different suit, hair still too long, but combed back. Is this a new version of Odell? You said that ya needed to change your ways." Sergeant Grundy stood in the living room of Lyle Odell's home and he scanned his friend and commented on his improved appearance.

Lyle Odell tilted the container of coffee back and took a long sip of the coffee.

"Thanks, George. Good morning. Damn good coffee from the corner store. I recognize the container. Still not too sure about changing my ways. I do know the Sonata performance last night was perfect. Just what I needed to restore my soul. I dipped in the Irish, but kept it under control. Which is good. Although, there might be one night this week, right before we make the arrest where I will flip back to my old ways and fall off the edge."

"Okay. Thanks for the warning, Odell."

George pointed at the overflowing ashtray filled to the top with spent cigarette butts.

Sergeant Grundy said, "You might have kept the Irish under wraps, but you sure tipped the scales on the smoking. Geez, Odell."

"It is a simple formula with me. I alternate bad habits. Yes, we need to pick up some smokes. On the way. Are Crump and Bradford meeting us? Did Bradford arrange for the housekeeper to meet us there?"

"Affirmative on the housekeeper, Lyle. The rest of the day is set, too. Crump and Bradford are there. Captain Moore will be there, too. Do you have your badge and weapon?"

"Badge, yes. Weapon, yes."

Sergeant Grundy could not hide his surprise at his friend's reply.

Knowing his ways, and Odell's penchant for only carrying his service weapon when he absolutely needed to do so, Grundy asked, "You have your weapon. Does that mean trouble for today?"

"Perhaps. George, when you get to headquarters, please put your body armor on. Have Bradford and Crump do so, too."

"Okay. You?"

"No, George. It restricts my aim."

"We would have been right on time, but Odell needed to pick up smokes for today. He smoked like a smokestack at a steel plant last night and ran out. Two packs burned to a damn crisp. Morning, Cap, Crump, Bradford," Sergeant Grundy said as he plowed into the conference room at Mohawk City Police Headquarters. Captain Conner Moore looked at his watch and shrugged his shoulders.

Moore then said, "Good morning. It is only four minutes after the hour. In Lyle Odell's world, that is on time."

Odell wandered in on the heels of Sergeant Grundy.

Captain Conner Moore spoke and then looked up and leaned back in the conference room chair in a display of some surprise at Lyle Odell's somewhat squared up appearance. Moore waved in the air in the direction of Lyle Odell and spoke with a hint of a smile on his face.

"You are looking rather unlike Detective Lyle Odell this morning, Lyle. I rather like the change going on here."

Odell stopped before he sat down and pointed at his own self.

"Weapon, check, and badge, check. I need a haircut and I still am not at regulation, but at least, I combed it back to fool people that my hair style is under control. My suit is wrinkled, my necktie is too short and not tied correctly and my pants are too big and kind of falling down around my waist. My shoes are not shined, too. But overall, I have an improved appearance. Confession is very good for the soul. And, today, at least, right now, I do not smell like a combination of Irish whiskey and cigarettes. I just smell like stale cigarettes. A random person that met me on the streets might actually believe that I am a police homicide detective. In my world, that is major achievement."

Captain Moore scanned Lyle Odell and nodded his head and said, "Points well-taken. Considering your past appearances. I have to agree. You have your service weapon on today. Interesting. Might I ask why?"

"The killer is on edge, Cap. On edge. He feels us on his heels."

"Okay. I understand."

"Captain Moore, I listened to an amazing Sonata last night that rejuvenated my soul, dipped in only a little Irish, did smoke like a chimney, but woke up to some clarity. This is a critical day. We need to be on our toes today. As I mentioned, the killer is now on edge. The funeral is tomorrow. Ordinarily, I always attend the murder victim's funeral because it reveals so much evidence. But I feel the crowd gathered outside the Townhouse unit on the afternoon of the murder achieved the same revelations to me as the funeral crowd will. Still debating whether I will attend or not. By the end of today, I will decide. Anyway, Crump, please have your photographers take photographs at the burial site. The usual method. From afar. No disruptions to the honoring of the dead man and his family in mourning."

Sergeant Oliver Crump said, "I will have my two best snappers there, Odell."

"Thank you, Sergeant Crump."

Lyle Odell placed his now empty coffee container in a nearby trashcan. He pulled a chair out from the conference room table and sat down next to Captain Moore. Sergeant Grundy sat next to Lyle Odell, with Sergeant Oliver Crump and Officer Miles Bradford on the opposite side of the table.

"I would predict that this new appearance might have some bumps in the road. Depending on this case. I predict a slip or two. Before the arrest."

Captain Moore nodded, as did Sergeant Grundy.

Captain Moore said, "You are entitled to that, Odell. I understand."

"Thank you, sir. Let's get to it. I don't want to keep the housekeeper waiting too long. Poor woman has been through enough as of late. Bradford, does she have her daughter with her?"

"Yes, she does. More for comfort than translation since they both know that I speak fluent Spanish. I will let her daughter lead the conversation and translation. I think that is best."

"I understand. Please bring them in here. I think this room is more comfortable than an interrogation room is. When you do gather them up and bring them in here, please explain to her in Spanish that she is not a suspect. We appreciate her coming in here and just have a few questions for her. I don't mind if the daughter translates back, just need ya to listen carefully to make sure nothing in the translation is twisted or turned. Not that the housekeeper is a suspect. At all. Just don't want to miss anything. My Spanish sucks."

Officer Miles Bradford nodded, rose from the chair, and walked out of the conference room to bring Mrs. Perez and her daughter into the conference. They both walked in and were wide-eyed as they scanned the conference room table. Officer Bradford pulled two chairs out next to him and spoke in Spanish for them to sit down and to relax. Once they were seated, then Officer Bradford explained in English.

"Detective Odell and the team here, out in the hallway, I told Mrs. Perez and her daughter, Rosie, that all is well here. She is not a suspect, just a few questions."

Mrs. Luna Perez was a heavy-set woman of about forty-five years of age. She had long dark black hair with some whispers of grey along the edges and she pulled her hair behind her into a long weave of a hair that tumbled down her back, almost reaching her waist. Mrs. Perez had a kind face with wide dark brown eyes and a gentle sloping nose and thin lips on a gentle mouth. She was very attractive and her daughter closely resembled her mother, except she was thinner and her hair was lighter and it was not as long as her mother's hair was.

They both had worried eyes.

Detective Odell waved in the air in the direction of the guests and said, "Thank you, Officer Bradford. Please introduce the team and tell Mrs. Perez that we know how difficult this is for her. Then, please allow Rosie to translate. I agree with you that we do not want this to be imposing."

Rosie smiled and whispered a gentle, "Thank you."

Officer Bradford nodded and told them both exactly what Odell said and introduced each member of the police team seated at the table and what their individual roles were.

"Please, Rosie, tell your mother that she is very good at her job. Then ask her when was the last time that she emptied the trash in the kitchen trashcan."

Rosie nodded and translated the words to her mother. Mrs. Perez first smiled at the compliment of her work, thanked Detective Odell, and then answered the question.

Rosie said, "Last Friday. My mother worked every other day during the week, but she worked both Saturday and Sunday."

"Thank you. Did she feel that Doctor Gilding was a nice man? Did he treat her well?"

Rosie translated and then said to Detective Odell.

"She liked Doctor Gilding and he spoke Spanish and he was very nice to her, paid her well, but my mother says that he liked many women. Too many. She did not enjoy cleaning up after he had the women over. It was . . . messy and . . . unpleasant."

Odell closed his eyes and did not say anything for a few minutes.

He was very deep in thought and then when he suddenly opened his eyes, Detective Odell said, "Bradford, Mrs. Perez said, what exactly? I think our gentle Rosie was a little shy in the translation."

Bradford nodded and said, "I agree."

Rosie nodded in agreement, too, as Officer Bradford relayed the exact words of Mrs. Perez.

"She said it was messy after Doctor Gilding had sex with many women and she had to clean the bedroom, empty used condoms from the trashcan and do his laundry with the bed linens and clean other dirty items."

"Gotcha. Thank you. No harm. No foul, Rosie. I understand. Crump, please, the pictures that I marked up. Please hand them to Rosie. Please, dear Rosie, and then show them to your mother and then ask her if any of the persons that I circled were over at Doctor Gilding's home often enough that she noticed or saw during her duties."

Oliver Crump produced the pictures and, after a careful study of them by Mrs. Perez, she placed her finger on all of the circled persons except for Mr. Larry Hicks.

Rosie then said, "These three people. The photographer guy. Ms. Fuentes and Ms. Maguire. They had this reading group a few nights a week. But Ms. Maguire was always there. My mother knows that she was having a sexual relationship with Doctor Gilding because my mother unintentionally walked in on them in bed together. My mother knocked and knocked, but they never answered because they were too busy. The bedroom was very large."

"Ha!" Sergeant Grundy piped up. "Looks like Larry Hicks was right on about his chickee-poo messing around with ole doc bedroom. This Gilding guy was a real pip. I would have quit if I was your mother, or asked him for more dough."

Rosie smiled and said, "Well, my mother said that he gave her an extra bonus for that day."

Grundy smirked and said, "Oh, well, then. Okay. Gilding was a horny jerk, but at least he was a generous one, too."

Odell patted his pockets in search of something, and then he stopped as he lifted a finger in the air. A thought interrupted his unknown quest.

Odell said, "Three more questions. One, did your mother

operate the alarm system? If so, when was the last time she operated the alarm? Finally, does she think that Doctor Gilding was having an intimate affair with Ms. Fuentes?"

Rosie translated and then replied with her mother's answer.

"Yes, on the alarms. But it often was not used. The last time she used it was last Wednesday. Doctor Gilding told her that it was broken and the alarm required service. She is not sure about Ms. Fuentes. But my mother said Ms. Fuentes was very nice but way too friendly with other men for a married woman."

Odell smiled, rose from his chair, and leaned over the table, and extended his hand to Mrs. Perez and Rosie. As they all shook hands, to everyone's surprise, Odell spoke in fluent Spanish. Both Rosie and Mrs. Perez answered Detective Odell in Spanish, then they too rose from their chairs, greeted each of the team and, while escorted by Officer Miles Bradford, they left the room.

Captain Moore asked Odell, "I thought that your Spanish was lousy, Odell? I know very little Spanish, but it seemed good to me."

"I said that my Spanish sucks, not that it was lousy. Exact testimony counts, Cap. I am a detective. So, Crump, what-cha got?"

Sergeant Crump slid the booklet of his report over to Odell and said, "Just as you predicted. Not too much, Odell. I am sorry."

"Not your fault, Crump. Let me guess about the laptop. The screen shot and files on the screen were moved there by the killer. He slid the laptop over to the new location on the desk, in the direct sun, after Doctor Gilding died. You are sure that Doctor Gilding was browsing digital versions of photos on the laptop when he was confronted, attacked, and killed. You found the photographs of Ms. Maguire on there and there are photographs of Ms. Fuentes. Both seated on the desk in the office or seated in the office chair at that same desk. Beautiful portrait shots of two very beautiful women taken by a skilled photographer. Pure art. Very lovely photos of lovely women. Ms. Maguire showed a lot of her body, mostly, if not totally naked, and a ton of skin in the photos, but Ms. Fuentes did not.

Fuentes is fully-clothed and they are mostly portrait shots of her face and upper torso. And there were photographs of the now infamous reading circle attendees. Those will be very helpful. I need those. I suspect Mr. Aki is the photographer. We might need that search warrant, Captain Moore. Might."

While he shook his head back and forth in a display of amazement at the testimony of Detective Lyle Odell, Oliver Crump commented.

"I am not sure why you even need me, Odell. You are spot on. As usual. How did you know about the photographs and the subjects of them?"

"What? Are you kidding me, Oliver? I need you more than I can ever tell you. I need you and your team to verify everything. The photographs were obvious—I knew because of the blue tape on the floor in front of the desk. Perfect location to shoot from in that room and the room has wonderful natural light for photography. At one time, I dabbled in a little photography. These two women love to tease men and since they are both gorgeous, I can see Doctor Gilding studying their beautiful portraits and dreaming of them. These photographs of the women and the bookcase behind the desk and of the attendees of the reading circle are of vital importance, Crump. Vital. I do not think we even need the photographs from Mr. Aki. Maybe we just need to verify his equipment matches the digital footprint on the photographs. How about fingerprints? Anything else?"

"No fingerprints of any use or what we feel is a potential killer's prints. Mostly the housekeeper's prints, prints all over the place in the bedroom and the master bathroom, which we feel is from the woman he had sex with, and Doctor Gilding's prints. No shoe marks. No unusual evidence. Nothing wonderful. The DNA from the hair in the shower matches the DNA from the hairs in the bed. The urine in the unflushed toilet did not yield any results. DNA on the used condom matches the hair DNA and, of course, it is Doctor Gilding's semen. The alarm was purposely disabled. As Mrs. Perez said, it had not worked in a few days. Interesting to note that the mother board had an integrated circuit clipped out of it. No fingerprints inside or outside. Only on the keyboard. Doctor Gilding and Mrs. Perez. You were, of course, correct on your calculations of the height of the killer. Based upon your requested measurements of the sweep of the knife blow to the head of the victim to the bookcases, and our calculations, the killer is indeed right-handed, and as long as they stood in the location that you detected on the floor behind the victim, the killer is at a minimum, six-feet-three inches tall. So, there you go."

Odell did not say another word. He was intensely focused on the report. His eyes darted back and forth as he read the words and flipped the pages.

As he read the report, Odell did not look up from the document, but he asked, "Bradford, the ex-wife has an alibi, as does Firefighter Colombo?"

"Correct. The ex-wife lives in California and has had zero contact with her ex-husband since the divorce and does not intend on even attending the funeral. She had no kind words for Doctor Gilding. Her employer vouched for her attendance in work all last week. They even worked last Saturday in their headquarters building on a special project. Ten employees worked together and all of them verify that she was there all day. Firefighter Colombo worked a normal three-day shift at his duty station. Never left the station unless they went on a call. His chain of command verified his presence."

"Thank you, Miles. Excellent work. As poor Colombo saved lives, his wife contributed to a person losing one."

Odell shook his head a few times, and he closed his eyes and went silent for a few moments. It seemed as if his statement affected his emotions.

Upon recovering, Detective Odell directed his attention to Sergeant Oliver Crump, and he asked, "Sergeant Crump, how did you make out at the local store with the condom purchase and the security video?"

Crump nodded his head. He pulled at the cover of a report booklet he had in front of him on his desk and said, "Great. The store manager was very cooperative. He told us he has a nephew in law enforcement and he respects our work and supports the law. He allowed us full access to the cameras and video and the system. From the sales receipt and the date and time stamp of it, we were able to find exactly what we needed. Here are screenshots of the key frames of the video. Doctor Gilding plucking his condoms from the aisle, then grabbing a random box of cereal, then waltzing up to the cash register to pay. All with the company of a lovely young woman on his heels. You are the great detective—not me—but I am not sure what this all means in the case. But take a look for yourself."

Crump slid the photographs of the key frames over the table for Odell to look, and at first, Odell did not look at them. The detective placed his hand on the photographs as if to cover up the images, and he ran his fingers through his hair and mussed it up once again. Odell momentarily lifted his eyes to Crump as he removed his hand from the photographs and then he gazed at them for the first time.

"I respect that, Crump. Thank you for your honest assessment and the hard work. I know that I can be . . . confusing and a little eccentric."

With those words, Sergeant Grundy sighed and mumbled, "Ya think."

Odell smiled but did not miss a beat in his further comments about the store visit and the photographs.

"Let me see now . . . yes, shopping for condoms with Ms. Kathleen Maguire and picking up a random box of cereal to offset and cover the purchase of two fifty packs of condoms while with a beautiful young woman. The old embarrassment at buying condoms trick. A prop. This is a vital, vital key to this case. A clue of the highest importance. Because of this incident . . . Doctor Gilding is dead. Horribly murdered."

Captain Conner Moore seemed very surprised and deeply intrigued by Odell's statement, and the commanding officer leaned in over the table and asked, "How so, Detective Odell? A shopping trip for condoms and a box of cereal, used as a prop or not, leads to murder?"

"Yes, Cap. Because whoever the sex-crazed doctor told about this little excursion . . . or in fact, bragged about it . . . and heard about other sexual conquests and intentions that the doctor had planned became enraged enough to kill Doctor Rochester Gilding. That is one of the questions we need to ask, Ms. Maguire. Despite all of this," Odell waved his hands over the photographs and then continued to explain, "Ms. Fuentes was not having an affair with Gilding. Maguire, yes. Fuentes, no. Yet, Fuentes is the key. The woman is the ultimate tease. Dangerous tease. Ms. Maguire had some other iffy ideas and actions, too. We will get to them. Anyway, I will need to suck down some Irish and connect the dots. Soon. Right now, I need coffee and a cigarette. I need to step out. Before I do, one more thought. Crump, I see where that bag in the trashcan in the kitchen had the muffin in there and the coffee container. The crumbs under the desk match the crumbs in the bag. But only one coffee container. Doctor Gilding's last meal?"

"Yes, his saliva DNA was on the container. His fingerprints were on the outside of the container. Doctor Kent states in his autopsy report that his last meal was coffee and a muffin."

"I see the bag and container came from that fancy joint out on the main drag near Gilding's home. That overpriced franchise bullshit place. Asteroid Coffee."

"Correct."

"Excellent work, as usual, Crump. Amazing. Thank you! We are on the game now. Lookie here, let's get coffee and I need to smoke and we will roll. Crump, please bring your fingerprint kit. Let's saddle up and go speak with Mr. Aki, Ms. Maguire, and Fuentes. Sarge Grundy will request you guys to suit up in body armor. I will meet you outside."

"Wait! Odell!" Captain Moore quickly stood up from his chair and grabbed Lyle Odell by his arm and stopped his progress. "Body armor, Lyle?"

"Yes, Captain Moore. As I said, the killer feels us."

"I am coming with you guys."

Odell looked over at Sergeant Grundy and then at Sergeant Crump and finally to Officer Bradford.

Grundy spoke first.

"As you wish, sir. Captain Moore, please, sir, just suit up. Okay?"

"Yes, suit up, Cap. You are too important to us. To your family. To everyone," Sergeant Crump added.

"I will. Thank you. Detective Odell, you are not wearing any body armor. Are you going to the locker room to change?"

Lyle Odell mussed his hair. It stuck out at all angles now. He patted his pockets and without any assistance from George Grundy, he produced a pack of cigarettes from his inside shirt pocket.

After shaking one loose and sticking a cigarette in his mouth, Odell said, "Negative Cap. Unless you order me to do so. I rather not. It restricts my aim. Besides, I have George, Miles, Oliver, and you to back me up. The best of the best."

Captain Conner Moore nodded and smiled. He knew of Odell's expert marksman capabilities and the fact that Homicide Detective Lyle Odell could easily handle tactical encounters on his own. He was the best shot in the entire Mohawk City Police Department. His hand-to-hand combat skills were unparalleled. He was the most decorated police officer in the entire department. The most honored. Despite his flaws and messiness; Odell was the most respected.

"Not an order, Lyle. A suggestion, but not an order," Captain Moore said.

◆ ◆ ◆

"Pardon the interruption at your workplace, Ms. Maguire, but we need to ask you a few questions based on your relationship with Doctor Rochester Gilding. This will not take too long. I am Officer Miles Bradford of the Mohawk City Police Department. This is our commanding officer, Captain Connor Moore, this is

Sergeant George Grundy, Sergeant Oliver Crump, from the Crime Scene Investigation Department and this is Homicide Detective Lyle Odell. Detective Odell is heading up the investigation into the brutal murder of Doctor Gilding on last Saturday."

Kathleen Maguire stood and listened in the breakroom of her workplace located on the first floor of the sprawling office building. She folded her arms across her chest. As her on and off boyfriend, Mr. Larry Hicks, accurately described, Ms. Maguire had generous and very full breasts, and she was full of curves. She was about five feet eight inches tall, had perfect facial features, full lips, sea-green eyes, brown medium-length hair, and she was stunning in appearance. Something about her was Germanic in appearance and something about her was Irish.

Ms. Maguire spoke with her arms still folded across her chest.

She was going to cop an attitude; not exactly knowing who it was that she was dealing with now.

"Wow! Why so many police officers to interview one little woman? On television and in the movies, it is always one detective and one other guy."

Detective Odell stepped forward and her eyes scanned over, Lyle Odell. He had become a messier version of Odell than he previously was. His combed hair had now fallen away, and it hung in many different directions. He had worked at his tie so that the knot was now loose. His suit jacket always appeared to be two sizes too big for Odell; therefore, he easily concealed the multiple gizmos and gadgets contained therein.

Ms. Maguire said, "Well, you certainly are not the stereotypical police detective now, are you?"

"Very true, Ms. Maguire. This ain't television or the movies. I often wish that it was. Say, I see a side exit door right there that leads outside this room. Can we all step outside on that patio and talk? I need to taste a cancer stick."

Ms. Maguire turned and looked at the door in the break room. She nodded and pointed and said, "Sure. It is not too cold today, and there is a heater out there, anyway."

The police officers and Ms. Maguire walked to the door and

went outside on the patio while Odell straggled behind as he fumbled in search of his cigarettes and Grundy assisted with the location.

"Inside right-side shirt pocket, Odell."

"Thanks, George. I just need to taste it. Ain't gonna light it."

Odell stuck the cigarette in his mouth and it firmly glued to that familiar spot on his lower lip.

Once outside, Ms. Maguire leaned on the wall of the building and faced the team led by Detective Odell.

"Please, Bradford, take notes. So, Ms. Maguire, did you know, Doctor Rochester Gilding?"

Ms. Maguire answered right away. It was difficult to look away from her. She was a beautiful woman. Her voice was soft and seductive, with a gentle rasp to it. Officer Bradford paused over his notepad, his pen in hand, and waited for her testimony.

"Yes, I knew him. I guess that I knew him . . . very well. Met him one day when my sort of on and off-again boyfriend, Mr. Larry Hicks, and I were walking his dogs on the grounds where Larry lives. In that townhouse development that is still under construction. Doctor Gilding had the fancy unit. One of the original units in the first wave of construction. The most expensive one of all. He had tons of dough. Handsome guy. We kind of hit it off. That place is full of nosey people. You step outside and in ten seconds, a bunch of nosey bastards all clamor outside to greet you. It is rather creepy. I did not kill him. Don't know who did. That is all that I have. You get nothing else from me. Anything else, then I will need to get a lawyer. You can speak to my lawyer. Not me."

Despite her statement to the contrary, Lyle Odell sensed that Ms. Maguire would not hesitate to answer more questions. Odell was very, very good at his job.

The cigarette danced as Lyle Odell asked, "Please. Define very well."

"What do you mean?"

"You just said that you knew him very well, but you paused after him and before very well, as if you searched for the proper words. You are leaning on the outside wall with your arms folded across your chest. It is not cold today, but you folded your arms across your chest inside, too. You are very lovely, you should not have self-esteem issues, so . . . to a detective such as I am, that indicates uneasiness in the situation. You are containing yourself. And despite your previous statement of not saying anything else, I think you want to answer more questions and assist us in this investigation."

Ms. Kathleen Maguire stood away from the wall and she dropped her arms to her side and tried to hide a smile.

"Wow! You are good. As in, very, very good. You are kind of rugged and sexy, too. Handsome, but not in a movie star sort of way. Hard-boiled. We should spend some time together, Detective Odell. Sure, I mean, yes, that I want to assist you and answer a few more questions for a few reasons. I think you are sexy and I like being with you and I, too, know body language and you know that I did not kill, Rock. You are a straight-shooter and most men these days are not. They are all phony frauds. Big babies. Nothing about you is phony and you certainly are hard-boiled and very sexy."

Odell did not react or speak; he simply stood and studied her.

"Rock and I were great friends in a special sort of way, and I will miss him. I had a good cry over it and now it is time to move on. I will attend the funeral, pay my respects, and life goes on. I hope you find the killer and lock the killer up forever."

"We will find the killer. But suppose I said to you that I feel as if you and Doctor Gilding were very intimate and passionate lovers. You routinely had sex many times during the week. Particularly during lunch hours when your sort of . . . as you stated, on and off-again boyfriend, Mr. Hicks, was working his day shifts and you could safely meet the educator of many things for some mid-day fun and still keep old Mr. Hicks on the line. You did not want to lose, Mr. Hicks, nor piss him off because he is sort of a big guy with lots of bluster and muscle. It is only eight miles from your workplace to Doctor Gilding's unit. Eight minutes with no traffic. Plenty of time for a quick roll in the sack and then back to work. Gilding often left work at lunch. The high school and his district office are only about ten miles from here, but he did not give a damn about taxpayer's money. We already investigated his patterns and actions. You are very proud of your beauty and do not mind proudly showing it off by displaying it. Nothing wrong with that on the surface. You are very lovely and you could easily be a highly paid fashion or photographic model. You posed for some portrait photographs and some naked body photographs on Doctor Gilding's desk and in the chair behind the desk. Mr. Aki, the local photographer, took the pictures for Gilding and for you. My guess is that Gilding paid him and paid you very well. I love art and admire art and photography can be very fine art. He paid for them. He got what he paid for. Beauty."

Odell removed the cigarette from his mouth and dropped it in his right-suit-jacket pocket and mumbled the location before speaking again. Ms. Maguire leaned in closer to Detective Odell as if she was intrigued by the messy and unorthodox genius of the man. Odell could smell her perfume hitting him in seductive waves.

Ms. Maguire watched Detective Odell, and she sensed his pause and said, "Yes. Rock and I were lovers. He paid me very well for the modeling work. Paid Mr. Aki very well, too. Doctor Gilding was rolling in dough. Yes. I posed for the photos and I am very proud of the photos. It is beautiful art. People generally say that I am beautiful and I have a great body. Money is money and that, mostly, was easy money. Although Mr. Aki is a pro and he works you hard when you model for him. This pose—that pose—this twist, that turn. Hard work, for sure. It was good money and I am not exactly rolling in it these days. If you have it—then use it."

"I understand. Money is money. A question. Did you ever go shopping with Doctor Rochester Gilding for condoms and supplies?"

Ms. Maguire answered immediately.

"Yes. I do not believe in unprotected sex."

Odell almost smiled and said, "Good practice. Why would he

purchase fifty packs of condoms? Any ideas?"

This time, Ms. Maguire did not answer right away. She folded her lip and bit it and then stopped when she noticed Detective Odell carefully watching her and her resulting actions.

Kathleen Maguire then shrugged her shoulders and said, "Not sure. He was a very sexually active man. I was not his only lover. Maybe he got a good deal in buying them in quantity, Detective Odell."

Odell closed his eyes for a few seconds and then opened them and said, "I doubt he was shopping for bargains. The guy had a ton of dough. Shifting gears. What if I said to you right now that I feel as if you had dinner with Doctor Gilding last Friday night? You went back to his unit, had sex two times in his bed in the master bedroom, then you both fell asleep and slept together. In the morning, you had sex one more time, then you showered and left around ten in the morning and left Doctor Gilding sleeping in his bed. Or was he at his desk and you cut his throat and stuck a knife in his skull and then you left? Or did Larry Hicks find out about your trysts and, in a rage of jealousy, kill his gal's side lover? We have medium-length brown hair in the shower that we pulled DNA on and it matches medium-length brown hair in the bed. We have DNA on used condoms. We have fingerprints that we believe are from a woman all over the master bathroom and bedroom."

Detective Odell turned to the team of his fellow police officers; he waved them over and explained, "You asked why so many officers? In theory, once you do what you have to do for legal protection of your rights, or you wave them, then Officer Crump is here to obtain a DNA and fingerprint sample from you. Captain Moore is here because we might need a search warrant to your house if you do not consent to any samples. Officer Bradford is the detailer and Sarge Grundy is the muscle. I am, well, a mess." Lyle Odell finished speaking, and he ran his hand through his hair and it stuck out in all directions again.

When Ms. Maguire's eyes went to his hair, she smiled and pointed and said, "Ha! You are such a sexy beast, Detective Odell.

I think that I am in love. Your hair is sticking up and you are so cool. Yes, Detective Odell, you are a mess and that just makes you sexier. There is no need for legal wrangling or warrants and other bullshit. I would willingly give you one of my strands of hair from my head and yes, you can take my fingerprints. I have nothing at all to hide. You are one-hundred percent correct in everything that you said except for the killing part. That statement was just a silly detective ploy to trip me up when I already know that you are sure I am not the killer. I left at ten in the morning and Rock was sound asleep in the bed. I did not see anyone. I did not set the alarm because Rock said it was not working. I left through the rear garage door and went and picked up coffee at Asteroid Coffee out on the main drag, then I went home to my apartment. I went through the drive-thru lane—there are cameras there. I bet you could confirm it on their video. Larry Hicks is not a killer, either. He is an ex-cop and protects justice. Sometimes, he is a little harsh and rough when doing so, but he is a protector. I like Larry. A lot. He is handsome, has the body of a god and is kind to me. Actually, he is a much better lover than Rock was, but Rock had the money. I just did and do not want to be exclusive with Larry. He knows that fact, and is uncomfortable with that, but he is in love with me and holds out hope that he is eventually going to be the one. Maybe and maybe not. Right now, I am intrigued by this messy genius of a detective in front of me and I am hoping you will ask me out to dinner. Honestly, I have numerous lovers. Rock was one of them. One of many. I guess one could say that I am a beautiful woman that likes to throw my body and love around and play the field. That is not actually proper behavior and I need to stop it and grow up because, as you can see, it leads to troubles. I would not be here if I behaved properly and kept things in order and under control."

"Your words, not mine, Ms. Maguire. I am not a judge, or a clergyman—just a detective. Yet, you make a good point that I suppose you should consider. Self-examination is productive. Since you decided to answer questions, and for that we thank you, a few last questions and we will let you get back to work. Thank you for your time and yes, I believe that you are not the killer. Neither is Hicks. Do you know, Ms. Christina Fuentes?"

As Odell asked the question, Ms. Kathleen Maguire threw her head back and laughed and then covered her mouth.

"Sorry, Detective Odell. Of course! Everyone knows Christina! She is a social butterfly and, is always over at Rock's place with his reading circle. Now there is a player. All the men. Young and old. Kind of loose with her words and her attire and actions for a married woman. She is in an unhappy marriage. She is nice, just was competition for Rock's heart."

"Interesting, Ms. Maguire. Do you think they were lovers? I mean Gilding and Fuentes."

"Please, Lyle, call me . . . Kathleen," she said with a wink. "No. Rock was after her big time. He wanted to bed her for sure. All the men do after she teases them. She is very beautiful and exotic. As I already mentioned, Rock had many, many lovers and I was always very careful in having only protected and careful sex with him. Fuentes played him as she did many others, especially those young men in that reading circle, but I do believe she is not a cheater on her man. That guy works all the time, and that is the issue for her. It allows her to run wild. She craves attention. Do you want my phone number, Lyle?"

Odell smiled and said, "Thank you, Ms. Maguire. You have been amazingly helpful. There is no need right now for those hair samples and fingerprints. If needed in the future, Sergeant Crump will arrange an appointment with you. Accordingly. Officer Bradford will record your contact number and we will be in touch if we need any more information or anything else. Ah, let's see now. Right-side-suit jacket pocket."

Odell fished around in the pocket, plucked a twisted cigarette from it, and then produced a lighter from the same pocket, turned, waved, and said, as he lit up the cigarette, "Let's go, men. Bradford, please write down Ms. Maguire's number. After that, we are done here."

"Ms. Maguire. Thank you for your time and for your

contact telephone number. What is it?" Officer Bradford stepped forward and asked with his notepad in his hand.

As Bradford recorded the contact number, Odell lit his cigarette. He leaned in for a few long drags and exhaled the smoke into the air as he left the patio.

He suddenly turned around and waved in the direction of Ms. Kathleen Maguire, and said, "Oh, Ms. Maguire. It is, and maybe."

Ms. Maguire narrowed her eyes and shook her head a little in a reaction to Odell's words. It was one of those typical Detective Odell puzzles that only Odell was tuned into.

"It is, and maybe what, Detective Lyle Odell?"

Odell took another puff on the cigarette and blew the smoke into the air with some words to follow the smoke's exit.

"It is rather creepy. I agree with you about that crazy neighborhood over there with all those wacky-ass neighbors. That kind of living is not for me. Leads to meddling, and as you can testify to . . . troubles. They are a bunch of nosey bastards that all clamor outside to greet you. Your observations are correct and right on. You are very brilliant and intelligent and highly confident. Solid skills and attributes to have these days in this crazy world. It is rather creepy. And maybe we can go to dinner someday. Maybe."

Ms. Maguire's face lit up, and she smiled widely.

"I will look forward to it. Lyle. Call me. Please."

Captain Conner Moore caught up with Detective Lyle Odell as they made their way to the parked police vehicles. Odell finished up his smoke and tossed it on the ground and ground it out, picked it up, and stuffed it in that same blessed right hand-suit jacket pocket.

Captain Moore needed to question his coveted detective. Not because of doubt; partly because of his position, and mostly, because of his curiosity. He was still learning the nuances of the eccentric Homicide Detective Lyle Odell.

"Odell, I am going to let that potential of mixing business with pleasure with Ms. Maguire ride because I respect you too much. I also feel that I do not completely understand your investigation methods and that the potential of you accepting a dinner invitation might be part of your master plan. Or you are uncovering something beneath the covers."

Odell looked at his commanding officer and smiled. After mussing with his hair, Odell said, "She is very smart and beautiful and intriguing in a beguiling way. Thank you for letting this unfold without your judgement of me. Maybe, Cap. Maybe not. Stay tuned."

"Odell!" Larry Hicks bellowed out as he stormed out of the front door of his townhouse unit. "Thanks for dragging me into your case of bullshit! You owe me a set of tires!"

Lyle Odell and the team had just pulled up to the townhouse unit of Mr. Hiro Aki to interview him, and Mr. Hicks spotted them and stormed out of the house while bellowing.

"I was just calling it into the police right now, when I saw all of you guys pulling up. No doubt to interview Mr. Aki and pull him in on the bullshit, too!"

Lyle Odell looked at Sergeant Grundy and he shrugged his shoulders as he stuck another cigarette in his mouth. Sergeant Grundy walked over to Mr. Hicks while waving his hands in the air to calm down the enraged ex-police officer.

"Easy there, Hicks, here is that angry bullshit surfacing again," Sarge Grundy preached.

"Oh, bullshit, Sarge Grundy! Do you have a grand sitting in ya wallet for new tires that you want to give me?"

"Not really, Hicks. I cannot even afford a grilled cheese sandwich and a few beers. I have these damn student-parent loans to pay off. Otherwise, I would be retired."

Detective Lyle Odell and the team walked over, and Odell stood next to Grundy while puffing like a smokestack on his cigarette.

Odell said, "Ya wanna tell us what the hell ya ranting 'bout,

Hicks? Timing is everything in life. This is Sarge Crump from C-S-I, and this is my commanding officer, Cap Moore. So, straighten ya ass up. This is a potential audition. Sorry for dragging you into this mess, but now I think you might have turned the tide of this case. Explain, please."

Larry Hicks ran his hands over his shaved head and then waved his hands in the air toward Detective Odell as he walked down his front steps and toward the team of police officers.

"Okay, I gotcha, Odell. Gotcha, Grundy. You are right. Nice to meet you, Sergeant Crump, and Captain Moore. Sorry for the outburst. It has been a sucky kind of day. First, my gal called me and said he does not want to date me anymore. Second, my car was parked in the driveway overnight. I worked a double shift because I have terrible employees that don't show up and call out if they have a hangnail. Got up in the late morning to go and get some coffee and breakfast and every damn tire on my car had a knife stuck in it and was flat. I have no exterior cameras. The dogs did not bark. I have nothing but the knives. And a much poorer wallet and bank account."

Larry Hicks looked up and scanned the team of police officers.

He then said, "I am still a cop, guys. Always will be. I know this is because whoever whacked Doctor Screw-A-Lot knows that I met with you guys the other day and spilled some kind of beans. The killer is trying to warn me to shut my trap. Ha! The killer messed with the wrong guy. I could give jackshit 'bout him."

Odell walked up to Mr. Hicks and said, "It's okay, Larry. We respect you. I plan to speak to Captain Moore about you once this case is solved. Did you preserve the evidence? Military knives or otherwise?"

"Otherwise. Hard edge. Commercial quality kitchen knives. I used gloves. I have them in my house. I can give them to Sarge Crump to check for fingerprints. I doubt there are any, but I did not screw up any potential evidence. I know what I am doing. I appreciate the respect. Sarge Crump, if ya wanna gather up ya evidence bags and such, I have the knives on my kitchen table."

Sergeant Oliver Crump waved and said, "I will be right there.

Let me get my kit."

Captain Connor Moore walked up the front walkway and extended his hand to Larry Hicks. Until now, the commanding officer had stood silently on the sidelines and not said a single word.

The two men shook hands and studied one another.

"Thank you, Mr. Hicks. I appreciate your efforts here and I am sorry about your misfortune and your tires. Once this case is complete, I will be anxious to speak to Detective Odell and learn more about his thoughts concerning you and your career."

"Thank you, Captain Moore. Nice to have a formal meeting with you, sir. Detective Odell, I just wanna say, I know that you are meeting with Mr. Aki. His part-time job is photography. His full-time job is working as a sushi chef at that fancy Japanese restaurant downtown. He has lots of knives. Commercial quality. Kitchen knives. Just sayin'."

"So noted, Hicks. Your assistance here has been invaluable. Believe me. You are still a police officer. A damn good one, too. I plan to get into Mr. Aki's part-time work and his photography of the reading circle and the beautiful chicks. Before, when we met, you mentioned a young buck, or as you described him, a punk, or a thug, that got all hot and bothered when you were speaking with Ms. Fuentes . . . one day. Could you describe him or identify him if we had a photograph of him? White, black, Latino, Asian, or otherwise? Tall, short, heavy-set, or thin?"

"Black man. Young. College kid. Big hair—like out of the 1970s. He never left his car, but if I had to guess, he was tall and sort of athletic. I would have ripped him apart if he stepped out and lipped off at me. Sorry. I know, calm down the anger. Odell, I was wrong about you. I do like you."

"Easy now, Hicks. Don't go getting soft on us. Very few people like me. How tall is tall?"

"At least six-feet- four. Maybe more."

"Gotcha. Sorry 'bout your gal. We just met with her. She is remarkable and beautiful, too. In my opinion, despite her conflicts and loose ends, she is a gal worth fighting for. We will be right back. Give us an hour, at the most. Head on a swivel, Hicks. You need, as we all need to be, on very high alert. The killer is on edge. We are growing very close." Odell rolled his eyes and looked around, and said, "Damn, I need coffee. Any ideas. Anyone?"

"Thank you. Gotcha, Odell. I am on point and will stay on alert. I will put a pot of coffee on and brew it up. C'mon over when you are done with Mr. Aki. I have ya covered."

Odell smiled and Mr. Larry Hicks smiled back.

CHAPTER EIGHT

Gunfire

"Officer Bradford . . . notes, please. Time?"

"Thirteen hundred hours plus sixteen minutes."

"Thank you. Mr. Aki, thank you for your time." Mohawk City's best, and in fact, their only homicide detective, the good Homicide Detective, Lyle Odell, stood in the living room of the townhouse unit of Mr. Hiro Aki. A few doors down from the unit where Larry Hicks lived, and about ten units away from where Doctor Gilding died as a victim of a brutal murder.

Odell ran his hand through his very messy hair. A comb was a mile away by now. Odell badly needed a haircut.

Lyle Odell spoke in a low voice, "Mr. Aki, we appreciate your time. Thank you. I just introduced the team. Please, you are not in trouble or a suspect in the case. Officer Bradford here will take notes. We promise not to take up much of your time. We know that you primarily earn a living at preparing sushi and other foods at a successful Japanese restaurant in downtown Mohawk City, but you also make some side jingle with some photography."

Odell turned and pointed at the walls of the room and waved his arm at the many framed photographs gracing the walls.

"Beautiful work. Landscape, portraits, objects, dogs, cats, women, trees, flowers, everything. You are very skilled. Photography is your hobby, or is it a part-time gig for you?" Detective Odell asked Mr. Hiro Aki as the group of police officers stood in the living room of Mr. Aki's townhouse unit. Sergeant Oliver Crump was missing from the team as he worked to collect any potential evidence or clues from the knives that flattened

Larry Hick's tires.

Mr. Hiro Aki was a slender man of medium height, about sixty years of age, with distinct Japanese features, a clipped accent that altered between Japanese and English, and he was bald, and slightly nervous and very soft-spoken.

"Thank you for the compliment. Very glad to help, Detective Odell. I am very sad about the horrible murder of Doctor Gilding. Oh yes, a part-time job, for sure. But lucrative. I have many clients. Some weddings, some events, special photoshoots. Client appointments to fulfill visions. I began my love of photography as a young boy . . . in Japan. Yes, my full-time job is working as a sushi chef. Previously, I owned my own Japanese restaurant. It was very successful but I grew too old for the stress of running a restaurant and sold it. That money bought me this lovely home. Now, I am very happy to just work as a sushi chef."

"I have noted that . . . ya are good with knives. Huh?"

Odell spoke; he lifted his eyes to gauge the reaction of Mr. Aki.

"Very good with knives, Detective Odell. I prepare sushi. I have to be good. But I am not a violent man. The last thing that I would do is harm someone! Plus, Doctor Gilding was a . . . good customer. He paid me very well for my work."

Odell nodded and said, "Relax, Mr. Aki. I already said that you are not in trouble and you are not a suspect here. In fact, so far, I will share with you that you have played an important role in working this case to a solution. I understand about Doctor Gilding being a very good customer. He paid you very well to take photographs of the reading circle of reading students and of the beautiful young women that he entertained."

Mr. Aki seemed surprised that Detective Odell knew of his photographic work.

Observing his surprise, the good detective quickly followed up his statement and added, "Our elite C-S-I team found the photographs on Doctor Gilding's laptop. Tell me, Mr. Aki. . .." Odell's voice trailed off as he suddenly began to tap his pockets while everyone watched the ritual. Odell mumbled, "Right-side-suit-jacket pocket," and he reached down into the depths of spent cigarette butts and mixed ashes to produce a twisted old replica of a cigarette. Finding it, Odell stuck it on his lower lip with the now familiar magical "Odell Lip Glue."

Mr. Aki immediately began waving his hands frantically in the air while proclaiming, "Oh, no, Detective Odell! Please! No smoking in my house. It disturbs my energy and stinks up my house with nefarious odors."

The cigarette danced with Odell's words.

"Relax, Aki. I ain't gonna light it—just taste it. It upsets me, too. Not my energy, although, I am sure it stinks up my house with nefarious odors, too. But primally it upsets the living hell outta my stomach. Lately, if fact, always, I feel as I will puke my guts out when I smoke. Yet, I do it, anyway. I need to research that fact and the fact that the word . . . nefarious . . . seems to pop up frequently as of late. To get back to it . . . now, can you confirm that you took these photos? Officer Bradford, please set aside your notepad and please give Mr. Aki the photographs. Thank you."

Bradford nodded and tucked his notepad and pen in his uniform pocket and dug down into his backpack and produced a folder. From that folder, Officer Miles Bradford took the photographs that Sergeant Oliver Crump and his team provided and the officer handed the photographs off to Mr. Aki. Mr. Aki studied each of the photographs and nodded and handed them back to Officer Bradford.

"Yes, I took them all. On one of my best cameras. The reading circle is interesting. Great light in that room. Natural light. And the young women are gorgeous. I am very proud of those portrait shots."

"Yes, gorgeous. Great work. Great art. I love art. Very beautiful and tasteful shots of stunning women. It is a very important fact and a turning point in this investigation that Doctor Gilding was studying them when he was murdered."

Mr. Aki took a few steps back from where he stood and held his chest with both of his hands.

"Really? Oh no! My work? Why?"

"Because he was a woman-chaser and worked hard at bedding every possible woman that he could. C'mon, now. You know that, Mr. Aki. I mean, did you like the guy?"

"Well, he certainly *was* a womanizer. For sure. He was always trying to persuade Ms. Fuentes to pose nude for me to shoot her naked. Obviously, as you can see, Ms. Maguire was open to it and she is very lovely and a great model. Ms. Maguire could make a fortune as a model. I think that eventually we would have scheduled those nude sessions with Ms. Fuentes, just never got around to it. Now, for obvious reasons, it looks as if we never will. Ms. Fuentes, because of her husband, who she suspected was not so keen on it, was a little apprehensive, but she is quite lovely and because I am not into women in my love life, I have a way of putting the models at ease. I think eventually, in the correct setting, she would have done it. I am an artist and could have done wonders with those women in photographic circles. Made them superstars and I would have made a lot of money, too. Done correctly, nudes are spectacular."

"I agree, Mr. Aki. Many moons ago, I dabbled in a little photography myself. I appreciate art in all forms. Something tells me that old Doctor Gilding was not into art. He was just into hot chicks and their bodies."

"No, art was not his bag. Pure lust was. I am afraid he had other intentions for those photographs. It was a progressive fling with him. Did I like him? He was okay. He was just a womanizer. Made a lot of enemies with the men around here by chasing their women. I bet a jealous man killed him. He was very wealthy, successful, charismatic, and handsome. A perfect mixture for the women to find irresistible."

"Actually, Mr. Aki, it turned into a lethal combination. What do you think of Ms. Fuentes?"

Mr. Aki smiled and said, "Very nice. Very friendly and very lovely. Gorgeous woman. Exotic looks. Great lips and facial features and a flowing and graceful body. All photographers and artists can feel energy and flow. She has great flow. Nothing clunky or clumsy about her. She is very flirty with all the men.

Too flirty in my opinion. She seems to fall in love with every man she meets. Not proper behavior for a married woman. I am not sure why she is even married. I make no secret of preferring the company of men—not women—and she even flirted with me!"

"Gotcha." Odell removed the dancing cigarette butt from his lip and he held it in his hand as he spoke. "Can you produce the original photographs for me to study? I mean, from the original files? I need to study them. On your computer, or a laptop, or a large monitor, or however you view your work to determine the quality shots from the lousy shots. If you can, it will be a great time saver and time is of the essence. Then we will be out of your way."

"Yes, of course. I want to cooperate, Detective Odell. Please find this way to my small study in the living room here. I have my photographic business set up in there. I use a desktop to view the original files for editing and adjustments. I have a large monitor. The original files are in RAW format, so they do take up a large amount of hard drive space."

Odell stuck the cigarette back in his mouth, just as there was a ring of the doorbell of the townhouse unit. Sergeant Grundy looked at Mr. Aki and said, "Most likely Sergeant Crump, joining us. Mr. Aki. Do you want me to check?"

"Yes, please Sergeant Grundy. I feel very safe with all these police officers here and I am not expecting any visitors. Detective Odell stood for a minute. He closed his eyes, fiddled with the cigarette butt in his mouth, opened his eyes, then turned to George Grundy and said, "Sarge. Ask Crump to go get Larry Hicks and bring him over here. Please. Thank you. We will meet you in the office here."

About fifteen minutes later, when Larry Hicks, Sergeant Grundy, and Sergeant Crump joined them in the office, Odell was seated behind the desk with Mr. Aki standing next to him as they went through the photographs on the desktop monitor. Odell furiously fiddled with the cigarette butt in his mouth and mumbled, "Geez, I need to light this sucker soon."

Officer Bradford stood on one side of the desk and Captain

Connor Moore stood on the other side, and Moore had a view of the photographs on the desktop monitor.

Detective Lyle Odell became very excited as Mr. Aki flipped through the photographs.

He almost shouted out as he spoke. "Bradford, please take copious notes. Please! Aki, these are from the Wednesday before the homicide. Correct? I mean the last reading circle event?"

"Yes, Odell-San," Mr. Aki reverted to last names, too; he added the Japanese show of respect to it, though. He was fitting right in now. Odell picked up on the respect and it followed Mr. Aki's lead.

"Please, first, the photograph of Ms. Maguire sitting on the desk. Then, Ms. Fuentes. When was that photoshoot?"

"About three weeks ago. Ms. Maguire came after the reading session. She did not attend the circle—she was not interested in reading classic literature. I only attended sparingly. I did sit in for that reading session. Mostly because I had the job to do afterwards. I like to read, but usually not the classics."

"And who was there for that session? I mean, other than Gilding, you, and the two women?"

"No one."

"Was there alcohol involved and snacks served?"

"Yes. It was a photoshoot session. Wine, whiskey, tequila, and expensive finger-food sandwiches and sweet treats. All very expensive and catered by Doctor Gilding. He usually spared no expense. It is work, but it is also a party time after and during work. It was a paid event for the models and for me, but it is meant to be fun. Keep it loose. The best shots are when you and the models are loose."

Odell nodded, then he stood up as his eyes remained glued to the screen with the photograph of Ms. Maguire displayed on the screen.

He removed the cigarette butt from his mouth and dropped it in his suit jacket pocket and mumbled, "Right-side-suit-jacket-pocket. Now, where is my magnifying glass?"

Everyone watched as Detective Odell began a furious pat down of his various storage places in search of his trusty foldable magnifying glass.

Odell looked at George Grundy for assistance, and Grundy shrugged his shoulders and said, "Sorry, Lyle lost track of it."

"Here, Detective Odell. You can use mine. I keep it in this drawer here. No offense, but you are rather absent-minded for a detective."

"Thanks, Aki-san. I am never offended. Can't use yours. Sorry. Has to be mine. I am used to it and using another glass will upset my energy."

Mr. Aki laughed aloud at the play on his own words, just as Odell produced his magnifying glass from the deep recesses of an inside suit jacket pocket. Odell unfolded the glass and zoomed in on the screen. Rather meticulously, Odell poured over the entire screen and studied it carefully with his glass.

Captain Moore commented, "My goodness. She is a stunning woman. A goddess. That is magnificent work, Mr. Aki. Magnificent."

"Thank you, Captain Moore. She is beautiful, as is Ms. Fuentes."

Odell waved and pointed at the screen and asked, "Please, Aki-San. Quickly, before my focus leaves. Ms. Fuentes."

Mr. Aki nodded and clicked the mouse button to change the photograph on the screen. He selected a photograph of Ms. Fuentes. Her beauty appeared on the screen.

Officer Bradford moved to study the screen, and he mumbled, "She is even more beautiful than Ms. Maguire is. The nude art is spectacular for obvious reasons, but this woman, fully clothed is magnificent. You are very, very talented, Mr. Aki. Just my opinion."

Mr. Hiro Aki stood up tall and then he folded his hands and, in a typically Japanese gesture, he bowed at the compliment from Officer Bradford and said, "Thank you."

Odell repeated the previous study with his glass on the new photograph and then leaned back and he almost smiled.

Lyle Odell looked at the group as he ran his hand through his hair and said, "The Holmes book is not there in the bookcase behind the women. I am convinced that the killer placed the book in the bookcase is a display of rage and a dose of ironic spite as he watched Doctor Gilding bleed like a river of blood and take his last breath. Ms. Fuentes needs to know who took her book, and that is another potential clue to the identity of the killer."

George Grundy jumped into the investigation and added his thoughts.

"Are you sure that Fuentes is not involved, Odell? Will she tell us that information? Or maybe she does not know who took her book. You mentioned the book on the day of the murder, when we first spoke with her and she did not say anything about the book. It does seem as if you are correct that Fuentes is the central figure in all of this mess. But why? We have to speak with her. I mean, she could have been there with the killer and not actually swung the knife."

Officer Bradford looked at his watch and said, "Well, it is almost five o'clock now. Our appointment with Ms. Fuentes is in fifteen minutes. We will know more very shortly."

Mr. Larry Hicks spoke for the first time.

He waved his hand in the air and said, "Nah. She loved the guy. She loves all men. She would never have killed the jerk or put someone up to doing it for her. Too violent. Lots of rage in that homicide. I see where ya going with this, Odell. The killer was wildly jealous of Doctor Gilding, but that makes up like half the population of the entire community of men here and every other man who knew him. I told you all he thought of was luring women into his lair. Married, single, attached or otherwise. He did not care."

Odell looked at Larry Hicks and he blinked a few times and stopped mussing with his hair and attempted to smooth it out. "Correct, Hicks. One of our key witnesses at the high school told us that he was a sexual predator. I agree with that label. Eventually, maybe, Fuentes would have broken down and slept with Gilding. Had an affair. Her marriage is not a happy one. But not then and certainly not . . . now. The book ties this to Fuentes. She is next on our interview list, but first, Aki-San.

Please, the photos of the reading circle group. Hicks, please, this is the moment. Concentrate on this photograph. Mr. Larry Hicks nodded and moved into position behind the desk as did the entire group as Mr. Aki hovered the mouse and clicked on the file for the reading circle group.

"Please study it, but everyone . . . do not say a word. Only answer my questions with correct, or yes or no or if I ask for more detail, then please do so. Do not expand your thoughts. Thank you, but it causes my mind to wander in focus and in a search for an answer, and this is the key moment in the case," Odell said as he studied the photograph with his magnifying glass. As he did so, and Mr. Hicks also studied the screen, Odell mumbled, "Mrs. Amanda Sheffield, then, an unknown young woman. Maybe a college student, then another middle-aged woman, then Fuentes, then a young man—college age with his leg touching Ms. Fuentes on her leg. Side-by-side. Close. Very close. Then, another young man, with another young man, then Doctor Gilding with a book in his hand, another young man, and in the last chair is Mr. Aki."

Odell looked up and asked Mr. Aki.

"Camera set on timer and a tripod, so that you could be in the circle?"

"Correct."

"What was the book you were reading and studying that day or week?"

"It's slipping my mind. I was only there for work and to do the photoshoot session. I would sit in and listen to the discussion when I attended, but I did not read the books. I am only being honest."

"Gotcha. Love the honesty part of that statement. Aki-San, please, can you zoom this part in here?"

Odell put his finger near the screen and then he zoomed in with his magnifying glass and focused on the book in Doctor Gilding's hand as Mr. Aki fiddled with the picture to increase the zoom.

"The book is *The Strange Case of Dr. Jekyll and Mr. Hyde*. Many people have dual personalities these days. Interesting choice of books. Zoom out again to capture the group. Mr. Aki, can you name these people apart from Gilding, Mrs. Sheffield, Fuentes, and you?"

Mr. Aki shook his head and said, "No. Can I expand on the details, Odell?"

"Yes, please do so. Thank you."

"I cannot identify all of them. The young woman is from the high school. I think she is a senior, but I do not know her name. I think the middle-aged woman lives in the community, but again, I do not know her name. The young men all are from the local college where Doctor Gilding taught. They all were there because of Ms. Fuentes. They all were obviously infatuated with her, and she hung around them all the time. They would act like young guys courting an older woman. Skateboarding, smoking weed, laughing it up, sitting in the courtyard all night, around the firepit. A married woman acting foolish and flirting with young men. Playing them for fools and for the attention. How her husband allowed that behavior is beyond me. But he is a firefighter and always working weird shifts. The one sitting next to her was especially so. He always was next to her. I think they all were in love with her and she played them all, as she does all men, like a fine violin. They are just young guys. Hormones bouncing and they were looking to have sex with her. Just being honest, but they couldn't give a damn about books. Especially classics. I know that the young man sitting next to Ms. Fuentes is Mr. Alan Hudson. He is a college student, but he also works. . . ."

Detective Lyle Odell held his hand up in the air, and Mr. Aki stopped speaking. Odell jumped up and frantically waved his arms in the air, and then he dug into his right-suit-jacket-pocket and found a twisted cigarette and stuck it in his mouth.

"Please, I can tell you where he works and I will do so. Aki-San, thank you. You have done us a great and immense service, and I will put you and Hicks here in for a community award. Mr. Alan Hudson. He looks very tall. Lean but powerful. Big hair teased up. African-American or some type of mixed Latino and African race. Hicks, this is it. Any of these young guys . . . is one of them the young guy who got raging mad at you when he pulled up and saw you speaking with Ms. Fuentes?"

"Yuppers, Odell."

"That is him, Alan Hudson. Right there. That is the thug punk-ass young buck who narrowly escaped with his teeth still intact in his dopey mouth that day."

Odell sighed. He placed both his hands on the desk. He closed his eyes and then opened them. The cigarette danced on his lower lip as Odell spoke.

"Aki-San, you were about to tell me when I stopped you that Alan Hudson works at the Asteroid Coffee shop. Right out there on the main drag. Where everyone who lives here goes for coffee and snacks. Like blueberry muffins."

"Correct. In the drive-through window."

"Is he tall?"

"Very tall. Very tall, indeed."

"Damn, Odell," Sergeant Oliver Crump said, "Gilding's last meal. The coffee container. The muffin crumbs. The container is from Asteroid Coffee. Hudson is tall. Hard to tell from the picture—but at least six-feet-three-inches. Hicks here thinks he is even taller than that. Hudson is powerful. Sounds like he has a bad temper. Damn. A college kid is a brutal killer."

"Yes, he is. Now, we just have to prove it. Right now, we have nothing but ideas and theories. Cap, Bradford, Crump. I need everything in the world on Mr. Alan Hudson. Everything. In. The. Entire. World. His family, his friends, what he studies, where he rides his skateboard. What he eats, where he sleeps. I will find out if he ever had sex with Ms. Fuentes. Everything. Then we will need a search warrant for his home and his car. If he actually has a car. Or maybe we can lure him out. I need to smoke this cancer stick and then tonight, grab some Irish and break my recently acquired, better habits. I need to study the situation very carefully. First things first. Let's go speak with Fuentes. Heads still on swivels, men. Aki-San. Thank you."

Detective Lyle Odell faced Mr. Aki and folded his hands and

duplicated the previous Japanese display of respect and thanks by bowing and thanking Mr. Aki. Mr. Aki reciprocated the gesture.

"Aki-San, please, do not venture out too much in the next few days. Keep your eyes peeled. Hudson knows we are here. He knows that we met. He knows."

"Oh, my, Detective Odell. This is very upsetting. Maybe I will head out of town for a bit. Visit my brother in Connecticut."

"Not a bad idea. If you do so, please give Officer Bradford your contact information. If you are uneasy or decide to stay here, Captain Moore can arrange for police protection. Please let us know. Hicks, you too. Same offer."

Hicks scoffed at Lyle Odell's suggestion.

"Bullshit, Odell. Bring the punk-thug on and I will handle it. With my last throws of anger."

"Your choice, Hicks. Please go home now and be careful. We will stay in touch. Just be careful because ex-cops are not bulletproof or knife-proof. None of us are."

"Oh, yes, Aki-San."

"Yes, Odell-San."

"I am not."

"You are not what?" Mr. Aki asked as he was puzzled as to the nature of this typical Odell-like conversation.

"Absent-minded. I am confused and fuzzy from too much Irish whiskey, and long days, and walking where phantoms tread, and the brutal horror of homicides, but not absent-minded."

Mr. Aki nodded his head, then bowed his head and sunk to his knees. As he knelt, he closed his eyes as he folded his hands in front of him in a form of prayer.

After a few brief moments, Mr. Hiro Aki lifted his head and said, "You are a great man. A genius. Please, go in peace, Lyle Odell. Find justice. May all the gods protect you and your friends. Go get the bad guy."

"Oh! Hi there! I am usually late for everything but it is only five o'clock now! I am so proud of myself. I saw all the police cars parked here, so I decided to walk up and meet everyone. I figured it was you, Detective Odell. I hope all is well with Mr. Aki. He is so sweet. I love him."

Ms. Christina Fuentes yelled and waved as she bounced her way up the sidewalk in the direction of Mr. Aki's townhouse unit as the group of police officers and Mr. Larry Hicks made their way down the sidewalk in front of the units. She was very outgoing and social. Ms. Fuentes was always and continually gregarious in her nature and she looked devastatingly beautiful, dressed in a tight sweater, a black denim jacket, and black jeans that hugged her curves and figure in a very alluring manner. Her long hair flowed behind her and her dark eyes flashed underneath her eyeglasses. Detective Odell stopped puffing on his long-sought after cigarette and exhaled the smoke in the air.

As the smoke circled his head, Odell commented, "Your love seems to be the weapon here, Ms. Fuentes. You love too much."

Just as Odell finished speaking, the sound of a rifle shot rang out. A single bullet hit the dirt right in front of where Ms. Fuentes walked and then another shot rang out and hit in the dirt just behind her. She screamed and Sergeant Grundy yelled out.

"Down, Ms. Fuentes! On the ground! Now! Gunfire! Take cover!"

Grundy immediately drew his service weapon and ran in the direction of Ms. Fuentes and hugged her, tackled her, and rolled over to protect her with his huge body.

Sergeant Oliver Crump drew his weapon and ran for cover behind the parked patrol cars, as did Captain Moore and Larry Hicks ran full-speed in the direction of Sergeant George Grundy. Another shot ran out, and it hit Grundy just below his right shoulder as he covered the screaming Ms. Fuentes. Grundy screamed out in pain as he collapsed and went limp and continued to cover Ms. Fuentes to protect her with his body.

Larry Hicks ran at full speed, and he dove over the top of the fallen Sergeant Grundy. Initially, Larry Hicks wanted to reach for Grundy's now dropped weapon to return fire and afford some type of protection, but seeing the amount of blood emitting from the wound on Grundy's back, he decided to forgo his own cover, and his own life, and administer first aid, instead.

As Ms. Fuentes screamed in horror, Larry Hicks took control of the situation.

Hicks screamed out, "Sarge took a hit! GRUNDY IS HIT!"

Larry Hicks pointed in the direction of where the rifle fire emitted and he screamed, "The shooter is in the new construction! On the second floor! High-power rifle fire! Officer is down! I got him! Heavy blood! Applying pressure!"

Larry Hicks ripped his muscle tee shirt off and wrapped it around his hands and dove into the wounded area on Sergeant George Grundy's back to apply pressure to the wound that spitted and flowed blood.

Officer Miles Bradford knelt in the driveway behind the parked car of Mr. Aki, and from behind cover, with his weapon drawn, Bradford made the call on his hand-held radio, "Unit 110 to headquarters. We are taking gunfire! Officer down! Sergeant Grundy is down! Need back up and medics! STAT! Raintree Townhouses. Active shooter on the second floor of the new construction on Raintree Drive! Corner of Fairview Drive. East side!"

The answer came immediately over the radio.

"Roger, Unit 110. Help on the way. Dispatch is immediate. Hold tight! Dig in! Many units are close to your location!"

Suddenly, the rifle fire in and around, the now wounded, Sergeant Grundy, and around Ms. Fuentes and Larry Hicks, stopped and now the gunfire was pointed in a different direction.

A new target.

A diversion.

When the gunfire subsided, Ms. Christina Fuentes crawled out from underneath the cover of the wounded body of Sergeant George Grundy and the protection of Larry Hicks.

She sat on her backside on the sidewalk and covered her eyes as she sobbed and then cried aloud, "Larry! Save him! Please save him! He saved my life!"

"I am doing all I can, honey. All I can!" Hicks replied as he worked to keep constant pressure on the wound on Sergeant George Grundy.

The shirt was already soaked in blood.

As the group of police officers looked up, they watched as Detective Lyle Odell sprinted like an Olympic sprinter directly in the direction of the shooter and into the relentless fire of the rifle bullets. More bullets hit the ground in and around Odell as he wove, and hit the ground, rolled, and then stood up, and made a serpentine path on his way toward the shooter. As Odell ran, he fired relentlessly from his service weapon.

"Odell! Damn! What the hell? Get down! Protect yourself!" Captain Moore yelled out, but Odell ignored his commanding officer.

Detective Lyle Odell expended one full clip and while still sprinting full speed, with the twisted cigarette still hanging on his lower lip, Odell ejected the spent clip, and in one fluid motion, dug into one of his many pockets, and he produced a fresh clip. Odell inserted the new clip, aimed, and fired off more shots.

"We need a rifle. Odell is outgunned and so are we! Damn! No time to grab it! Over the top, men! Cover Odell! Let's go!" Captain Moore commanded and waved and Officer Bradford, Captain Moore, and Sergeant Crump jumped to their feet and followed behind the still sprinting at full speed while simultaneously firing his weapon, Detective Lyle Odell. All three police officers ran full speed behind Odell and they all relentlessly fired their weapons in a barrage of ammunition in the direction of the shooter, who seemed to be hiding in a hole of the new construction, perhaps, within a rough-framed window opening, now some fifty or so feet away.

The rifle fire suddenly stopped.

Sirens screamed in the background of the city. Police cars, medical assistance, fire trucks, ambulances. Mayhem!

Odell stopped at the base of the new construction, right underneath the opening that the rifle shots emitted from. Odell scanned the area with his weapon drawn as the rest of the group caught up with him.

Odell said between great heaves of his chest, with the cigarette still dangling on his lower lip, "He fled. We needed a diversion. I was the diversion. We were sitting ducks. George is down. God be with him and comfort him and heal him. I did not hit the shooter. Too far of a distance, and my bullets could not penetrate through the wood and shell of the building. Quick, men. He is exiting out from the rear or wherever. We need to split up. If the shooter makes it to the main drag and into the confines of the city then, the shooter is gone!"

Odell looked at his commanding officer, and the fire and pain were both deep in his eyes. Odell expertly ejected a clip and effortlessly dug in and around within the vast confines of his seemingly endless pockets of tools, plucked another clip out in one smooth motion, and he loaded it into his weapon.

With great respect in his voice, Homicide Detective Lyle Odell said, "Cap! Call the strategy. Sir."

Captain Connor Moore nodded, quickly scanned the building, and then waved and pointed in the air with his free hand while he held his weapon at his side.

"Bradford, right, Crump left. Odell, work the center and get up in the building just in case the shooter is hiding out inside. I am heading for the main drag to intercept any potential escape paths. Bradford, you have the radio. Call in the extra firepower to the main drag. Looking for a young man. African-American with a mixed race of Latino. Big hair or wearing a hat to cover it. He most likely has ditched the rifle. No one dies here, men, except this son-of-a-bitch that hit George. Circle back here in no more than five minutes. Check your watches."

Odell tossed his cigarette aside, and for once, he did not try to retrieve it.

The police officers jumped into action.

Homicide Detective Lyle Odell set out on his mission. He held his weapon out in front of him, with his right hand on the weapon and his left hand cupping the handgrip of the handgun. He was steady; concentrated and determined, although he was wounded on his right leg and the blood and pain flowed from his leg and the pain from his soul. Odell's chest heaved while trying to capture air, and his mind raced with thoughts of his best friend fighting for his life. Odell did his best to block them all out as he crept into the building, and he kept his ears and eyes trained for any signs of the shooter fleeing the scene. Step-by-step, Detective Odell carefully crept through the rough construction of the building. He found a center staircase and continued to creep and search and listen. His focus was wide, then it was narrow. His eyes trained. His weapon was ready and pointing in all directions at once. Amidst the sawdust and grit of the new construction, Odell took careful steps while keeping his weapon out in front of him and ready to fire within seconds of spotting his target. Higher and higher, Odell climbed the staircase until he found the exact spot that the shooter stood and fired and tried to kill Ms. Fuentes, and then he tried to kill them all.

And from where he wounded George Grundy. . ..

On the third floor of the structure. There were four floors in total.

Odell spotted the shooter's weapon; dropped on the floor amongst the sawdust and the grit. The good detective did not dwell upon the spent weapon; instead, he trained his eyes upon where the shooter stood, aimed, and fired from. Convinced that the shooter had fled the scene, Homicide Detective Lyle Odell shouldered his weapon and dropped to his knees. His keen eyes scanned the scene for clues, but Odell knew there were none. He did not even need to enlist the aid of his various gizmos and gadgets to determine that this was a dead end.

Odell mumbled, "We did not even hit 'em. No wounds. No blood. Fired and fled. Hit Grundy. Lucky-ass bastard. I am coming for you now, ya son-of-a-bitch. No place left to hide."

He rose to a standing position and sighed as he looked at his leg and the blood running out of his pants leg, over his boot and onto the bare wooden floor. Odell needed to move. He did not want his blood to mix into an investigation. Odell turned and walked down the same staircase that he climbed, his eyes and reactions ready to draw his service weapon . . . if needed. He knew it would not be so. Yet, when he arrived on the first floor of the new construction, Odell still felt as if he needed to retrace the potential routes of the exit of the shooter. Lyle Odell walked slowly, scanning the many points of exit and potential entry for clues. Near an exit; a roughly framed glimpse to the outside world, but still lacking a door, Odell spotted something. A set of keys on the floor. Amidst the sawdust and the grit. He limped forward; blood leaking; back screaming; Odell bent at his waist and then he carefully knelt on the wooden floor of the structure and he studied the keys on the floor. The good detective almost smiled, but the combination of the pain and the emotion would not allow him to do so.

Odell mumbled as he stood up and flexed and grimaced from the pain in his lower back from dashing and running, and the wound on his right leg from the bullets.

"Finally. Game on. Game up. We gotcha now."

Meanwhile, while Odell searched the new construction and the active scene of the shooter, and the rest of the team split up into alternate directions around the building, Captain Connor Moore raced to intercept the shooter. He could still sprint very fast and as he sprinted along with his service weapon drawn, his mind raced with flashbacks of military combat; of dodging bullets, and of explosions, and of his brothers in arms, blown apart. When you think about it; living and dying actually go together. It is a very fine line that separates the two of them. Only God knows where the line begins and where it ends.

Captain Moore was a fearless man. He held it together.

Moore tried hard not to focus upon those thoughts, but to remained focused on the mission at hand. This was real, and this was now; that was all in the past. He hoped his combat-related PTSD would not haunt him. His team counted upon him. Moore raced ahead, his weapon drawn out in front, ready to fire. As he turned the corner of the building and arrived onto the busy city street that sprawled in front of him, for a fleeting minute, Captain Connor Moore caught a glimpse of the shooter. The shooter's long hair waving in the wind as he raced into the maze of a busy city street at the height of the activity of a busy day.

Moore aimed his weapon at the shooter and screamed, "Halt! Police! Stop! Now! I will shoot!"

The shooter ignored his commands and his warnings and instead, he raced at full speed away from where Captain Moore set his legs into a tripod of a shooter's stance, and aimed his weapon and prepared to shoot. Moore's eyes and his brain captured the moment and all the different aspects of the surroundings.

'A baby in a stroller being pushed by parents. An elderly man walking down the sidewalk with his cane steadying him. Cars, shoppers, a taxi picking up a fare while parked by the sidewalk. Too many innocents.'

The shooter disappeared into the maze of the city. Panic amongst the by-standers ensued. People screamed and ducked. Moore shouldered his weapon. His chest heaved and his mind raced. Captain Connor Moore knew that he made the proper decision. His breath caught and shuddered. The shooter escaped.

After about five minutes, the police officers met once again at the agreed rendezvous point. They were all covered in sweat, panting for air and exhausted. Captain Moore was the last to arrive, and he looked at his troops and shook his head.

Captain Moore said, "I thought that I initially had a shot at him. I was wrong. I could not take it. Too far away and I only have a vague description of him and caught a vague glance. Long hair. Tall. Great athlete. A very fast runner. There were too many civilians in the way to take a chance at a shot. Too far.

Yes, indeed . . . to reiterate . . . he has long hair and can run really, really fast. I am sorry. He escaped. Let's call it in and have the extra uniforms close this entire facility down and label it as a crime scene now. The press is already here out on the main drag. Damn shooter just fled and they are already here. Sergeant Crump, it is all yours now for your team and you. Hopefully, you find something."

Detective Lyle Odell seemed hardly out of breath. That was remarkable; considering the exercise and scope of the adventure that he had just performed.

Odell bowed his head, lifted it, and then Odell said, "Sarge Crump. I worked my way through the entire building. Up to the location where he shot from. Third floor, near the southwest corner, opening for a window. I can see our spent bullets on the floor. We missed him. I am sure of it. Cap's testimony confirms that he can run fast. Either he is not wounded or he is superhuman. I will go with the fact that he is not wounded. Yet, I think there might be some items for your team to capture and inspect. Might be very fruitful for evidence. Pay no attention to the blood on the floor of the scene. The blood there on the floor is mine. Not his. The shooter fled in terror. He is a poor shot. Most likely a hunter. Or he is not used to the weapon. That is why I am still alive. I feel as if even an average shooter could have and should have easily dropped me. A bullet grazed my right leg. A mere flesh wound, as they say. Over there. Across the pond."

All eyes of his comrades in arms glanced at his right leg and noted the tear in his pants right around his calf muscle and the puddle of blood pooling on the sidewalk right next to his boot. Detective Lyle Odell did not miss a beat in his continued testimony.

"There is a hunting rifle on the third floor. Near to where the shooter setup to make his kills. The shooter ditched it because he needed to split the scene very fast and he knew he could not hide a rifle out on the main drag. Nor could he carry it, so he ditched it. I did not touch the rifle. I suspect it is fully empty of ammo. I also found a set of keys on the first floor near an exit from the building."

Odell turned and waved in the direction of the structure and continued to explain.

"I suspect they were hanging on his hip on a typical belt holder and he bumped into the wooden frame of the construction as he frantically fled in haste and they knocked off their belt holder. They look commercial in nature. Might be keys from the construction, but I do not think so. I don't see any locks on this place. It is just a rough frame and core and shell construction project right now. The keys could be for toolboxes, but they appear to be door locks and store keys. My guess and my hope are that they are keys that fit locks at the Asteroid Coffee out here on the main drag. My hope is that the manager of that coffee shop was dumb enough to entrust this punk-ass kid, a killer, with responsibility. If I am correct, it might give us enough to open this case wide open. I can show your C-S-I team where the keys are. I did not touch the keys, either. Chances are, he wore shooter's gloves and the serial numbers are filed away from the rifle into oblivion. I would like to examine, with my methods and my various gizmos and gadgets, the shooter's firing position with you and your team. Other than that, I have nothing else to add to this mess of a day. As Captain Moore testified, this guy is an athlete. In very good shape. He got away. This time."

Sergeant Oliver Crump walked over to Lyle Odell and he put his hand on Odell's right shoulder and gripped it tightly in a show of emotions, teamwork, and of respect.

Crump said, "Lyle, I know what you did for all of us there. For George. For the team. For the mission. We are on it, Lyle. All over it. Of course, we will not miss anything. Sounds as if we might have something this time. Check it out when you are ready. My team is on the way. We will work on your orders, and Cap's orders, and the usual protocol. Glad you are okay. But you do need to have that right leg looked at. Pronto. That is not just a mere flesh wound . . . you are bleeding heavily. You took a bullet. EMTs and the medics are right over there. With George."

Oliver Crump's emotions broke up and he gripped Detective Lyle Odell's shoulder even tighter and looked to the sky, then wiped at his eyes and gathered his words and emotions.

"George is gonna be okay, Odell. He is Grundy. He is the man. Those were some crazy few moments there. You ran directly into the line of fire."

Officer Bradford caught his breath and seemed able to speak now. He stood up tall. Very tall.

He looked at Captain Moore and asked, "Permission to speak, sir."

"Of course, Officer Bradford. Go ahead."

"Thank you, Captain Moore. The radio chatter is that Sergeant Grundy is already in an ambulance on the way to the hospital. Elite medical assistance for sure from those first responders. We will all pray now. To address, Detective Odell. Detective, that was the bravest thing that I ever witnessed. Sir. Your athleticism and bravery are amazing. You ran so fast. No body armor. Yet, you had all of us wear it. You created a diversion to save our lives. Once more, what is it that you did in the Coast Guard? Sir."

Odell nodded and said, "Thank you, Crump. Thank you, Cap. Thank you, George. Thank you, Hicks. Thank you, Bradford. Sometimes in life, you do what you have to do for the people who do for you. Someday we will all be ashes and dust in the wind. It was what we did between those some days, and before the dust arrives, that counts the most. To answer your specific question. I did investigations, Bradford. Investigations."

Odell then looked at each of his comrades individually and then focused his gaze on his commanding officer. Odell wiped the sweat away from his eyes and what appeared as if were a mix of tears and sweat streamed down his cheeks.

"A person with nefarious intentions . . . shot, George. Captain Moore, sir, God help the shooter now. I am gonna get the shooter. Katie bar the door."

"I understand, Lyle. I will do the paperwork for today. Odell, please, no holds barred. I will cover every sin that you think about or might commit. God will cover the rest. Go get this son-of-a-bitch."

"I will, Cap. I will."

Odell stood back and upright. He snapped off a proper salute to his commanding officer and then returned to a standing position and an at ease position and he spoke almost in a whisper.

"For, George."

Captain Moore properly returned the salute and echoed Detective Odell's words.

"Yes. For, George."

Homicide Detective Lyle Odell was good at his job.

Very good.

So was Captain Conner Moore.

So was the entire team.

CHAPTER NINE

Love

"I know that you met with Marjorie and George's children. It was very much appreciated, Lyle. I too met with them, and afterwards, I thought it best that we sat out here and allowed them the private time in the separate waiting room. Even if you are George's best friend and likewise. Time as a family without all of . . . us all around them. Especially if we begin to speak about the investigation." Captain Connor Moore spoke to his team and the visitors, as the emotions of the moment obviously took their toll on him.

"I agree. Great call, sir. I did my best, Captain Moore. It was rather . . . difficult," Odell replied. "I told his wife . . . Marjorie . . . and his children, how much that George means to me. How much I love him. How great a man he is. And yes," Odell glanced over his shoulder to where Ms. Christina Fuentes sat in a chair in the waiting room, "we will talk a little business here."

The usually unshakable Homicide Detective Lyle Odell was shaken. His voice reflected the fact.

"You did great, Odell. Wonderful. Thank you. Is your leg, okay? Did the medics stop the bleeding?"

"Thank you. Yes. I am fine, Cap. Just a graze. Lots of blood, but no bite. I will numb the pain tonight. The pain of my wound and the pain in my soul. With lots of Irish. Promise on that one. I am sorry. Falling away and I am just being honest, Cap. Please. You will need Officer Bradford to come and wake my drunken ass up in the morning. I gave him an extra key to the front door. My cellphone will not be charged—in fact, I am not even sure where it even is right now. Home. Maybe on my end table. I will listen to a glorious piece of classical music on my old radio. Einaudi. Primavera is on the playlist tonight. Out of Philadelphia. A fine symphony that one is and an equally fine conductor. The New York Rovers have a game tonight. Philly. How ironic. It seems to be a Philadelphia type of night looming. I will tune that in after the concert. Going to keep my optimism going here and predict that I will be home in time for these events. I will dive deep into the Irish whiskey and find the final pieces of what we need to do to solve this puzzle and make a solid arrest. I want to attend the funeral tomorrow and then we can meet up afterwards. My prediction of days for an arrest might be delayed. I did not . . . anticipate . . . George being wounded. Of course, this is all depending upon . . . tonight."

Captain Conner Moore smiled. He nodded his head, walked over to where Detective Odell sat, placed his hand on his shoulder, and spoke.

He spoke almost in a whisper. "I understand, and I have you covered. Do what you need to do, Lyle."

Captain Moore then released his grip on Odell and took a seat amongst his troops.

Detective Lyle Odell, Sergeant Oliver Crump, Captain Conner Moore, Officer Miles Bradford, Mr. Larry Hicks, and Ms. Christina Fuentes sat in a group, in chairs, in a waiting room, in the Mohawk City Hospital. Waiting on the word of how Sergeant George Grundy was doing. The doctors and nurses told them that George Grundy was in critical condition and he was now in surgery.

Ms. Fuentes insisted on sitting next to Detective Lyle Odell. She looked at Odell and smiled, and then she closed her eyes and opened them again. Her dark eyes flashed, and Detective Lyle Odell caught the flash. Momentarily. Very, very momentarily. If he could have held it in his hands, then he would have, but he could not. The flash escaped him. It was very elusive, as all beauty is. It was a just a fleeting moment in time; a moment that mixed in with many others in his life and, sadly, the beauty faded into the midst of a career of chasing phantoms, evil, horrible homicides, and various criminals and others laced with only nefarious intentions.

At the very least, as best that he could, he held the beauty of her eyes in his mind's eye. Forever. At least he had that. Regrettably, given his lifetime commitment to fighting crime and tracking down the evil in the world, Odell suddenly understood why the killer had killed a man within the competition for her love. Amid her beauty. In order to remove any love that could have stolen her from him.

"Ms. Fuentes, I need to tell you this. I am quite sure that your young friend, this young man . . . Mr. Alan Hudson is the killer of Doctor Rochester Gilding. He tried to kill or wound you, he wounded Sarge Grundy and he is on the loose. He killed out of jealousy over Doctor Gilding's attraction to you and maybe some other influences and because of your interactions with, as you called him . . . Rock. Hudson's raging temper got the best of him. He felt that if he could not have you, then no man can. Maybe."

Shock at Odell's testimony rippled through her lovely face as Ms. Fuentes said, "Alan Hudson? Oh my! Alan? I cannot believe that he is a killer! But I am a married woman! He already cannot have me, Detective Odell." Ms. Fuentes shook her head and then covered her face with her hands. She was silent for a moment or two, and then she began to sob a little as Odell continued to explain his theory.

"With all due respect, Ms. Fuentes . . . and, please keep in mind that I am only going on the testimony of your friends and neighbors and some of my own preliminary observations. You hardly act as if you are married. My intention is not to make you sad or to feel guilty. Although that will obviously be an unavoidable by-product of my statements and observations. I only am speaking factually as a homicide detective. Flirting with every man, spending time with Hudson and his young group of men. Flirting with the known player of all women, Doctor Rochester Gilding. Acting like you are romantically interested in each and every one of them. Playing them and leading them on. Especially Hudson. You are a very beautiful woman, Ms.

Fuentes. Your beauty has immense power. In this case, it turned into an evil power. Not that you ever intended it to do so, but actions either good, bad, or indifferent, all have consequences. The young man fell head over heels in love with you, became obsessed, and went off the deep end. It happens. I have seen it many times in my career. Your fun-loving attitude on life and on people, your desire for attention and your alluring behavior turned a young man into a monster over love. Love is a powerful emotion. Only loneliness exceeds love's power in our mind and soul. Perhaps Alan Hudson felt there was a chance for you two someday."

Ms. Fuentes had uncovered her face and now she looked at Detective Odell as all eyes in the circle of men remained silent as they all stared in on the powerful scene.

She wiped at her eyes and flicked some tears away before she spoke.

"I never cheated on my husband. I never would do that. Despite the many offers. I just love the . . . attention. I need therapy. I am sure of it. My husband does not support me emotionally or physically, but he does financially. His family is very wealthy . . . but he does not take a penny from them. He works all the time, and like all of you do . . . sees awful things at his job. It turned him dark and I need light. He is on shift today and called me when he heard of the shooting. Do you think he would leave work and check on me? Comfort me? I was just shot at and a brave and fearless police officer and Mr. Hicks saved my life! Nope. Heard that I was okay and that the shooter missed and he stayed at work. I guess that I should be thankful that he even called. Said to me, the shooter was going after the cops. Not me. I was just there. Can you imagine? I love my husband. Or at least, I think that I do. Or I did. I am not sure right now. At one time, we were hopelessly in love. We could not stand to be away from each other's arms for more than a few hours. It was amazing. Oh damn. My goodness, Detective Odell. Have you never been hopelessly in love? Let me tell you about it. That is, if you do not know already that it is hopeless. The only reason that I know I am in love is by the pain that I feel."

Detective Odell did not comment, he simply lowered his head and listened and allowed Ms. Fuentes to vent a little and heal her soul through some self-awareness of her own behavior and actions.

She continued to do so.

"Anyway, back to me and my woes and issues. It is the same old story. My father left our family when I was a young child. Daddy issues. How sad of me . . . how stupid of me to do this. To act like this. To be like this. I did play, Alan. My actions implied many things. I play with many men. Doctor Gilding was all over me. Pressuring me to have dinner and to have sex with him. I should have never got involved with that reading circle. But he was so attractive. . .."

"You are not stupid, Ms. Fuentes. Far from it, in fact. You are very intelligent. I sure as hell am not a priest or a pastor or a good person to seek advice from. Lord knows my sins lie deep in the comfort of those bottles of Irish whiskey. That is for sure. So, take these words or leave them—you just need to change your ways. Recommit to your husband and your marriage. Ya married the guy for a reason. Find that reason once again. Let me ask you this? Does Mr. Hudson have a temper? Did he take the Sherlock Holmes book? Was that a trigger in some way? Since you never slept with him or with Gilding. I need a trigger."

Her answer was immediate.

"Oh yes! He has an awful temper. If he does not get his own way or things go sideways for him. He is a huge complainer, and it is always someone else's fault or the world dragging him down. If I would tell him, we could not hang out because my husband was off shift for two weeks, he would pout and text and call me and eventually begin to yell at me. We all suggested books for the reading circle sessions and I love Sherlock Holmes books. I love detective stories. I guess that I am living in one right now."

She worked a smile into the edges of her mouth, and then it quickly faded as she realized the implications of her thoughts and words.

"I bought that one book and brought it to the reading circle as my suggestion for us to read. Rock snubbed it. He was a literary snob. He did not like Conan Doyle as an author and thought the stories were too simple in construction and composition. Besides, my book was a paperback. Doctor Gilding only allowed us to read from hardbacks." He used to say, 'Paperbacks are for dime stores and drug store racks. Not my reading circle. 'Alan was enraged at him. I guess he felt as if Rock disrespected me."

Odell nodded and spoke in a low voice as he mussed his hair and then tugged at his already loose necktie. "There is the trigger for sure. Hudson is a raging maniac. We will dig into him as soon as we can."

"Can't you just arrest him now, Detective Odell?"

"Nope. Nothing concrete to go on yet. Only my theories and my gut-instincts. Cap Moore and I can't go to the D-A with that. It won't stick. Sergeant Crump and his elite C-S-I team found some items at the construction site. We will know more shortly. He is very smart. Right?"

"Oh, yes. Brilliant. He excels at his college studies but is a classic underachiever. Alan started college late. He is older in age than you think he is, but very immature. Just goofs off. Works a few shifts at the Asteroid Coffee Shop out there on the main drag. The manager always wants him to cover more shifts, but he does not like to work. He studies a little. Mostly, does not have to study to get good grades. He smokes weed, and skateboards all around. Alan thinks that he will eventually become a professional skateboarder. About the only thing I ever heard him talking about doing with his family was deer hunting in the fall and winter with his father. He never mentions his mother, and he is an only child. Yet, he is very, very smart and had a good job working with his father in the family business that he said was too dirty of a job and too hard."

Odell lifted an eyebrow and asked, "Family business? Dirty and hard. Let me guess here. The father owns an electrical contracting business or does alarm and security camera installations."

"Why yes, exactly. How did you know that?"

"The alarms and cameras at Gilding's house were broken for days before the homicide. Crump feels that a professional disabled them. Most likely, Hudson snuck out during a reading circle break or used some excuse to take out the systems."

"Oh, wow! Yes, he would be capable of that. Alan quit that work, but he knows it backwards and forwards. As I said, he is very brilliant and can do anything that he sets his mind to. That is part of why I am . . . well, attracted to him. As a friend. Only."

Odell huffed and then leaned back in his chair and said, "Right. *Only* as a friend." Odell tried to smooth his hair out and then sat up in the chair and asked, "Do you think Hudson read that Holmes book? I ask because it is one of the few Holmes stories that cover murder. One victim is stabbed. As you might recall from reading it."

"Yes. It is the first Holmes and Watson adventure. Yes, Alan read it. He told me all about it and that is why he advocated for the book in the reading circle. My goodness. What a mess this is now. And poor Sergeant Grundy. And Doctor Gilding to die in such a horrible manner. Alan is a monster. What have I done?" Ms. Fuentes finished speaking; she bowed her head and folded her hands together as if in prayer.

"Ms. Fuentes, he could give a hot damn about that book. He only advocated for it because it was your suggestion. He will do anything to impress you."

She lifted her eyes, and the beauty within, and she spoke gently; almost in a whisper to Homicide Detective Lyle Odell.

"I am so sorry that this all happened because of my silly behavior and my wayward ways. Silly and flirtatious behavior has ill-fated repercussions. I know that now. Unfortunately, a little too late. The stupidest wish that I ever had in my life was when I was a child—when I wished that I was an adult. I still act like I am a teenager. It is time for me to grow up. I am thirty years old now." Ms. Fuentes swallowed and you could track the movements in her throat as her swallow pulsated her graceful throat and it continued a rather painful and interesting journey down her throat and into her lower body.

In the end, we are all so fragile.

Fragile.

Both in our bodies, and in our mind, and in our souls.

She closed her eyes and then opened them again and said, "I know that Sergeant Grundy is your best friend. I am so, so, sorry. He is going to be okay. I can feel it. He is a hero. He saved my life."

Odell swallowed hard, and he said, "He is a hero in so many ways. A great man. A wonderful soul. Great humans never seek out praise. They always know their self-worth. Grundy knows his worth. His power overwhelms so many things in this ordinary world because he is so extraordinary."

Odell finished speaking and then he closed his eyes and he kept them closed for a few moments. The pain from his mind and his soul exploded into the air. It was so apparent. As plain as the nose. . ..

Then he opened his eyes and spoke once again, "Besides, he is also my only friend."

Ms. Fuentes reached out and motioned for Lyle Odell's hands and she smiled. Odell grasped her hand, and they held the grip for a few minutes. She was that kind of woman; where you always wanted to hold her hand and absorb her beauty.

The warmth of their grip warmed Odell's soul.

Ms. Fuentes said in a voice just above a whisper, "No. Wrong. Now, you have two friends, Detective Odell."

Odell grasped her hand, and he smiled and said, "Thank you, Ms. Fuentes. Much appreciated. Someday, when you are old and worn out by life as I am and your remarkable beauty is fading, try and not to be an aching soul like I am. Like the rest of us are. Now, I am just an ugly mug and an aching soul. Please keep that in mind."

"You do not have an ugly mug, Detective Lyle Odell. In fact, you are ruggedly handsome. Typically, dark Irishman features. Classic. I will keep all of your advice in mind, Lyle. I will."

Odell placed both his hands on his knees and used his arms

to lift himself out of the chair. He did so with a little moan and groan.

"Good. Well, thank you for all of this. It has been invaluable and vital to the solving of this case and has closed many of the loose ends. Too bad this testimony was not in your living room as we had originally planned and instead, it is here in a waiting room while we worry about the status of George. Damn shame that I let this happen. I have to do better. Now that we know the identity of the killer, we just need to find something concrete to pin on this evil punk. I need to suck on a cancer stick. I gotta find the smoking area around this joint. Since this is a hospital, it might be in Ohio."

Sergeant Crump rose from his chair and he said, "I will join ya, Odell. Want to run some stuff by ya."

Larry Hicks jumped up from his chair and Hicks said, "I don't smoke, but some air sounds good right now. Looks like ya ass is dragging Odell. And ya got a bad limp and blood seeping through on ya pants." Hicks pointed at Odell's right leg as it was very apparent that the bullet caught Odell very hard. It was more of a severe wound than Odell admitted to. Odell ignored it and he had already begun his patting routine in search of cigarettes and a lighter.

He looked down at his leg and said, "I am sore. Tumbling around and running and hitting the ground hurt. The leg is fine. No big deal. I have the remedy at home. Some wild tonic concocted over in Dublin. The bullet did not kill me, so I might as well spin the big prize wheel of luck and give the Irish and the cancer sticks a whirl or two. Go down swigging and smoking."

Suddenly, the door to the waiting room opened and, bursting through the door, was Mr. Hiro Aki.

He rushed over to where the three men stood and immediately asked, "How is Sergeant Grundy? I had to come! I was horrified at what happened. Right outside my door. I heard the gunfire and ran and hid in the townhouse unit for the entire gun battle and when Sergeant Grundy went down, I cried. I cried and prayed."

Mr. Aki looked over at Ms. Fuentes and nodded, and then he looked at Larry Hicks. He reached out his hand for Mr. Hicks and Larry did the same.

The two men clasped hands and shook hands as Mr. Aki said, "I saw what you did, Larry. You are a very brave man. An honorable man. Perhaps everyone has misjudged you. You are a hero, as is Sergeant Grundy."

Larry Hicks stood up a little straighter on the realization of his actions. Perhaps some pride was now seething through the intense emotions of the day.

Hicks spoke in his characteristic growl.

"I did what I had to do, Mr. Aki. Thank you. I am no hero. Just did what I had to do for a fellow police officer and to guard an innocent life. Grundy is the hero here. Not me."

Odell shook his head in a display of disagreement and said, "Nah. Hicks. Ya a hero, too." Odell then placed his hand on the shoulder of the gentle Mr. Aki and said, "I understand, Mr. Aki. Thank you for coming. We do not know anything yet. He is in surgery. His wife and children are in a private waiting room. The doctors will visit them first. I am sure we will know shortly afterwards. Please sit and join us here. In retrospect, I didn't need to smoke, anyway."

As the four men stood in the center of the waiting room, the door to the main hallway opened once again and in walked Mrs. Marjorie Grundy, followed by her two children. George Junior and Claire Grundy. Marjorie was a stunning woman. As she grew older, as women often do; she only became more beautiful. The children were the spitting images of their parents. George Junior looked like his dad did. Handsome, tall, muscular, dark hair cut short and close to his head, and he had wide and observant eyes. Claire looked like her mother. Short and lean, with a wonderful figure, brown hair wrapped up in a ponytail behind her back, Claire had beautiful facial features and a smooth flow and glide to her walk. Homicide Detective Lyle Odell was always on the job. He was always and forever observant in every detail of life and of human beings and his surroundings. Odell's keen skills at reading eyes and body language kicked into high gear as he studied Marjorie's face and then glanced at the children. Odell smiled as Marjorie rushed in and wrapped her arms around Odell.

"Marjorie. George . . . is going to be okay. Right? I am correct? Right?"

Tears streamed down her face and she announced, "Yes! Thank God! George is going to be okay, Lyle. The body armor nicked the bullet just enough that as it went into his body, it diverted in direction and slipped into his armpit rather than into his main chest cavities. The bullet, even though it was a heavy caliber, slowed in its travel to stop short of his heart and lungs. And the first aid, the pressure by Mr. Hicks, saved his life, too. It stopped him from bleeding out until the medical team arrived. Plus, the surgeons said that George is so strong and powerful that was a lot of muscle for the bullet to pass through. As you and I and everyone else know just how strong he is! My George is the man! He is going to be okay, Lyle. Oh, praise God. He is going to be okay!"

"That he is, Marjorie! That he is," Odell said as his eyes filled with tears of joy. In fact, there was not a dry eye in that entire waiting room. Even the seemingly perpetually angry and determined and hard as nails, Mr. Larry Hicks wiped tears away from his angry eyes.

The children gathered around, as did Ms. Christina Fuentes, Captain Moore, Oliver Crump, Mr. Hiro Aki, and Larry Hicks. Captain Connor Moore was a church-going man and a praying man, too. At his direction, they all formed a circle and reached out their hands and clasped them in unison.

"Let's bow our heads and pray together. Lord, Father in Heaven, we thank you and praise you for healing our beloved comrade and our wonderful friend. A brave and outstanding police officer. A fine man. Father. Husband. Please be with George Grundy and all praise to the doctors, nurses, and others, whose marvelous skills contributed to his health. May you continue to heal him as he recovers from a blow of evil treachery.

Comfort George and his family at this time. Amen."

"Amen" was the proclamation within a blessed unison.

After the prayers and exchanges of good will and joy amongst the group, Mrs. Grundy walked over to Larry Hicks with her children at her side and Mrs. Grundy asked, "Are you, Mr. Hicks?"

"Yes, I am, Mrs. Grundy. I am Mr. Larry Hicks. I am very happy to hear that Sarge Grundy is going to be okay." Hicks growled in response.

Mrs. Grundy motioned for Mr. Hicks to hold her hands and for him to lean over a little. Mr. Larry Hicks was a very tall and very large man. As Hicks did so and Mrs. Grundy clasped his hands, she gently kissed the right cheek of Mr. Larry Hicks.

His anger softened.

"Thank you, Mr. Hicks, for saving our beloved George. You, sir, are very brave and are forever our hero. Where did you learn to perform life-saving first aid like that? While under gunfire from a rifle. Amazing! Were you in the military as a medic or a corpsman?"

"Well, no, Mrs. Grundy. I mean, yes, I was in the military. Army. But I was a tanker in the Cavalry, not into the medical stuff. Aside from some routine stuff, we were taught in basic training. I am an ex-cop, though. Learned the medical stuff and first aid training from that career."

"Well, thank you for you. Seems as if you should consider going back to being a police officer. You are certainly brave enough."

Captain Moore walked over and placed his hand on Larry Hicks' shoulder and said, "I agree with Marjorie. Besides, Odell, here has been advocating for you since he met you. Once this mess is over, Mr. Hicks, then we need to talk. I am not sure exactly what went down there on the island a few years or so ago, but we need to talk. There are two sides to every story. If you are interested in joining us here in the Mohawk City Police Department, then we are interested in talking to you. I think we need a great and brave man such as you are—and we need you to not be an ex-police officer, but an active-duty police officer."

Larry Hicks smiled and shook hands with Captain Moore, Hicks said, "I would love to talk. Sure. I am very, very interested. Thank you, sir."

Mrs. Grundy then confronted Detective Odell and spoke to him as she waggled her fingers in front of Odell.

"I heard what you did to create a diversion away from Mr. Hicks, and George, and the young woman here. You are a hero, Lyle, but you know that when George is better that he is going to give you hell for what you did. Insisting that everyone else wears body armor and you do not. Then running straight into gunfire from a rifle! Armed with only your handgun. Foolish, Lyle. This world needs you. I need you. George needs you. Don't take chances."

"Marjorie. It was George there with a bullet in him. George. I did what I needed to do and I know that George is going to give me hell for this. He is gonna make me buy all the pizza and the beers, and the grilled cheese sandwiches at Gulliver's Bar and Grille, too."

Mrs. Grundy laughed as did her children, and she hugged Lyle Odell and said, "Odell. I love you so, so much. But George would make you pay for everything, anyway. Those damn student-parent loans. Ya know!"

Odell's voice softened, and he fumbled with his suit jacket and checked his pockets for no reason or purpose other than habit or to quench his nerves.

"I am so sorry that I pull George into my cases and that this happened. If George had. . .. Geez. I cannot even imagine what a mess that would make me. I am a mess now. Can you imagine? No! We can never think like that! Marjorie, George Junior, and Claire. So sorry. It is not his job to assist me with my horrible world and investigations. I am the homicide detective. Not George and this time, he almost lost his life. I need to stop pulling George into my investigations."

George Junior shook his head and spoke for the first time, "Hell, no! Detective Odell, my dad would never allow that. You are the only homicide detective in the department. A one-man band. My father loves you, Odell. Like a brother, and he would never allow you to take on a huge case like this without him. He saved your life in the serial killer case and you helped to save his life here today. You know that Dad would never leave you alone."

Everyone agreed.

Odell nodded his head and seemed to accept the testimony.

Then he asked, "Marjorie. Can I see, George?"

"You are not the only great detective around here, Odell. I knew you would ask that. He is in the intensive care unit. He is still in critical condition. Stable but critical. He is out of it on pain medication right now and only family members can see him. But I knew you would ask and I also know that my George, even if he is out of it, will know you are there. I might have fudged some orders with the nurse's station. As in you are his step-brother. Different mothers sort of thing. Sorry Cap. I know that sometimes in investigations, ya gotta bend the truth a bit to get to the heart of the case and get the bad guy to confess. Odell taught George that, and my husband taught me."

Captain Moore playfully put his fingers in his ears and said, "I never heard a thing."

Homicide Detective Lyle Odell stood next to the hospital bed where George Grundy lay. Grundy was full of monitors and tubes and wires and next to his bed was a stacked array of electronic equipment, with beeps, and heartbeat sounds and other interesting, yet threatening and ominous noises emitting from them all.

Odell gently reached out and felt for Grundy's hand underneath the layers of blankets, and he found it and clasped it.

"George . . . Sergeant Grundy. Maybe you can hear me. Maybe you cannot. I hope you can. You are my greatest friend. It has been my honor to have you in my life. I am so glad that we did not lose you, George. That I did not lose you. That we did not lose you. That this world did not lose you. I am sorry for dragging you into this case and putting you in the face of danger. Let me tell you that I now realize that time is our most precious possession. It is more valuable than gold is, or any precious metal is, or any amount of money is. We cannot regain time. Nor can we bank it or add to it. Let this all be a lesson to me. To all of us. I need to do better and be better. Be sure as life goes on—to spend time with those that you love. Hold their hands, absorb their love, and feel their warmth. Because all too soon . . . time is gone. And so are they. By the way. The Rovers play tonight. Home game against Philly."

When Odell finished speaking, Sergeant George Grundy's eyes flickered a little and Odell felt his hand gently squeeze his hand.

Odell smiled.

◆ ◆ ◆

Homicide Detective Lyle walked out into the main lobby of the hospital and he was looking for Officer Bradford, or Captain Moore, or Sergeant Oliver Crump to hitch a ride with back home with. Instead, to his surprise, he found Ms. Christina Fuentes waiting for him.

She smiled and her beauty and her smile and her energy warmed up the room.

"Need a ride? I told Officer Bradford that I would wait for you. I have a feeling that you need to ask me more questions."

Odell smiled back and tried to smooth his hair down.

"I need to get a haircut. On this Friday. After the . . . arrest or the climax of this mess."

He glanced at his watch.

"Yes, please. No more questions for you. Promise. I have all that I need. For now. I just need a plan for a trap or a confession, but that is a tomorrow thing, or if you are up for it—maybe a tonight thing. Say . . . it is a little later than I anticipated. Gonna miss the classical performance on the radio but not the hockey game. At least we might catch the final period. You said your husband is on shift tonight. Do you like ice hockey? Do you like pizza and beer and Irish whiskey?"

Ms. Fuentes smiled back and reached out her hand for Odell's hand. He took it and enjoyed her warmth. Odell knew from her warmth and from the ripples in his soul with their touch why Hudson killed for her. Not that he condoned it; he just knew.

"This way. I parked my car right over here."

Christina Fuentes pointed at a door on the east side of the lobby to show the way to her car.

"I absolutely adore pizza and beer, too. Pepperoni is my fave. Yes, my husband is saving lives tonight and I need to love him and respect him for that fact. He is a hero, too. I never watched hockey, but I understand soccer and I have to think they are similar. Never had Irish whiskey. Willing to try them. Both."

"Okay, sounds good."

They clasped hands once again as Odell said, "Thank you for the ride and company. It is going to be a long night and I will get very sloppy. By the way, Ms. Fuentes, I have."

Ms. Christina Fuentes stopped short and rather abruptly in her steps. She was not yet used to Odell's eccentric behavior and his wandering ways within his genius mind.

While still holding Odell's hand, she asked, "You have what, sir?"

"Been hopelessly in love. I was and am, a lucky man. Her beauty fills the entire world. She never leaves my dreams, my mind, or my soul. Some day she will, and maybe, I will find another love and lover. But not right now. Although I might, I truly feel as if I will never replace her in my heart. Perhaps remembered, but never replaced. Ms. Fuentes, one request, please call me, Odell, or Lyle, or Detective Odell. Please never call me, sir. Bad vibes from the past."

"Understood, Odell. I will respect and honor that request. Please call me, Christina. And never call me late for pizza. Pepperoni or otherwise."

CHAPTER TEN

Odell Closes In

Sergeant George Grundy used to refer rather jokingly, to waking Detective Lyle Odell up after a night of dipping into the Irish while dodging phantoms and solving the clues and puzzles of an investigation, and digging deeply into the minds of criminals with only nefarious intentions, was as if you were raising Lazarus from the tomb.

Officer Miles Bradford was now pinch-hitting for Sergeant Grundy.

Officer Bradford was slightly alarmed at the car of Ms. Christina Fuentes parked in front of Odell's house. Bradford was an excellent police officer, and he recognized the professional firefighter license plates. Yet, he knew that Ms. Fuentes offered to drive Odell home, so perhaps, therein, was the clue. Maybe they worked all night exchanging testimonies and ideas on the case and Mr. Alan Hudson or they partied or a combination of the two. Knowing Odell and his testimony of dipping into the Irish whiskey to find the answers, Miles thought that he would go with the combination thereof. Miles Bradford received no response when he rang the front doorbell at Detective Lyle Odell's home. Yesterday, Detective Lyle Odell had warned him about this exact scenario. No answer at the door. No answer to the cellphone and it would go directly to the voicemail. The final attempt at contact was to be a knock. Two loud knocks are what Odell told him to perform. Hit the door hard. And always bring coffee. From, the corner store at the end of the block where Odell lived. Black for Odell. Whatever coffee he wanted. Coffee money is in a metal coffee can in the cupboard in the kitchen. The right side, directly above the coffeemaker and to the left of the stove. If the knocks do not work in raising Lazarus from the tomb, then it is time to use the key and hold on tight for what you might see, because it is generally not pleasant.

Officer Bradford used the key, and spun the lock, and it snapped, and he opened the front door. Odell, of course, never minced his words. As Officer Bradford scanned the scene in the living room, in front of him, he thought for a moment or two that Detective Lyle Odell might have under-described the potential impact of the situation in his warnings of the situation to the police officer. Officer Bradford blinked a few times and then he gazed upon the scene.

Detective Lyle Odell was asleep, or so it appeared as if he was asleep in his easy chair in the living room. As he gently closed the front door behind him, Officer Miles Bradford's eyes scanned around the living room and he thought how it was so threadbare. A bare minimum amount of furniture, no art on the walls, the old television with the rabbit ear antennas, and Lyle Odell asleep in his chair. The old end table had an ancient table radio perched upon it that was playing classical music at a very low volume. Next to the table radio was an ashtray piled high with spent cigarette butts. Bradford could smell them even from where he stood. There were two empty pizza boxes strewn at his feet around the chair. One box was open and there were two slices of pizza left in there.

Pepperoni slices.

There also was a pile of empty beer bottles. Mexican cerveza. Bradford noted how Odell wore the same suit he wore yesterday except for his necktie, which lay haphazardly across the top edges of the table radio. Odell's right pants leg was rolled up past his wound and the bandages were missing from it. It looked very nasty, and not only was the wound exposed and oozing some blood, Miles could see a large bruise forming around the wound on the muscular part of Lyle Odell's leg.

As Officer Bradford took a few more steps to where Odell sat in his chair, the classical music stopped playing on the radio and Lyle Odell's eyes immediately snapped open and he said, "Serenade No. 13 for strings in G major, by Mozart. Wonderful piece and one of the most famous pieces of all time. Used in television shows as backdrop music. I think that was the symphony out of London."

Odell motioned for Bradford to remain quiet as Odell turned the volume up on the radio and listened as the radio announcer confirmed the exact name of the musical selection and the artists. Indeed, it was the symphony out of London. Odell nodded in a slight acknowledgement of his correctly identifying the music and the symphony, and he snapped off the radio. The dial lights faded in a glowing blink.

"Good morning, Bradford. Thanks for the coffee. Feel free to grab some dough from the coffee money can. You know where it is there. I gave you the location yesterday."

"Good morning, Detective Odell. Here is your coffee. Black. From Joe's Corner Store. I am good. The least that I could do is to buy you some coffee." Bradford handed off the coffee to Odell, who immediately flipped the plastic tab on the lid and took a sip of the coffee as he leaned back in his chair.

"Say, there were a bunch of media hounds out there on the street in front of your home. I chased them off. I am doing my best Sarge Grundy imitation here. But there is only one George Grundy. Are you okay, Odell? It looks like you had an interesting . . . evening. Are you hungover? That leg wound looks nasty as hell. Maybe you need to see the doctor instead of the medics? Did they really release you for duty with that wound? I mean, you were wounded on the job."

"Yes, George is the best. I appreciate the effort on the imitation. Ya doin' great. Oh no, never hungover, Miles. Ya . . . kinda, sorta. . . asking me too many questions, Bradford. Too early for a ton of questions . . . and I have not had any coffee yet. I am fine. Had to get some air on this wound. I will redress it in a few minutes. We don't worry our ass about work releases and all that injury paperwork bullshit, Officer Bradford. I am not gonna lie to you. The medics told me to go see the doctors for a sick call. You now see the wound. We both know that this is not a flesh wound. They would pull my ass from active duty and that is not gonna happen. Unless I was dead and pushing up daisies. We have a job to do. Please, keep this between us. Okay?"

"Okay, Odell. I understand."

"Great. Thank you. I do not mean to put you in a bad spot, but this is about so much more now. It is about Grundy. Ms. Fuentes stayed over. She is asleep in the spare bedroom upstairs. She was in no condition to drive and her husband was still on shift at his station for another two days. I thought it best if she was not alone these days. Not with Hudson out there on a rampage. I discussed with her that we are going to assign some police protection to her. Please work with Captain Moore on that one and have a uniform or two guard this house until she rises and heads home and then we can guard her Townhouse unit. At least, until Firefighter Colombo returns home or we have Hudson neutralized. She ain't going to the funeral today."

"I will arrange it all, Detective Odell."

"Aside from asking a shitload of questions early in the morning, before I have had coffee, you're a good man, Bradford. Been a huge help to me and to us in this case. Huge. Let me tell you, Bradford, that woman can eat. Loves her pizza. Pepperoni. The Irish not so much. She needed to relax and talk 'bout the case and other things. We watched the hockey game together with George in mind and in our prayers. We both needed this. I have a solid plan now."

"Thank you, Detective Odell. I see that you had a great time last night," Bradford said as he sipped his coffee. "It is a mess in here. Good call on Ms. Fuentes. Yesterday was quite the day. Any word on Sarge Grundy?"

"Marjorie Grundy called me at around eleven last night. Before my cellphone went dead. George is now stable and all his vitals are looking very snappy. The plan is for him to move out of the intensive care unit and into a regular room. They will slowly remove him from his medication, and knowing George, he will wake up very hungry. I hope that the chow hall is prepared for feeding a ravenous Sergeant George Grundy. It is not a pleasant sight or experience. It will be like unleashing the Furies of Hell. Or worse. He will be in the hospital for at least a week. I think. All in all, we were all very lucky."

"Great news! For sure. We were very lucky. So, what is the plan? The funeral? Then what? Captain Moore told me to tell you that he is standing by to bring some updates to the D-A or arrange for the D-A to go to the bench for a search warrant for Hudson's house and such. Cap is getting some heat now from the Gilding family for justice. They are wealthy and connected and running it up the political flagpole. Sergeant Crump said you were correct in identifying the keys found at the construction site yesterday as to fitting commercial locks, but no fingerprints or identification. Just some sort of numbering system on them. From C-S-I's point of view, right now, there is no way to tell what locks the keys control or where these locks are or if they even are Hudson's keys. I suspect you have a solid idea on tracking the keys, though. As far as the weapon goes, nothing significant on the rifle. Standard hunting rifle. No numbers. All numbers are ground off clean to the metal with a grinder. No prints. No traceable assets or evidence."

Odell continued to sip on his coffee, and he motioned for Officer Bradford to pull over one of the folding chairs from the table in the nearby dining room.

"Gotcha. Numbers on the keys. Interesting. Might be important to establish an issuing of the keys. Facilities maintenance departments usually use a numbering system on keys. Hopefully, the Asteroid Coffee shop does, too. Thanks for the update on those items. Sit down, Bradford. Enjoy your coffee. Relax."

Lyle Odell went silent for a moment. He closed his eyes, his fingers tapped on the top of the end table amidst the scattered mess generated by last evening's activities. Officer Bradford now knew of some of Odell's eccentric ways and he stood and remained silent for a moment and then he reached down to the floor and began to pick up some of the bottles and mess around

Odell's easy chair.

Immediately, Odell's eyes snapped open, and he said, "Please leave it, Bradford. Sit down. Relax. Thank you, but I will clean that up. Yes, please make a call and lay the groundwork for a search warrant request. We will seal the deal and make the final request once we confirm the match with the keys to Hudson and his workplace. Then please call the request for a search warrant with the chain of command and they will send it to Captain Moore to bring to the D-A. I want a search warrant for Hudson's home. Thank you. I want his skateboards, too. Particularly any skateboards they find. Looking for the victim's blood. Blood is our best bet to find. Should have done it sooner. Maybe. Yet, he might have fled. I doubt myself, but now it's the time. Spring two traps at once and minimize any chance for Hudson to target more people with his lunatic rage. There must be blood. Maybe it dripped on the skateboard and Hudson missed it and never cleaned it."

"I can't sit down and relax, Odell. Too much happening. I am thinking about all the angles. Understood on the warrant. Got it. I will call it in and give the chain of command on duty today a head's up on what is coming."

"Good. Thank you. I like that, Bradford. You can't sit down and you think while standing up. I sit down and think. We make a solid combination because one of us has to remain standing. My thoughts are wondering aloud here, Bradford. Please hang with me here. I understand about the Gilding family and their political connections. Politicians are not detectives, and that bullshit is what they pay the police chief for. He has to plow that road. I ain't worried 'bout that. That was a brutal murder. Had to have some blood splattering around. But this young man is very smart. The clothes he wore are burned. The sneakers, too. He showered after the homicide. Not at his house. Most likely at a gym or at his college after pretending to work out. The murder weapon, the knife, he ditched in a random lake, river, or pond somewhere. It will take too much time to search for that or trace a path of possibilities. I am not sure if Hudson even owns a car. Hicks testified to us that when he confronted him, Hudson was in the passenger seat of the vehicle. Could be one of his friend's cars. Hudson walks, mooches a ride, or rides his skateboard around like some teenage punk. I guess we could go after the origins of the knife stuck in the skull of Gilding. Maybe we find something there, but as I said, this Hudson guy is no dummy. He is not stupid enough to have paid for the knife with a credit card or a check. He paid cash for it at a flea market or some other random place. Most likely that open market down in Colonie. That is where he probably picked up the knives that he used to trash the tires on Larry's vehicle. Amateur move. More anger. More uncontrollable rage that makes him act like a nutcase. Hudson is also not stupid enough to have stolen the murder weapon from somewhere or borrowed it from a friend's collection. Nope. Tracking down the knife and pinning that on him would take up a terrific amount of time. Right now, time is not something that I want to play with."

Odell nodded toward Officer Bradford as if he was looking for a response. He sipped his coffee, with his eyes peering out of an early morning haze combined with an all-night adventure with pizza, Irish whiskey, and beer, mixed with a beautiful woman. Odell gazed over the top of the coffee container while carefully studying Officer Miles Bradford.

Officer Bradford took the hint.

"How so? You think he will try another kill shot or two, or three?"

"No question. This guy is full of rage. All we need is for something to trigger him like some random guy checking out Ms. Fuentes, and off he will go in revenge of his precious and demented love for Ms. Fuentes. The guy is a treacherous loon. Do you have the report from Sergeant Oliver Crump on Mr. Alan Hudson's background from his team's research, from the files and the profiler? I had asked for everything that we could find on this guy."

Officer Bradford was very efficient. While he stood somewhat stoically in front of the chair and the strewn mess and evidence of Detective Lyle Odell's journey into clues, sprawled all around the base of the chair where Odell sat, Miles Bradford removed a folded paper from his uniform shirt, and after unfolding it, he began to read.

"Yes. Mr. Alan Hudson. No middle name or initials. Age, twenty-six. Born in Mohawk City Hospital. His parents are. . .." Odell held his hand up, took a sip of the coffee, and then interrupted Officer Bradford.

"Nah, too much detail. My mind will wander. Nuthin' personal. Let's see how I do, Bradford. I don't need all the scoop. Fine work by the team and by you, too. Much appreciated. By the way, I want to read your notes on the way to the graveside service at the burial site. College student, now. Just part-time. Majoring in liberal arts or some other useless degree. Attended Mohawk City High School, but he was prone to fights and anger. Did not play sports despite his athleticism, size, and height. Coaches tried to recruit him, but he did not play nice with others. Expelled a few times for violent actions. Yet, he is extremely smart . . . borderline genius . . . yet very manipulative, and he did not apply himself to his studies. A classic underachiever. Minor arrest record . . . maybe possession of a low quantity of weed. Just a hand slap from some liberal judge and off he goes. He went to work in his father's business. Electrical and electronic contracting. Alarms systems, cameras, access card systems, that sort of thing. He quit to go to college and works part-time at the Asteroid Coffee Shop. Manager says he is a so-so employee. Habitually late for every shift. He yells at co-workers, and has a terrible temper, but he is fairly efficient on the job when he is not too high on weed and is focused. Lives at home with his parents but often bunks in with his skateboarding buddies. He hangs around the local skateboard shop dreaming of glory as some kind of skateboarding magnate. How did I do, Bradford?"

Odell asked as he cleared a little path in the debris on his end table and set his coffee container on an open spot on the end table. He then stuck his head down and rather determinedly searched the ashtray of spent cigarette butts. Detective Odell mumbled as Officer Bradford watched in a mix of awe of his genius mind and abhorrence of his rather grimy habits. Odell poked around the ashtray and picked out a half-smoked cigarette.

He mumbled, "Running low. Need to stop for supplies."

Odell plucked a butt from the ashtray, stuck it in his mouth, and then grabbed his lighter and lit the smoke. After a few puffs, Odell turned his gaze to Miles Bradford.

"Your testimony is amazing, Detective Odell. Dead-on. I must say that," Bradford waved at the ashtray and the cigarette episode and continued, "was rather disgusting."

"No question it was, Bradford. I am a mess. As far as the testimony goes on Hudson, well, I might have had some help from Ms. Fuentes. Anyway, after my studies of last night, it is very clear in my mind without any hesitation that Hudson killed Doctor Gilding after his Saturday shift at the coffee joint ended. Hudson most likely brought Gilding the muffin and the coffee, too. He did not have to worry about the alarms. Hudson already disabled them on the Wednesday of the last reading circle session. We already know that he is a professionally trained alarm and security technician from working with his father. Just too lazy and immature to work at that business."

Odell waved his left hand in the air to Bradford, as if to dismiss those options for pinning the murder on Alan Hudson. Odell was very passionate at this point as he laid the case details out for Officer Bradford. It seemed as if there was a two-fold reason for Odell sharing so much information with Officer Bradford right here and now. Perhaps Odell needed to talk out what he studied the previous evening in one of his whiskey-enhanced study sessions, and perhaps he was teaching Bradford some of his methods. Regardless, Detective Lyle Odell, uncharacteristically, went on with his ideas and theories. Odell usually remained rather close to the cuff with his theories until the end of a case.

"Big deal. He knows alarms. Means nothing. We cannot prove

anything. Evidence is non-existent or destroyed."

Odell finished his cigarette and ground the spent butt into the pile of mess in the ashtray.

"We found Asteroid Coffee remnants in the trash there. Gilding could have bought it himself. One thing in our favor is that this punk has no alibi or a weak one. He will say that he rode his skateboard home from work during the murder time and that is the truth, except he also rode his skateboard over to Doctor Gilding's home, killed him and then rode home. Someone will vouch for seeing him going down the main drag on his skateboard and seeing him shower at the gym or school. Crap alibi, but not enough for us to pin it on him. This punk reads Holmes novels, and he is brilliantly smart. He thinks he knows how detectives work."

Odell paused and smiled at that thought and ran his hands over his head to smooth out his bedhead hair. He then began to explain some more of his thoughts to Officer Bradford. Odell looked awful this morning.

"Maybe he does. Maybe he doesn't. I dunno. He is not going to flee or take off because he cannot stand leaving his true love here. Married to another man. Colombo will be next on the kill list. For sure. I guess we can arrange protection for him, too. Yet we cannot protect the entire world. We have nothing to go to the D-A with. Nope. Cap will be wasting his time."

"Okay, so what's the plan, then? You said to me that you came to some conclusions last night."

"No, that is not what I said, Bradford. Words and attention to detail are important in investigations, Miles. What I said is that I have a solid plan. No conclusions. Not trying to be harsh with you, Miles. Just teaching. I ain't gonna be around forever. Maybe ya got some detective in ya someday."

Odell studied the police officer for a reaction to his words.

Miles Bradford waved and nodded and said, "Thank you, Odell. I understand. Maybe. My wife might not like that, but we will see."

"Sure, we have a motive because Rochester Gilding was not

the consummate professional that everyone thought he was. We can provide countless testimonies as to his sexual predatory ways and methods. Love and jealousy. The motive behind countless homicides. That would work if Firefighter Colombo was the killer, but not for Hudson. Hudson was just a friend. A fellow reader and student and worshipper of the great Doctor Gilding. Fuentes might have led him on and hinted and pretended that they could be lovers, but she never slept with him or consummated the relationship. She said she never even shared a hug or an innocent kiss with the guy. We must lure Hudson into a confession or trigger his anger into another nutso rage attack in order to bring this entire mess to a conclusion. Fuentes is the key because of his wild infatuation with her. We will use that to our advantage. First, we attend the graveside service just to confirm that he is there. He will be there because he thinks that Ms. Fuentes is going to attend. Remember this, Bradford. Always attend the victim's funerals and-or grave-side burial services. It can hold vital clues to body language, reactions and the killers are generally heartless bastards that attend their victim's funerals without any apprehension. In this case, we have Crump's team of photographers detailing the event and attendees for us. Stick close by me and head on a swivel today, Bradford. More note taking for you, Bradford. I know that I already mentioned it but please remind me to read your notes on the way to the cemetery. I need to rehash the details with the words."

"Gotcha, Odell. Wow! This is all so amazing. Thank you for sharing this, Detective Odell. I am fascinated."

"Well, my liver took a few more hits last night to work all of this through. We book out from the funeral, grab the keys out of the evidence locker, then head for Asteroid Coffee and interview the store's manager. We'll test the keys to see if they work, check the numbering system to see if it's coded, and ask the manager if they were issued to Mr. Alan Hudson. Bang! We have a serious clue and a piece of the puzzle at the scene of the shooting of Grundy and us. Good, but not great. But getting better and better."

Odell picked up the coffee, and he took a long sip of the coffee, moved some items on the end table, and placed the coffee container on the end table. He then worked at his pants leg to slip it down over his wound and he slowly groaned and stood up.

"We need more coffee and I need more cancer sticks. Got to get moving, Miles. I am a stiff mess here."

Odell began to clean up the mess on the floor and carry the items to the kitchen to the trash.

"I see. Let me call in some uniforms to protect the house and to stay with Ms. Fuentes. I will also make the call on the preliminaries for the search warrant request."

"Thanks, I will clean up in here while you do that. Get my joints moving a bit."

Miles Bradford keyed the radio on his hip using the microphone on his uniform lapel and, within a few transmissions, he arranged for additional police protection. After Officer Bradford made the radio calls and the phone call to the duty of the day's chain of command, Odell returned to the living room after completion of his cleanup mission.

Officer Bradford walked over to Odell and pointed at his wounded leg.

"With all due respect to our mission, I still say you should see a doctor on that wound. Once the case is closed. When is the last time you even had a checkup or saw a doctor, Odell?"

Odell shook his head, fussed with the waistline of his wrinkled pants, and said, "I will have the wound taken care of once we make this arrest. As far as a checkup goes. No can do. The poor doctor's stethoscope would melt from the alcohol intake. Might burst into flames."

Miles Bradford smiled. He withheld a laugh, but in observing the evidence and remnants of Detective Lyle's evening bender and his present appearance, somehow, Bradford felt as if Lyle Odell might be correct in his joking statement.

"Okay, well. Keep it in mind. We could have the fire department stand by the doctor's office. So. The plan. For today.

After the coffee shop, where do we go?"

"Fuentes knows the plan, as does her husband. So does Larry Hicks. They are all in. We worked it all out last night and spoke with Hicks and Firefighter Colombo on the phone to work out the details. Christina wanted her husband to know that her flirting with Hicks was a ploy and that while she might be in danger, we have her covered. He agreed to the plan. I think they are serious about recommitting to each other. That is good stuff. It makes my heart very happy. Parts of the conversation were in private and Fuentes seemed to be pleased with the change in their marriage and attitudes. Everyone wants this Hudson guy. Fuentes is going to contact Hudson around noontime today. She will tell him that she is recommitting to her marriage. She loves her husband and knows that she was wrong in leading Hudson, and all these other men on, and that is actually the honest truth. She *is* adjusting her priorities, but I am afraid it is much too late to save Hudson. Very sad situation."

Odell paused in his words and shook his head in sadness and then he continued to explain the plan.

"Christina will tell Hudson that since the reading circle is over, there is no reason for them to see each other again. She will tell him to come by and pick up the rest of his Holmes books and that is the end of it. They can no longer be friends sort of thing. Jilted lovers that actually were never lovers at all! She makes an appointment to meet Hudson at her unit. We tail Hudson the entire way, lay in the weeds and watch. Alan Hudson pulls up, and he is all fired up already over losing his true love, and we duplicate the rage scene with Hicks. Hicks and Fuentes will be outside the unit. Talking and laughing it up. This time, Hicks, and Fuentes juice it up a little. Maybe a little quick and covert touchy-feely as they duck under the cover of a front porch, a hug, a grab or pat on the butt, and Hudson sees it. Fuentes just told him they were done, and she loves her husband and here she is playing Larry Hicks. Hudson goes nuts. We move in and tell him that we found his keys at the scene of the shooting of the construction site and that we know he was not at work during that time. We lay it on thick with other teasers of what we have on him and a bunch of other yackity-smackity to convince him that he is dead in the water, and hopefully, he confesses."

"Hopefully. Captain Moore is not going to like pulling civilians into danger. What if Alan Hudson doesn't go nuts, Detective Odell?"

"You are correct about Captain Moore. Cap will protest, but I have done this same game plan before. It is really the most efficient way to capture this guy. If we drag it all out looking for the perfect evidence to bring to the D-A, then Hudson will try to kill again. And this time around, he might be successful. Again. I will clue Captain Moore in on the plan on the way to the burial. Besides, Cap wants this guy very badly too, for what he did to Sarge Grundy. Captain Moore will plow the road for us, and knowing Cap, he will join us for the final confrontation. Larry Hicks is an ex-cop, who hopefully, will be on our police force very soon. We will have tons of uniforms there, along with Cap, Crump, you, and my old ass. If he doesn't go nuts? Well, then, the cat does not catch the rat and we go another route. But ya know, something, Bradford? You just mentioned your wife and how she might not like a change in your career path. Women guide our moves. It is a powerful force between a man and a woman. I am betting that his testosterone makes him go nuts. Hudson might just slip up and lose his mind over the situation and bring a weapon. That would be dangerous. For him. Hopefully, we have the proper trap for the rat and he confesses quietly."

Officer Miles Bradford nodded and said, "I have it all, Detective Odell. I understand the plan."

"Good. Let me shower quick, put on another suit, not exactly a fresh suit, but a suit. I will get my act together and we can get out of here. Are those uniforms in place to guard Ms. Fuentes? She is knocked out. Might not get up until noontime when she makes the call to Hudson."

Detective Lyle Odell took a few steps up the main staircase of his home and then he stopped dead on the second stair.

Odell looked at Officer Bradford and said, "As I said before.

Head on a swivel today, Miles. Weapon loaded and ready. I will bring mine, too. I cleaned and dressed it out last night after all that firing and smoke and gunpowder. As you know by now, I seldom carry my weapon until the bad guys are ready to surrender or fight. Today . . . Hudson will either surrender or he will fight."

Officer Miles Bradford tapped his weapon holster and his right ankle.

"I have two weapons today. One here and one down there. Just in case. And my body armor."

Odell nodded and then climbed the stairs with a decided limp and a much slower paced climb than his usual manner was. You could hear his footsteps on the stairs until they slowly faded away.

CHAPTER ELEVEN

Rat in a Trap

"There he is. Just beyond the inner circle, Bradford. I have studied his every move. His every action. His nervous fidgets. His use of his feet. His use of his hands. The way he flexes his neck. Always study body language, Bradford. Make note of a person's movements. It is very important to determine evidence and expose nefarious intentions. Yet, despite his actions, I must say that in a strange sort of way, Hudson looks so comfortable standing there in front of the casket of a man that he ruthlessly killed in cold blood. With a knife. A very, very sharp knife. Humans are strange creatures. They are adaptable depending upon their emotions and can be comfortable in such unusual surroundings."

Detective Odell spoke to Officer Bradford as the two police officers stood on the top of a sloping hill and looked down at the gravesite below them. There was a huge crowd surrounding the graveside burial service.

Doctor Rochester Gilding and the entire Gilding family were wealthy, popular, and very well connected.

Officer Bradford nodded and said, "So noted, Lyle."

Detective Odell looked over at Miles Bradford and he noticed how the police officer turned the collar up on his police jacket and how he shivered a little as the cold November wind blew across the cemetery. Lyle Odell only wore his usual suit; this one was just as oversized, just as wrinkled, but a tad bit cleaner than the suit he wore the last few days. His hair stood in all directions in the wind and he made no attempt to smooth it out. A ragged, but unlit cigarette hung on his lower lip. Odell had respect for the dead and he was not going to smoke in the cemetery even if they were quite a long distance away from the burial service.

Despite the month of November's best efforts to interface occasional warmth into the mostly colder days, it is always so cold in cemeteries.

So cold.

No matter the season.

Odell spoke over the currents of the wind.

The cigarette dangled when he spoke.

"Hudson even wore a suit and tie. So respectful considering that he is the man who cut the victim's throat and drove a knife through his skull."

"Damn. I see that. Do you think he wore a suit and tie and rode a skateboard to the cemetery? How weird is this guy?"

"Very weird, but no. C'mon, Bradford. Wake up. He is a raging lunatic. A killer. I am betting that he borrowed a friend's car. I don't see any skateboards out there. All works in our favor because once Fuentes calls him, he will jump in that car and race like a madman to see his true love. Remember that true love bullshit is powerful, Miles."

"Understood. I need to think better. Hey, as a side note, I know about true love. I love my wife, Lyle."

"That's wonderful, Bradford. Sappy, but admirable. I bet ya do love her," Odell said, then he tapped Officer Bradford on his arm and said, "let's get the hell out of here. Crump's team will document this in photographs. They will let us know when Hudson leaves and what kind of car he is driving. Let's go get those store keys and test them. I wanna call Marjorie and check on George. Can I use your cellphone? Not sure where mine even is. I need to light this smoke or my head will explode. Do we need more coffee? We can buy it at that asteroid joint. I heard it is expensive, but good coffee."

"Never had it, Odell. Too expensive. My wife keeps me on a tight leash with money these days. We are saving our pennies for a house."

Odell seemed satisfied and rather pleased. His ensuing comments noted that fact.

"That settles that. Keys all fit. Glad the manager did not immediately change the locks out after Hudson reported them missing. He is watching his budget, so his chain of management does not ride his ass for overspending. Good for us. I think this is significant. Moreso in the fact that Hudson told him he thinks they are in his house and that he would bring them tomorrow."

Officer Bradford asked, "Is that significant, Odell? I mean, for evidence."

Odell's mind was wandering and it was obvious that he was off into another world of Detective Odell. Officer Bradford and Odell slowly walked back to the police cruiser parked in the parking lot of the Asteroid Coffee Shop and Bradford gave him time and some space to allow his mentor to ponder what it was that he was working on in his mind. After a few minutes and covering some ground, still, Lyle Odell did not answer Officer Bradford's question. Instead, he took a sip of coffee and managed to do so with an unlit cigarette stuck on his lower lip. Bradford was still amazed by some of Lyle Odell's eccentric behavior and odd ways.

"Say, Bradford, please make that phone call for the formal request for the search warrant. Explain that the keys are a match to Hudson and his workplace. It might be enough."

Officer Bradford nodded, picked up his cellphone and within a few minutes, the request was in place and more information obtained on the unfolding of the tactical plan.

"Done deal, Odell. Captain Moore is on it and running it to the D-A right now. The D-A will review all the information and if they feel it is good to go, then they will find a judge with an opening as soon as they can."

Odell nodded but did not speak.

Finally, Bradford spoke again since he had more questions on his mind, despite the fact that he could tell that Odell's mind was still in another place and time. The young officer was working hard and trying to contribute without interfering too much with Odell's methods.

"Did you find it unusual that the manager of that coffee shop was not even the least bit surprised that the Mohawk City Police Department had the keys issued to Alan Hudson in their possession and has been asking questions about him for a few days now?"

Lyle Odell was now using his one free hand while struggling to find his cigarette lighter and was in a frantic mode of pat downs of his body while the cigarette hung on his lower lip awaiting a flame.

"Try your inside suit jacket pocket there on the top left, Lyle. I think that is where you stuck it."

"Gotcha. Thanks, Bradford. Nah. Not surprised at all. He already told us the young man has anger issues and let's face it. The job doesn't pay too much. Hudson is a college student and the manager just plays the game with the employees that he can muster up. Geez . . . this coffee is strong as Hell. I will be up for a few days. Good thing the manager gave it to me for free. Ya wanna try a sip?"

Odell offered it to Officer Bradford, who shook his head but helped with Odell's struggles.

"No. But thanks. I need my sleep these days. Here, let me hold it while you light the cigarette. You really are limping badly, Odell, and you ought to cut down on the smoking."

Odell handed the coffee off to Bradford and leaned into the flame. Puffed a few puffs and then motioned for the coffee as he stuck the cigarette lighter back into the same pocket that he found it in.

"Go back in there until I need ya flame. Yup and yup."

Officer Bradford watched as Odell struggled with his eccentric manner of storage and he understood his answers to Bradford's observations, but the young officer did not comment any further on them. Instead, the young officer relayed the latest updates obtained from his telephone call.

"Captain Moore is heading to the townhouse complex. Units are all in place. Sniper units are hidden, ironically, in that same construction complex that Hudson fired down on us from his little nook. Hicks is wired and on-the-air on the tactical frequency."

Odell looked at his watch and took a giant drag on his cigarette and motioned for Officer Bradford to hand him the coffee back. Bradford did so and while walking around the side of the patrol cruiser and climbing into the driver's seat, Miles Bradford unlocked the passenger door and Odell climbed in, slipped into the seat, and then exhaled the smoke from the long drag on his cigarette. Odell then lifted his left boot and ground the flame out on the cigarette on the sole of his boot and then stuck the extinguished butt in his right suit jacket pocket.

"Ya nervous, Bradford?"

"No. My wife is. She rather me not be a police officer, but she married me . . . anyway."

"Gotcha. Well, be sure to call her right after this showdown. Oh yes, by the way, yes and no. But Hudson does not know those facts."

Officer Bradford was now very used to Homicide Detective Lyle Odell's eccentric ways and knew that he was replying to something that was said or asked many words ago. Or even days or hours ago. In this case, it was minutes earlier, and remarkably, Bradford recalled his question.

As he started the engine and put the cruiser in gear and began to head for the main drag, Officer Miles Bradford said, "I get it. Yes, it is significant. Not for concrete evidence, but for a possible tie to the shooting of Sarge Grundy scene. And of wounding you, too. Or he could just say someone stole his keys. Yet, you are going to use it to shock him into some kind of action. Force a confession. Thank you, Odell. I am beginning to understand your ways."

Homicide Detective Lyle Odell smiled widely. A very, very rare wide smile. He was very pleased. Maybe he had found a protégé.

"Bradford, that is a scary thought that you are beginning to understand my ways. Hey, let's go catch a rat."

◆ ◆ ◆

"Damn, Ms. Christina Fuentes really set this table! That woman is one hot, Latina. It is a cold and overcast November day and she still might manage to melt the damn sidewalk and peel some paint off the front of those townhouse units. I can see how a man could get lost in loving her. Oh, sorry . . . Cap. Sir. I could not hold it in."

Sergeant Oliver Crump was mumbling aloud while using his scope and peering in at the scene as he hid in a clump of trees on the edge of the Townhouse unit, in a common area about fifty yards away from the location where, Ms. Christina Fuentes was walking down the main sidewalk on her way to meet Mr. Larry Hicks. The trap was now set. All the team needed was the rat for the trap.

In the same coppice of trees, were the rest of the team.

Minus one team member. They were missing their muscle.

Or were they?

Sergeant George Grundy, according to the latest report, was awake, alert, and of course, he was . . . eating. His loyal wife felt as if a full recovery was on the horizon. Grundy requested an immediate update of the situation upon conclusion.

Officer Miles Bradford, Sergeant Oliver Crump, Captain Connor Moore, and Homicide Detective Lyle Odell all lay in wait and watched and waited for the rat to appear. Bradford, Crump, and Moore all used scopes to peer in on the scene.

Odell did not have a scope.

Scopes were not his thing; not in his bag of tricks.

He was fumbling to find a cigarette and going through his usual motions. . ..

Captain Connor Moore provided advice.

"Hold steady, Sergeant Crump. Although, looking through

this scope, in keeping this professional in all matters, and as Odell would do, look only at the evidence . . . I must agree. She is a knockout. I guess that is part of the plan. By the way, the D-A was confident to bring the search warrant request to the bench. I just got the word on another channel. Based upon the key evidence found at the shooting scene and the match of the keys to Hudson's workplace, the judge just approved a search warrant on Hudson's home."

Odell finally had a cigarette lit and hanging in its familiar location and he said, "Thank you, Cap. Yes, she is a beautiful woman. Part of the plan. We gotta pull out all the stops to lure the rat to the trap."

Crump peered through his scope and he commented once more.

"It worked. She is lovely. Hopefully, this plan makes Hudson lose his mind. I know that I might lose my mind, if she was my woman . . . that is for sure."

Ms. Christina Fuentes walked seductively down the sidewalk as she approached the unit where Mr. Larry Hicks stood on the sidewalk in front of his unit and watched her make her way down the sidewalk in front of all the units. It was a rather long jaunt; Mr. Hicks lived on the opposite end of the units from where Ms. Fuentes and Firefighter Colombo lived. It was a cold and overcast November day, but Ms. Fuentes wore a black overcoat over a very tight bright red sweater that hugged her chest rather tightly and displayed her "attributes." She opened the overcoat wide in order to openly display her glorious chest. Additionally, she wore a pair of black jeans that tightly fitted her curves and displayed her swaying hips and other features in an alluring manner. On her feet, Ms. Fuentes wore a pair of black low heels that clicked on the concrete while she made her way.

All in all, she made quite the appearance. To say the least.

Odell glanced at his watch and noted the time.

Between puffs of his cigarette, Odell mumbled, "Twelve hundred and forty-seven minutes. It is about twenty minutes from here to the cemetery. Any minute now. Damn. Nicely done.

Perfectly timed."

The radios crackled with a transmission and the earpieces in the ears of the team broadcasted the message. It was Larry Hicks.

"Here she comes. I suspect any minute now, this clown will appear . . . in fact, there is a car that just crawled into the main drag now. I think he spotted her. Car is crawling up the road now. Sarge Crump, ya C-S-I. C'mon, man, and please confirm this car is driven by the suspect. Ya gotta be on this shit and on ya game. Now it is not the time to be asleep at the switch. Key that friggin' microphone and give me the scoop."

Sergeant Crump did not key his microphone immediately.

Instead, he looked at his commanding officer and said, "I love this guy. I dunno 'bout his past baggage, but ya gotta hire him, Cap. The guy is friggin' fearless, and he is a born cop. Unarmed and standing tall and barking orders in a tactical situation where his life and other's lives are on the line. Love it."

Captain Conner Moore nodded and said, as Crump keyed his microphone, "I am working on it, Oliver. Right now, he is a cooperating witness and a civilian. Pease keep that in mind."

Crump transmitted on the tactical frequency.

"Car confirmed. Suspect is here, and he is the driver. Be aware, Mr. Hicks. Head on a swivel. Thank you for your service."

"'Bout damn time ya keyed in here. Roger. It is almost worth it. Fuentes is a super-hottie. No matter what happens, I am gonna enjoy this moment."

Humor and reality intact.

Captain Connor Moore keyed his microphone and transmitted the orders over the tactical frequency.

"Captain Moore here. Hold steady team. Hold at all costs. Detective Odell will lead the charge. Watch for his signals. Hudson has spotted her and he is creeping the car up the road. He is watching the scene unfold."

Ms. Fuentes could have won an award for her acting and when she closed the distance between her and Mr. Larry Hicks, she rushed up the sidewalk and met Hicks and gave him a huge hug. They held the warm embrace as Alan Hudson continued to cruise up the road. It was obvious that Alan Hudson was watching this scene unfold from his car. When Larry Hicks planted a gentle kiss upon the cheek of Christina Fuentes and he reached around, and pulled her in even tighter and more seductively, the rat sprung from his lair! The car driven by Mr. Alan Hudson abruptly stopped in the middle of the main roadway; he slammed the car in park; and he did not even shut off the car's engine. In one motion, he flung open the driver's side door and jumped out of the car. Hudson charged in the direction of Mr. Hicks and Ms. Fuentes. Alan Hudson still wore his suit that we wore to the funeral service.

As he ran, he screamed, "What the hell is this bullshit, Christina? You just told me how you are getting back with your husband and here you are, getting ready to smash it with this muscle head!" Hudson stomped across the road in the direction of where Fuentes and Hicks stood. Hudson waved his hands over his head and it was easy to tell that he was enraged. Instinctively, Larry Hicks pulled Fuentes next to him and then pushed her behind him as he shielded her with his huge body.

Hudson continued to make his way and as he did so, He yelled, "I am so tired of this bullshit, Christina. Of you playing me! Either you love me or you don't! If we ain't gonna be together, then no one else can have you! Only me! I am gonna kill this muscle head just like I killed. . .."

Hudson's voice trailed off as he realized his words and slipup and he stopped short of finishing his statement. Larry Hicks used his police training, and while still shielding Fuentes, Larry Hicks, screamed out his words.

"Like you killed, Doctor Gilding? You little punk-son-of-a-bitch. C'mon! Over here. Bring it on!"

Larry Hicks screamed and as Hudson stopped in his tracks and tugged at his jacket and seemed to use his left hand to feel the outside of his jacket and then he began to reach inside his jacket with that same hand.

After observing Hudson's actions, Mr. Larry Hicks pushed Ms. Fuentes to the ground and dove over her to protect her.

Ms. Fuentes screamed and began to cry out and sob as Hicks protected her.

Odell intensely watched the scene.

He mumbled, "Hold steady. Hudson is bluffing. He does not have a weapon. I can see that and I can feel it in my bones."

Odell pulled his last drag on his cigarette and ground the butt out on his weapon's shoulder holster and dropped the spent butt in his right-hand suit jacket pocket.

Odell keyed the microphone of his radio for the first time and transmitted, "Move out, team! Snipers hold steady unless I wave twice over my head with my right hand. Otherwise, I will take this punk-ass-thug on myself. He shot George. This is now very personal."

Homicide Detective Lyle Odell led the charge out of the hidden spot. Lyle Odell, even on one bad leg, could run very fast. Or he sucked up the pain and did not allow it to slow or bring him down.

Odell was the perfect combination of grit, surprising athleticism, and determination.

Detective Lyle Odell outran the rest of the team. Even the younger Officer Bradford and Sergeant Oliver Crump could not keep up with him as Odell sprinted off in the direction of the suspect and the pending final confrontation.

As Odell ran, he yelled out, "Mohawk City Police Department! Don't move a muscle, Mr. Alan Hudson. Not a muscle! Down on the ground! Hands over your head! Where we can see them!"

Within a few seconds, the team had closed the distance, drawn their weapons, and surrounded, Mr. Alan Hudson as he stood dazed, enraged, and confused by the surprise ambush of a team of police officers in the roadway in front of the Townhouse unit of Mr. Larry Hicks. Detective Odell stood next to Hudson as he disobeyed the detective's order and still held his hand on the outside of his suit jacket.

"Ha! Finally! We meet in person! The great Homicide Detective Lyle Odell," Hudson sneered as his face twisted into an anger-filled contortion of horror mixed with evil, "I know of you. You know of me. Alan Hudson is a better detective than you are. I am even better than Holmes is, too."

"Is that so, Hudson?" Lyle Odell spoke as he held his service weapon out in front of his body, locked eyes with the suspect, and slowly approached Alan Hudson. The good detective took his steps carefully, as he slowly placed one foot in front of the other in a slow step march towards where Hudson stood. The rest of the police officers did the same as they slowly encircled the suspect, who still stood in the middle of the roadway.

"One trouble, Alan. Holmes is fictional and I am not. Why did you not answer Mr. Hicks' question? Go ahead and finish the sentence and answer the question. It is a good question because I know that you killed Doctor Gilding in a fit of rage. A fit of rage . . . just like you displayed in front of all these witnesses. Now, hands over your head and slowly sink to your knees and this will all be over in a flash. No one else needs to die or be shot."

"Nope. Not gonna say another word about the murder." Hudson smiled and still disobeyed Odell's orders. He slowly shook his head back and forth and continued with his words.

"No, Detective Odell. I will not answer the question. You have nothing on me. Nothing. I know you are dead in the water with nothing to pin me with for the homicide of Doctor Gilding. Not that he did not deserve it. Not gonna take my hand off my handgun here in my suit jacket. I can legally carry this weapon. I have a permit for it. You got nothing. I will defend myself."

"Not true. I have plenty on you. A legal permit to carry did not come up on your background check. That is bullshit. As is most everything that comes out of your mouth is. Let me lay it all out for you, even though you think that you are a great detective. Step-by-step. Inch-by-inch. You murderous punk."

Odell was angry and his actions and his voice reflected that fact.

Detective Odell continued to speak with his service weapon trained on Alan Hudson. Their eyes locked together in a dance of good versus evil while Odell spoke.

"You knew Gilding was trying to sleep with Ms. Fuentes. It

enraged you. You felt that he was close to doing so and making the love of your life another conquest of his endless sexual appetite. You could not bear to think of that! Especially so because she would not sleep with you! Gilding slept with every woman that he lured into his den of sex and sin. Then he pissed you off even more because he rejected the Holmes book that Ms. Fuentes selected and you advocated for. A book, all about murder and a book where a knife was the weapon of choice. In your warped mind, the story planted many seeds of evil and how to kill and how to get away with it. You used your skills and training to disable the cameras and alarms and security system when you visited for the last reading circle session on the Wednesday before the Saturday that you killed Gilding. After your Saturday afternoon shift ended at the coffee joint, you skateboarded over to Gilding's house, like the little punk you are, armed with a surplus knife bought at a weapon's flea market sale a few weeks back down in Colonie, New York, and some more knives that you eventually used to trash the tires on the vehicle driven by Mr. Larry Hicks. Stupid move to try to frighten a very brave man. Dumb move there. So along with the murder weapon knife, you had the Holmes book in your backpack. You brought him coffee and muffins. You asked him one more time to consider the book for the reading circle. You caught him ogling over photos of Ms. Fuentes and Ms. Maguire. Doctor Gilding shared how he already bedded Ms. Maguire. He bragged about shopping with her for boxes of fifty condoms and planned to use everyone of them suckers. He bragged about bedding the gorgeous Amanda Sheffield and how he was going to have sex with Ms. Fuentes next. Ya know . . . guy talk. Testosterone flinging all around the room. Comparing, you know what's that are attached to your bodies. The only trouble is that Gilding did not know you were a ticking time bomb, who is head over heels in love and infatuated with a woman. A married woman, by the way. Might I remind you . . . just to burn your ass a little bit more that she is not married to you. You lost your mind and cut his throat, sunk the knife in his head. Put the book into the bookcase as a final act of spite. We have it all. Your strength allowed you to sink the knife into the bone of his skull. Your height, and your arm-span, matches the measurements from the desk chair to the bookcases. And we have the keys, too. The keys assigned to you for your job. The keys that you lost at the construction site when you shot at all of us, wounded Sergeant Grundy, and picked me off in the leg."

Odell nodded his head and continued the intense stare into Hudson's eyes. There was a burn in Detective Lyle Odell's eyes that displayed his intensity, his yearn to seek justice; his mission.

"Ya should have been a better shot and dropped me, Hudson. In trying to kill the woman you love in a demented fashion to try to prevent any other man from having her, you shot my best friend. An honorable man. A brave man, who defended that same woman from danger with his own life . . . if needed to do so. That was not the kiss of vengeance for you, Hudson . . . instead, it becomes mine. You might have well as put your head between your ass and kissed it goodbye, because, once you shot George, then I made it my mission to nail you. No question that it became my mission. Oh yes, and by the way, right now, we have an approved search warrant for your home. I know that you burned your clothes and sneakers and even your underwear from the day of the murder. You took a shower at any place but your own home. Yet, I have a strange suspicion that you forgot to wipe down the skateboard that you rode that day. Me thinks that our elite C-S-I team will find some of Gilding's blood on that sucker."

Hudson's eyes widened at the testimony of Detective Lyle Odell and he turned white.

Pure white.

His face was not ashen. It was white.

Odell knew that he had nailed him. Right then and there. Odell knew that he had his man.

It was over.

"Gotcha, huh? Missed wiping that down, huh? Honestly, you

did not miss much. But you missed that one. Too bad for you. A point for the good guys. For us. I can see it now. You are skating on your skateboard. Skating along to go and find a shower, maybe at your university or at a gym or a buddy's house. Then you need to find a way to burn your clothes. All the time, your mind is whirling with how to get away with this. How to hide your rage. How would Holmes approach the case? What would he look for to nail ya ass with the murder? Uncontrolled rage. Skating along, after you slit his throat, moved the laptop computer, then plunged the knife into his skull. Blood everywhere. On you, too. Blood from Gilding's body, dripping down from your pants, or maybe it is on your hands. Or on your arms. Remnants that a microscope can pick up and were erroneously left on your skateboard. When you make a deal with the Devil, then eventually the Devil comes to collect his soul. You are a ruthless killer. A young man who slit a man's throat and then drove a knife into his skull while he bled out. For the love of a beautiful woman."

Odell shook his head and challenged Hudson with his voice and with his words.

"Now, are you still a great detective? Or are you a raging lunatic? I am thinking you are ass at being a detective, but very good at being a homicidal manic and a looney-bird. Now . . . answer that question and Mr. Hicks's question. But before you do so, once more . . . hands up over your head and get on the ground. Sink to your knees slowly with your hands over your head. Last warning, Hudson. Otherwise, I am not responsible for what happens next. However, I am confident in what I know."

Homicide Detective Lyle Odell slowly dropped his service weapon, and he held it to his side in a relaxed manner. While doing so, he motioned with his head and his eyes for the team to keep their weapons drawn and focused on the suspect. Odell was confidently working some kind of angle.

Mr. Alan Hudson slowly and reverently recovered from the shock of knowing that Odell had him right where he wanted him and that his fate was now sealed.

Often, there is an unspoken respect between adversaries.

In desperation, Alan Hudson played one last card.

Still with a sneer in his voice and a burn in his eyes, he said, "I am now famous and we can die together. You have no idea of how I can kill and how much that I love my woman. I was willing to kill her and others . . . so no one else could have her."

Odell immediately answered, "Oh, I do. And you have no idea of how I deal with nutcases like you are."

"I have a gun inside my jacket and I will draw it out, shoot you, and then shoot myself. Gilding deserved to die. I did it and I am glad that I did so. It was worth it to see him choke on his own blood and for him to die in front of me. His eyes rolled back in his head and he spun around in his chair in pain until he bled out and died. He will never have another woman. He will never void another woman's virtue. I take joy in that fact. Most of all . . . he will never have my woman."

Odell stood and looked at Alan Hudson and then he shook his head with some tinges of sadness involved. He placed his service weapon in his shoulder holster and then mumbled, "Right side suit jacket pocket."

Odell fished a bent cigarette out of the pocket.

He stuck it in his mouth and said, "Damn. This one still has some smokes left on it. I wonder why I ditched it too soon? Huh? Oh well. Misjudgment on my part. For sure. I sure wish that I knew where a lighter was. I will find one. Anyway, Mr. Hudson, the gig is up. I mean, look around? There is now way out of this situation. You are the rat and you are caught in our trap. Gilding will never have her and neither will you. Ms. Fuentes is not your woman. She never was. As much as I would like to save taxpayer's money on a trial and I would not shed a tear, for obvious reasons, if you shot me, or shot yourself, we both know that is not happening. Not only are you too much of a softie to kill yourself, and we both know that you do not have a handgun hidden inside your suit jacket."

Hudson screamed out while his eyes darted around in his head as if he was looking for an escape path.

"Odell! This goes for any of you police officers! Do not come closer! I am warning you!"

"What is with that? Where are you going to run to? Just shows me even more how nuts you really are. Punk . . . give it up, sink to your knees and put your hands behind your back, and for once in your young life, be a man, and allow Officer Bradford to handcuff you, to read you your rights, and to arrest you. Because you are reaching for an invisible handgun with your left hand . . . and . . . you are right-handed. I would not worry too much. Some wacky head shrink in our system will determine you are a nutcase—a homicidal maniacal and you can plead temporary insanity. Most likely do twenty years in the clink and then get out and still be a young guy. Hopefully, you are no longer nuts. We shall see."

Odell fished around on his body, and he suddenly smiled as he successfully discovered a previously hidden lighter. He plucked the lighter from its lair and then flicked the lighter into a flame. In one smooth motion, Lyle Odell leaned into the cigarette.

After one glorious puff and an exhale, Odell looked at Officer Miles Bradford and said, "Officer Bradford. Please, without any further conversation or hesitation, read him his rights, cuff him, and arrest this suspect. He is all yours. This madness is over."

Lyle Odell tugged at the waistline of his pants and tried in vain to smooth out his hair.

He mumbled, "Now . . . I can get a haircut."

Sergeant Oliver Crump holstered his weapon and ran over to the vehicle that Alan Hudson used to drive to the location. Crump pulled out his gloves and slipped them on his fingers as he reached in and shut off the car. Crump immediately began to do his forensic magic. Oliver Crump was an investigative machine.

Captain Connor Moore stood by as Officer Bradford read Mr. Alan Hudson his rights, and handcuffed him, and made the formal arrest for suspicion of the murder of Doctor Rochester Gilding.

Additional Mohawk City Police Department cruisers sped into the roadway, lights flashing, and sirens blaring. As now, the crowd of on-lookers gathered to watch the scene unfold in front of their eyes and on their doorsteps. They all felt safe now to do so, rather than hide behind curtains and blinds and peek out.

Homicide Detective Lyle Odell turned around on his heels and walked away in the direction of where Larry Hicks and Ms. Fuentes stood in front of Mr. Hicks' Townhouse unit. Mr. Hicks warmly embraced the sobbing Ms. Fuentes.

Suddenly, a car sped around the corner and slammed to a stop right behind where the police cruisers were setting up a barrier. A tall, handsome man dressed in a Mohawk City firefighter's uniform jumped out of the car and began to sprint in the direction of the police scene, when the uniformed police officers stopped him.

Captain Moore looked over to Odell, who nodded and called out, "Firefighter Colombo. It's okay! Please let him through!"

The police officer allowed the firefighter to pass and when Ms. Fuentes saw her husband running to her, she thanked Larry Hicks with a quick kiss on his cheek and a whisper of thanks.

Ms. Fuentes ran full-speed to meet her husband.

They embraced and kissed on the front lawn of the unit and after they kissed, Firefighter Colombo said, "Are you okay, babe? You are not hurt?"

"I am fine. It is over, honey. Over . . . and I am so happy you came. I love you. I am so sorry for all that has happened. Between us and them. Please, let's make this work. Okay? I want to make us work."

"We will. We will. Sometimes it takes a bit of madness in your life to wake you up to what is really important."

"Yes. We are going to be okay. Now and forever."

They kissed again. Now and forever.

Homicide Detective Lyle Odell smiled at the scene.

He looked over to Larry Hicks and gave him two thumbs up as a signal to the resolution of everything. Hicks smiled, nodded, and returned the acknowledgement.

Odell then took a long puff on his cigarette and he exhaled the smoke into the air.

Lyle Odell mumbled, “I gotta call George. Give him the scoop.”

He then turned and slowly walked with a decided limp to one of the police patrol cars. There he sat on the ledge of the passenger’s side with the door of the car wide open on the patrol car and enjoyed his cigarette and watched the scene unfold. Blood ran down his leg and dripped next to his boot and it fell upon the asphalt. Yet Odell was oblivious to the pain and the blood and the madness of the situation. He had been here many times before in his long career, and God willing, he would continue to fight for justice and against evil for a little while longer.

Homicide Detective Lyle Odell was good at his job.

Very, very good.

CHAPTER TWELVE

The Return of George Grundy

One Month Later

It was 10:00 O'clock in the morning on a Thursday. It was now nearly Christmas. A simple wreath celebrated the holiday, and it hung on the face of the podium. A podium where the Mohawk City Police Chief of the Department, Chief Shea Kilpatrick stood behind, along with the mayor of the city and some other police brass and politicians who all stood next to the police chief for the ceremony.

The ceremony was in the auditorium for the Mohawk City Police Department Training Facility and it was packed to the rafters with attendees for the ceremony honoring the bravery, the service, and some promotions of a group of police officers with the department. And the appointment of a new police officer joining the ranks. Family, friends, local businesspersons, the media, and, of course, numerous politicians and state officials were in attendance. The cameras rolled, and the microphones recorded.

After some words by Chief Kilpatrick and some words from the mayor, Chief Kilpatrick walked across the stage and he first shook hands with Captain Connor Moore, and then, with the assistance of the police commissioner, Chief Kilpatrick first saluted Captain Moore. Moore smartly returned the salute and stood at attention in his immaculate blue dress uniform. The chief then removed a Police Meritorious Service Medal from a box and pinned it on the uniform of Captain Moore. Next to a large collection of awards and ribbons that were already proudly displayed on the chest of the uniform of Captain Connor Moore. Captain Moore then saluted the chief once more, shook hands with the police commissioner and he received the box from Chief Kilpatrick, and he walked across the stage and faced a line of police officers.

First in line was Lieutenant George Grundy, then Lieutenant Oliver Crump, then Junior Homicide Detective Miles Bradford, then newly appointed Officer Larry Hicks, and last in line was Homicide Detective Lyle Odell. The scene was breathtaking as Captain Moore shook hands with Lt. Grundy, then they exchanged salutes and Captain Moore pinned the Police Meritorious Service Medal, the promotion lieutenant bars, and finally a police purple heart on the uniform of Lieutenant Grundy. Grundy also received his new badge and his promotion papers. The crowd broke into heavy applause and Mrs. Christina Fuentes-Colombo and Firefighter Colombo (dressed in his smart blue dress firefighter uniform, too) and Mr. Hiro Aki, whistled and cheered for the heroism that Grundy displayed in saving the life of Mrs. Fuentes-Colombo. The scene repeated with Lieutenant Oliver Crump receiving the same medals, minus the purple heart that Grundy received, and his new badge, and the promotion papers.

Next in line was newly promoted Junior Homicide Detective Miles Bradford, who received his promotion papers, his rank bars and new badge, and the Police Meritorious Service Medal.

Officer Larry Hicks stood smart and proud and powerful as Captain Moore exchanged salutes with the hulking man. It seemed as Hick's uniform might have been custom made to accommodate his powerful chest. Officer Larry Hicks received his badge, his appointment papers, and the Citizen's Valor Award (technically, at the time of the actions by Mr. Hicks, he was a civilian) and a few loud cheers from the Fuentes and Colombo and Aki attendees!

Finally, Captain Moore approached Homicide Detective Lyle Odell, and he exchanged salutes with Odell. Odell stood proudly, stiffly, and he looked amazing. It was in stark contrast to his usual unkempt and disarrayed appearance. His new haircut displayed his rugged features. His hair was high and tight, he was clean-shaven, and his gray eyes were clear with no rims of redness or haziness from the whiskey or the bouts of all-night despair and struggles.

In the jam-packed crowd of seats in the auditorium, Mrs. Christina Fuentes-Colombo leaned into her husband and flashed her beautiful smile and whispered to him.

"Damn. Odell cleans up nice. I never would have thought it. He is a hottie with a body, too."

Firefighter Colombo frowned at his wife's words.

"Geez, Baby. We ain't gonna go down that flirting bullshit road again. Are we?"

She laughed a low laugh and smiled, grabbed her husband's hand, and said, "I gotta call at as I see it. Facts. Odell is hot as Hell. But no fears. You and I forever. Just wait until we get home. I will show you how much you mean to me."

Firefighter Colombo smiled at his wife's words.

Captain Moore reached into the box and removed the remaining medals. He then studied the uniform chest of Odell and smiled. This was going to be interesting to find a new spot to pin these medals on. Odell needed a larger chest. He was the most highly decorated police officer in the Mohawk City Police Department. By far. In fact, Homicide Detective Lyle Odell was one of the most decorated active-duty police officers in not only New York State, but in the entire country.

As the crowd cheered and clapped and the applause built to a resounding level, Captain Moore smiled and turned to the crowd and said, "My goodness. Either we need smaller medals or Odell needs a larger chest."

After a wave from Captain Moore, in a surprise move, Homicide Detective Lyle Odell's former commanding officer, the now retired Police Captain Lawrence Tucker, jumped out of his seat in the auditorium and he briskly walked across the floor then ascended the side staircase and joined the award ceremony. Captain Tucker was Odell's commanding officer for close to twenty-five years. Therefore, it was a warm and touching gesture for Captain Moore to invite him on stage for the ceremony.

After a warm embrace and a handshake or two, and a respectful exchange of salutes, the ceremony continued with both Captain Tucker and Captain Moore joining together in awarding Odell his newest honors.

Odell received the Police Meritorious Service Medal, the Police Purple Heart, and he received the Honorable Mention Ribbon with a Silver Star insert for extraordinary bravery while under imminent danger in the line of duty. About the only medal missing from his fruit salad display of colors and medals and ribbons on Odell's chest was the Medal of Valor.

It seemed as if that was only a case or two away.

The Mohawk City Police Department brass and city's politicians tried to promote Lyle Odell to the rank of Special Police Inspector. That rank would technically make him the highest-ranking officer in the department, serving in a special role of honor, reporting directly to the Police Commissioner, and by-passing the uniformed ranks of the police department.

Odell steadfastly refused the rank and promotion.

Upon refusing the rank and promotion, Odell said, "Nope. I am, what I am. I ain't interested in that bullshit. I report to Captain Connor Moore and work as a team with Lieutenant Grundy and Lieutenant Crump and Junior Detective Miles Bradford. We are a team. I will stick to the mission. Rank means jackshit."

The crowd went crazy when the final medal was presented to Odell. Even the media cheered! Tears streamed down the faces of Christina Fuentes-Colombo and Mr. Aki. Even Captain Connor Moore encouraged the crowd to give the team a standing ovation.

And they did so.

Willingly.

Two Months Later

"Oh geez, for the love of food, Fuentes! C'mon, already! C'mon, Mr. Aki! Geez, Louise! It ain't filet mignon! Damn! Tell me if I am right or not!"

Lieutenant George Grundy grew impatient with waiting for the opinion of Mrs. Christina Fuentes-Colombo and Mr. Hiro Aki on the quality of the grilled cheese sandwich washed down with the daily special of beer. A large group of police officers and civilians combined all sat at a table near the bar at the legendary Gulliver's Bar and Grille on Fifth Street and Main Street in downtown Mohawk City, New York, on Saturday afternoon around two o'clock in the afternoon. Most of the early conversation revolved around the question posed by Lieutenant George Grundy on whether the grilled cheese sandwiches at Gulliver's were the best damn grilled cheese sandwiches in the world.

Or not. . ..

Grundy adamantly proposed that they were and usually woofed down a minimum of three on each visit and drowned them out with copious mugs of the house special of ice-cold beer.

Usually, Lyle Odell and his best friend, George Grundy, sat at the bar; however, this gathering was too large for the group to settle in at the bar. They only did so, if their faithful bartender, Annie would wait their table. Annie was old, but very efficient.

Around the table was a large group.

Odell, Hicks, Grundy, Mrs. Grundy, Crump, Captain Moore, and retired Captain Lawrence Tucker, Mrs. Christina Fuentes-Colombo, along with Firefighter Frank Colombo, Doctor Patrick Kent, and Mr. Hiro Aki.

Old Annie was going to earn a hefty tip.

Odell faced forward in his seat at the table, in order to have a clear view of the front door to the restaurant. That was so that he could watch the front door. Just in case of a person or persons should enter who might have some nefarious intentions. Before he sat there, Odell also made a very careful note of the position and location of all the emergency exits. It was one of the little things that Homicide Detective Lyle Odell did to stay on top of the situation and he always tended to error on the side of caution.

Mr. Aki carefully chewed and savored the sandwich, as did Mrs. Fuentes-Colombo.

Mr. Aki waved his hands in the air in order to calm down the impatience of Lieutenant Grundy and, between chews, Mr. Hiro Aki said, "Calm down, George. Please . . . calm down. I am, and always will be, a sushi chef. Sandwiches are out of my usual expertise and cuisine. Please give me a minute."

George Grundy nodded and then he turned his eyes upon the also still chewing Mrs. Christina Fuentes-Colombo.

"Easy, big guy. I love you, but I am Mexican. This ain't no burrito or a blessed taco."

Doctor Kent chimed in, "I am a medical doctor. Savor your meal and chew it thoroughly. Eating too fast can lead to stomach and digestive troubles."

The tension was as thick as if the team members were waiting to diffuse a time bomb.

Mr. Aki swallowed, and he smiled. He held one finger up in the air just to indicate that he was not ready to comment.

Mr. Aki then reached over and took a big sip of beer from the mug in front of him while Grundy impatiently drummed his fingers on the table. "George," Mr. Aki said with the smiled still planted on his face, "you are correct. Best damn grilled cheese in the world. I love the burned edges of the melted cheese. It is amazing!"

Grundy pounded his enormous fist upon the table and everyone held onto their drinks so that the power of the big man did not topple them over.

George excitedly shouted.

"Hot Damn! I knew it! Now, Fuentes!"

Christina had finished her bite of the sandwich. She leaned in over the table and she, too, smiled a wide smile as her beauty lit up the table. "George, you are not only a lifesaving hero, you are my food hero, too. Let's come here all the time, snuggle up in a corner, and eat until our stomachs are bloated messes. Best damn grilled cheese sandwich in the world! By the way, my last name is now, Fuentes hyphen Colombo."

Grundy stood up from his barstool and clapped his hands and waved in the air as the big man did a little dance.

He then turned around and waved at Annie and said, "Okay! Yeah! Whatever, ya name is! I love this! A'nudder round for everyone, Annie. This one is on Odell's tab."

Lyle Odell mumbled, "I did not need to be a detective to figure that Grundy would say that. I think they all have been on my tab so far."

Mrs. Marjorie Grundy leaned in after George sat down and she flashed her eyes in the direction of Mrs. Fuentes-Colombo and cleared her throat and said, "Ah, Christina about the snuggle part with my husband. . .."

Christina waved and laughed and said, "Oh, don't worry, Mrs. Grundy. It is not an invitation for a date. Odell will be there, too. It is all on the up and up. Two foodies joining forces together. After all, someone has to pay."

Laughter, at the expense of Detective Lyle Odell, was all part of the group showing their respect and love for the brilliant detective. Odell took it all in stride.

Annie delivered a round of beers as Captain Tucker posed a question to Lyle Odell.

"Say, Lyle, how do you feel about correctly predicting the fate of Alan Hudson? I mean twenty years and they declared him temporarily insane and such? I mean, you called it."

Odell mussed with his hair, and then he smoothed it out. He closed his eyes for a second and then opened them. It was obvious that Odell was pensive in his thoughts and he was pondering hot to answer Captain Tucker's question.

Odell finally spoke. "Cap, I wish that I was wrong about that one. In my opinion, Hudson is a nut job and will always be a nut job. But the system is what it is. The facts are that he is brilliantly smart. Maybe reading those Holmes books really did teach him how to almost pull off the perfect crime. He did not really mess up at all and we had nothing until he blurted out his confession because of his kookiness and rage. I called his bluff on where he bought the knife used as the murder weapon and the knives, he used to trash Larry's tires, too. Just an educated guess on that one because I know of that military surplus marketplace in Colonie, New York. The irony of the fact is that the skateboards had no blood residue on any of them, but because Hudson never thought to check on it, he felt as if we had him. But we did not. It was the only way. To trick him because he would have killed again. No question."

"How did you know that it would take four days to nail him, Lyle?" Detective Bradford asked. He quickly added, "As your student, and a junior detective—I find that amazing. You predicted it right from the get-go and you were right on target."

Lyle Odell tapped his suit jacket pockets, and he nodded to Annie and made a motion of tipping a glass to the old bartender. Annie knew the Odell sign language. Odell wanted a glass of Irish Whiskey. Annie, the bartender, was old but very efficient.

After Annie acknowledged the order, Odell answered, "Easy. I had to make the arrest in four days to prevent more bloodshed. The horror of the manner that he killed Gilding told me that we were in trouble with this killer. He was full of rage. I figured two days to identify the killer. One day to narrow it down and have a plan to make the arrest and make it stick with the district attorney. Then one day to make the arrest. Because of the surface facts and the initial crime scene, I knew this was the first time that the killer committed a homicide."

Everyone leaned into the table and hung on every word of Odell's testimony and genius. The conversation was fascinating.

As he spoke, Odell had discovered his pack of cigarettes and he removed a crushed and twisted pack from his suit jacket pocket and he examined them and frowned at the sight of the condition of them.

"Must have sat on 'em. Anyway, the circle of suspects told me right away that this was a first-time killer. A violent person, but the first homicide committed by the killer. My experience and my studies tell me that, usually, these types of killers will not kill again quickly . . . not right away. Unless we confront them. They take a few days to figure out their next move and if the police have a trail to track on him or not. In this case, Hudson figured that his love for Christina would not allow him to flee. He either had to have her love, or no one else could have it. His warped mind led him to try to eliminate any competition, or in fact, when he realized the rejection and hopelessness of any prospects of love . . . Christina. But hey, that is enough of that. The case is over. I see the tears in Mrs. Fuentes-Colombo's eyes and the pain of this rehash. Let's enjoy our time together. I need to have a cancer stick while Annie pours me some Irish. Anyone care to join me in a slow march of death in a maze of smoke?"

Odell rose from the table and shook a single cigarette loose from the pack, as Christina Fuentes-Colombo rose from the table and said, "I don't smoke but I will join you."

Officer Larry Hicks stood up and he said, "Me, too. I want to puff on a cigar that I stuck in my pocket. Mine is not a twisted mess like yours is Odell. Why are your cigarettes always a twisted mess?"

"Lucky you. Hey, ummm, everyone," Odell said as he turned back to the table after taking two steps to leave via the side door to go and enjoy his smoke. "I just wanna thank everyone for their jobs, their courage, and their brilliance. No way that I could do without any of ya. I am thankful for the healing blessings of God for George and the protection that God afforded us. We are a team and I hope that George can settle in now, pay off those parent-student loans and enjoy the rest of his career as a lieutenant and not get sucked into my madness any longer."

No one said a word as they all turned to Lieutenant George Grundy for his reaction. Annie was delivering the glass of Irish whiskey for Odell and she huffed and let out a little cry at Odell's words as she carefully set the drink at the table position where Lyle Odell sat. Grundy was just about to take a bite of his fourth grilled cheese sandwich when he heard the words, and George set the sandwich back on the plate and stared intently at his best friend.

"Oh hell, no! Not that easy, Odell. These Louie bars on my ass don't mean jackshit. I know you have your mentor there in Bradford, but ya not gettin' rid of me that easy. Ya gonna need my brains and my muscles, too. The doctors are gonna clear me for active-duty next week and I am tellin' ya, Odell, that if a homicide comes in and ya need me, then I will be there. Besides, who is gonna teach Bradford how to deal with how weird you are or when ya fly is open?"

Odell smiled and smoothed his hair out. He tugged at his waistline and tried to tuck his shirt in as the cigarette dangled from his lower lip.

"Thank you, Annie. Good point, George. I truly thank you for that and for being my friend. Rovers game tonight. Face-off at seven. You and Marjorie coming over to my joint? Christina and Colombo, Miles and his wife are gonna be there. Are you two coming over?"

"Depends. Pizza from Frank's West and beers? On your tab?"

"Of course."

Grundy nodded and picked up his sandwich and held it in his hand, and carefully examined where to take the next bite.

"Yuppers. We will be there!"

Odell waved and Christina held out her hand for Odell to take it. He did so, as Hicks, Odell, and Mrs. Fuentes-Colombo joined together to go outside.

Odell suddenly stopped short and turned back to Grundy and asked, "Is it George?"

Grundy waved in the air and swallowed his bite of the sandwich, shrugged his shoulders, and said, "Is it what?"

Junior Detective Miles Bradford jumped in excitedly to the conversation. He was very eager to show how much he already had learned with the now-famous "Odellisms."

"No, your fly is not open, Detective Odell. You are good to go. Facts and details are very important in investigations."

Odell smiled and said, "I am gonna like working with you. Junior Detective Miles Bradford. Sounds smooth. Ya gonna be a helluva detective. Oh yes, and Officer Hicks, it is because I always sit on them. I put them in my rear pants pocket and I sit on 'em and squish the hell out of them."

Homicide Detective Lyle Odell was good at his job.

Very, very good.

◆ ◆ ◆

Three Months Later

"Oh, Lyle . . . I am so happy to be here. Out spending time with you. I actually thought that you were not interested in me and that you would never call me for a dinner date."

Detective Lyle Odell sat on a bar stool on the far end of the bar at the legendary Gulliver's Bar and Grille on Fifth Street and Main Street in downtown Mohawk City, New York. It was a gentle Saturday around three o'clock in the afternoon.

Odell sat at the far end where the bar was wrapped around and faced the front of the restaurant. The side exit was next to him and he could watch the front door of the establishment. Sitting next to Lyle Odell was the gorgeous and captivating Ms. Kathleen Maguire.

Ms. Maguire spoke again as she watched Lyle Odell fiddle with his cellphone. He jammed at the keyboard with his fingers and turned the device over and carefully examined it.

"I thought, perhaps, that because I was very promiscuous in my past and was with Larry Hicks, then you were not interested in me. Sure. I would understand that. An important law enforcement officer like you. Seen out and about hanging with a loosey-goosey chick. But I assure you, Lyle, that I have put all that behind me now. I have turned over a new leaf and life. Larry and I broke up amicably. We just were not going to work out . . . after all that went down."

Lyle Odell continued to fiddle with his cellphone. He mumbled while he did so.

"Oh yeah. No trouble. Sorry that I did not take you to a fancy joint. But I love this place. The grilled cheese sandwiches are the best damn . . .."

Ms. Maguire finished the sentence and as she did so, she looked at her wineglass and her empty plate.

"Grilled cheese sandwiches in the world. And the wine is wonderful. I love this place." Ms. Maguire looked over at Lyle Odell, who still had his head down and was still fumbling over his cellphone. She smiled and acknowledged his eccentricity and seeming ineptness.

Ms. Maguire asked, "Do you need some help with that, Lyle? You seem to be flustered."

Odell handed the cellphone off to Kathleen Maguire and said, "Sure. Thank you. I cannot get it to turn on and I need to call Lieutenant Grundy. Sorry for the interruption to our evening together and our first date. Police business and such."

"It's okay, Lyle. I understand how important you are."

Ms. Maguire took the phone and within a few seconds, she had the phone turned on and the contacts list exposed and she had dialed up Grundy. Odell downed the last drop of Irish from his glass, and Annie hustled over with a replacement. Detective Lyle Odell nodded and thanked Annie for the drink and Ms. Maguire for her assistance.

He took the phone and put it to his ear and said, "Ready. All is good to go, George. Thank you."

Ms. Maguire stared at Odell and asked, as Annie dropped a replacement wine for her to enjoy, "All is good to go? What is good to go? Or is that police business and confidential?"

Lyle Odell took a sip of his whiskey and said, "Oh yeah. It is a police business. Not confidential. At least, not to you. Ya see, Kathleen. It is a very strange sequence of events. So random.

When we found Doctor Gilding's body, the killer clicked on a bunch of files on the laptop on the desk where the body was. Gilding's laptop. The killer, Mr. Alan Hudson, who is now in jail and serving out his sentence, he clicked on any old file in order to conceal what he felt were intrusive photos of Ms. Fuentes and you that Mr. Aki took. Beautiful photos. You are very lovely. Gorgeous. Anyway, the killer clicked on files and randomly pulled up financial spreadsheets and records. Who would have thought that I would check them out? These random files. The files matched some other spreadsheets and records that Doctor Gilding had on his laptop hard drive when he got whacked by Hudson. Numbers. That sort of thing. Many, many numbers. For a business. Life is a funny thing. Oh, well." Odell lifted his glass and took another gentle sip of whiskey as he then lifted his eyes in the direction of the front door of the establishment. Lieutenant George Grundy and a uniformed Mohawk City police officer walk into the establishment.

Grundy looked around, spotted Odell, and nodded as he waved to the police officer in Odell's direction. Ms. Maguire nodded, and she calmed down in her body posture as if she knew what was coming her way. She lifted the wine glass and took a sip as she studied Lyle Odell.

Odell continued to explain, "Those financial files had tons of checks written to you. I guess as payment for your escort service. Ya know . . . the prostitution ring that you ran with Gilding. Sure, you two made love here and there and everywhere and had some fun. However, you primarily made money running a covert prostitution ring posing as a professional escort service. Gilding fronted the money and dipped his toes and another part of his anatomy into the pool whenever he wanted to do so. But ya also farmed out chicks to Gilding and others and he fronted the dough and had some you-know-what on the side. My old ass knew that no one, even Rochester Gilding, could use cases and cases of condoms up. Even with taking them herbal pills for his dinger to get, well, ya know. I mean, the guy was a stud, but he was human. I watched once again the video from the corner drug store showing you two buying two cases of fifty condoms . . . and a box of cereal. And laughing. You were laughing. Once I examined the financial records and did some digging and uncovered some names of clients and women who would testify and such, then we had the case signed, sealed, and shut. I am very sorry. The law is the law. Prostitution rings hiding as professional escort services do not make the cut."

Ms. Maguire nodded and seductively took another sip of her wine and set the glass down on the bar top.

"We did have some fun. Rock and I. And we made some side money, too. I did not lie when I told you that part of my life is behind me now." Ms. Maguire batted her eyes and then she sighed.

She carefully studied Lyle Odell and then she said, "I have to tell you this. I know men. I made a lot of money by studying men. You are a catch, Odell. It is easy to see that you are great in the sack. Maybe someday I will be lucky enough to confirm that fact. I bet you are an amazing lover, Lyle. Amazing."

"I appreciate the fact that when you are confronted with the truth you do not respond with hatred. So many people do. That shows that your true character is good. I believe you when you say that particularly nasty and unlawful aspect of your life is behind you now. I really do. It has been my experience as a homicide detective that it seems to be a lot easier to be tainted than it is to be virtuous. Perhaps, it is more fun to be evil and more adventurous. Virtuous might be boring. I am not exactly sure. What do I know? Yet . . . I do know . . . that if you choose to hang out with iffy people, who might, and do engage in iffy things, then sooner or later, it comes back to bite you right in the ass. A pretty ass or not. The bite really hurts. Bad. Always does. Folks get too cocky. Too smart and self-assured. Then it all crumbles down around them. Then they become sad. Very, very sad when I come calling. As far as lovers go. Maybe. Maybe not. In retrospect, I never had many complaints."

"You have me cornered, Lyle. In many ways, I guess that I deserved all of this and have learned my lessons. I guess that you are now going to arrest me now for my past endeavors? Yes. How sad. I thought we might have a good thing going here. I do admire you, Lyle, and find you very sexy."

"Oh no. Not Odell. Nah. Nope. I am a homicide detective. Vice is not my gig. That is why Lieutenant Grundy is here with the uniformed police officer. To arrest you."

Odell mussed with his hair and looked over at Ms. Maguire as Grundy and the police officer approached.

He gently sipped his whiskey and said, "Thank you. You are a beautiful and sexy woman. No worries. I know how these things go these days. Chances are . . . it will be a hand-slap, a suspended sentence, some community time. Get a good lawyer. Gonna cost ya a few bucks. No hard feelings. Please. It is my duty and my honor. I have to enforce the law. Maybe we connect when you get clear. Maybe we do not. Honestly, I am kind of stuck on a woman. A special woman. Life is a funny thing. Oh, by the way, I didn't."

"Didn't what, Odell?" Ms. Maguire shrugged her shoulders and asked with a puzzled look on her face.

"Call you for a date. I came to your office and met you and asked you there. I did not call you. Always remember, no matter what the circumstances are and despite any bombs dropping all around you . . . that exact facts and details are very important in investigations. And in our lives, too."

Kathleen Maguire lifted her wineglass and smiled. She realized that Detective Lyle Odell was a genius and a very special man. She downed the remaining wine and set the glass upon the bar top.

"Life is a funny thing. It really, really is Homicide Detective Lyle Odell. And you are a very special man. I hope you are still available when I settle my matters. It is with gracious and honest assurance that I tell you that I am a changed woman. No more iffy relationships. If you are not around or available, then so it goes. Life goes on and is a funny thing. So, I must think that this woman that you are in love with is a very special and amazing woman. I bet my beautiful ass that she is. All the best. I hope this woman knows that she is a very lucky woman."

She blew a kiss at Odell just as the law closed in upon her.

Odell nodded at Grundy and lifted his glass in the direction of and in honor of Ms. Maguire, and he downed the remaining whiskey in the glass. In one smooth motion, displaying his amazing nimbleness and surprising athleticism, Odell jumped off the barstool, nodded at Annie and gave her a hand signal, and Annie then intuitively knew how to close out the tab and apply her tip, and he turned on his heels and walked out the side exit of Gulliver's Bar and Grille.

He did not want to watch the actual arrest procedure.

Odell, rather briskly, walked out the side exit door and escaped into the night.

◆ ◆ ◆

That Same Evening

Odell had long since earlier settled into his easy chair. The empty pizza box from Frank's West Pizza shop sat at his feet.

There were two slices left in the box.

The ashtray on the end table overflowed with spent cigarette butts and an empty bottle of Odell's favorite Irish whiskey sat forlornly on the floor; on the right side of his chair. Odell's rather stubborn and tedious cellphone sat on the end table, too. It was on charge with the charger and that made this a very rare occasion. Usually, the phone was dead.

His old table radio hummed with some gentle violin strings and glorious sounds as Odell sat in his chair while he remained mesmerized by them. Odell waved his hands in the air in time with the music. He was feeling the vibe; the music; the flow.

Odell mumbled as he listened and waved in the air.

"Such as a sad, sad piece of music. I guess it fits my mood. I guess. Tchaikovsky. Serenade for Strings, 1st movement. Sounds as if it is Modesto. Out of California."

As the music ended, the radio announcer confirmed not only

the musical selection, but he also confirmed the symphony orchestra.

Odell, of course, was correct in both of his identification.

Odell leaned back in his chair as the announcer finished his work and he breathed deeply as the next musical piece began.

Strangely, Lyle Odell drifted off to sleep. He generally never fell asleep during these concerts. . ..

Odell's eyes glanced at his empty glass just as his cellphone lit up with an incoming call. His eyes widened and his heart pounded as he read the text associated with the call.

"Marlin Santini."

Lyle Odell picked up the phone, pushed the answer button, and said, "Lyle Odell here."

"Odell . . . Marlin here. Detective Marlin Santini. I just landed at Albany airport and I am hailing a taxi to your house. Right now. Don't argue. Don't piss me off. I will see you in 'bout a half an hour or so. Ya got some Irish? Pizza? Beer? Wine? Is Frank's West still delivering?"

"I just finished a bottle and I am half-in-the-bag. I have another bottle in the stash. Beer and wine in the fridge. Two slices in the box. I will order another pie right now. They are still open. Matty is on the job. He will deliver a fresh pie. For me. For you."

"Good."

"Why now, Marlin?"

"Because you need me and I need you. Duhhhh!"

"Yuppers. Gotcha."

"Lyle . . . I love you. We are gonna make love all night and into tomorrow. Maybe even into next week. I have court on next Tuesday. Gotta be back in time. Cracked a tough case. The guy is dead to rights. How is Grundy feeling?

"I love you, too. Marlin. George is great. He is cleared for duty. Good to go."

"I am gonna wear your old ass out. You do know that. Don't you?"

"Yes. Kinda countin' on it. Marlin . . . be safe. Be here. Be my love."

"Of course, Lyle. I am your love. Forever."

"Click."

The line went dead and Odell pushed the button to order a pizza pie from Frank's West.

The musical piece radio played loud and clear as Odell leaned in and listened as he waited for someone to pick up the line at Frank's West Pizza Shop.

"Oh my! Maurice Ravel . . . Jeux D'eau. Sounds as if it is out of Boston. So romantic. So ironic."

Odell smiled just as the person on the phone answered.

"Odell! What's up? Another pizza? Ya really hungry? Huh?"

"Yes, yes, yes. I have a special guest on the way here. Please, another cheese pie. She will be hungry. It was a long flight for her and many miles traveled. I will take good care of Matty for his efforts so late at night. Thank you."

Odell hung up the phone, and he smiled as his arms and hands waved in time to the music.

Lyle Odell mumbled, "A guest. A very, very special guest. My goodness. Life sure is funny."

Lyle Odell's eyes snapped open, and he gazed around the room. He mussed with his hair and kicked at the pizza box at his feet and he glanced at the empty bottle of whiskey. He then picked up his cellphone and fussed at the buttons and checked the recent calls. George Grundy was the last call received.

Incoming and outgoing.

No calls from Marlin Santini.

It was just a dream.

Just a dream.

Odell placed the phone back on the end table and he leaned back in his chair, and turned his ear to the radio. The concert was still ongoing, and, once again, Lyle Odell waved his hands in time to the strings and enjoyed the music.

"I did not miss too much of this performance. Must have only dozed for a few minutes . . . but somehow . . . it seemed so much longer."

Lyle Odell adjusted the volume on the radio and he took a deep breath and leaned back in his chair.

He whispered, "Damn. It is Maurice Ravel . . . Jeux D'eau.

Sounds as if it is out of Boston. So romantic. So ironic. Just like in my dream. I must have heard it even while I was asleep. Maybe. Oh well, yes, life sure is a funny thing. So many people with nefarious intentions in their hearts. So many. Too many."

THE END

EPILOGUE

In March

The wind blew strong, with just a hint of crispness buried within it. Winter had hit very hard in upstate New York. There were remnants of snow here, and there, and everywhere. It had snowed on Saint Patrick's Day in upstate New York and the snow still lingered as the month of March slowly crawled to a close.

Even on the warmest of days, cemeteries are cold places.

Mrs. Christina Fuentes-Colombo stood next to Senior Homicide Detective Lyle Odell as they both stood next to the grave of Doctor Rochester Gilding. Ever since, as she calls it now, "the incident" Christina uses her husband's last name, and she also uses the title of Mrs. to let everyone know that she is a married woman. Her life was very different now. Everything now changed for the better.

Sometimes, it takes a hard fall from the wrong direction in life to stand back up and go off in the correct direction. Lessons learned.

Odell had the ever-present cigarette dangling from his lower lip. It was unlit just so that he could taste it. The wind blew Odell's hair, and he mussed with it, but then gave up and allowed it to stand out in all directions. Christina's hair also blew in luscious waves and she used her hand and fingers to push it back from her face as the wind had its way with her hair. The two of them held hands as they stood there studying the gravesite.

"Lyle, do you always visit victim's graves? I mean the victims of your cases."

Lyle Odell answered her question right away.

"Only of the cases that I solve."

"Okay. How many victim's cases did you not solve?"

"I solved all of them. So far. I have not missed one yet."

Mrs. Fuentes-Colombo smiled and mumbled, "Of course you have. So, you have visited every victim of all the homicides that you have investigated and solved over these many years?"

Odell answered very matter-of-factly.

"Yuppers. Sure have. Not a single murdering son-of-a-bitch has escaped any of my investigations. I have zero unsolved cases."

"Amazing. Respectful. Totally Odell-like. And you are messy, as usual, but you do seem sober. Even though it was a late Friday night for you yesterday. I get it, but, I mean, why are we here? I mean, I guess to pay our respects? But Rock was, well, let's just say he had some major flaws and leave it at that."

Odell waved his hands in front of his body in a little waving motion.

As the cigarette bobbed and weaved on his lower lip, he said, "Confession. Borderline sober. And this suit is the same suit that I wore for three days now. It's heading to the cleaners on Monday. But I showered this morning . . . so I am sort of fresh. Yes, we are here to pay our respects. Lookie here, I am not going to speak ill of the dead, right here next to his grave, but well . . . no one deserves to die in such a horrible manner. So, we are here to close it out forever. Case solved. Bad guy convicted and locked up for a long time. We are also here to say a silent prayer."

Initially, Mrs. Fuentes-Colombo seemed surprised by Odell's statement. Then she studied his body language and relaxed as she asked a question.

"Pray? So, does that mean that Detective Lyle Odell believes in God?"

"I do. Yes, I do. There is no way that I could deal with the evil bullshit of this sad-ass world without God. I will not be so bold as to predict God's reactions to all of our humanely nonsense, but since Jesus once was human, I will venture to say that Jesus weeps at our behavior. He wept when Lazurus died. I am sure he weeps now. The most powerful two words ever written down.

Jesus wept. Wars, blood, famine, murder. Horrible behavior. I will say that some people might consider me to be a Catholic . . . I am more inclined to classify Lyle Odell as simply a believer in God. I do go to Mass once in a while and take communion. Just to keep me grounded in faith and attached to some formal ceremony of religion. The ground underneath the cross of the sacrifice and the pain of Jesus is even. Everyone has a chance. Even the chronic sinners. My job seems to be, while it pays some of my bills, is that I identify and bring the sinners to Earthly judgment, but I don't judge 'em or hand out any final punishments. I let the judges, and the juries, do their things, and then ultimately, I let God judge 'em. Not in my pay grade to make any final calls. So, let's pray, Christina."

The wind blew hard and Mrs. Fuentes-Colombo shook her head and smiled.

She mumbled against the wind.

"You are so layered in complexity that I am continually amazed by the depth of the genius of Homicide Detective Lyle Odell. Yes. Let's pray. I like that. Let's pray for Rock. Together. I hope his soul rests peacefully."

Odell nodded, and they joined hands, bowed their heads and prayed silently amidst the gusts of the cold wind. After they prayed, Odell tugged at her hand and led them both off in the direction of Mrs. Fuentes-Colombo's car. She shivered and Lyle Odell detected it, and he felt her body ripple. He pulled her in close to his body and they wrapped their arms around each other to share some warmth.

While they walked together to the vehicle, Christina asked, "Do you ever get lonely, Odell? Do you ever grow tired of all the pain of these horrible murders?"

"Yes, and well, yes. But someone must do this. Walk around where the phantoms of evil tread. There are so many evil people with nefarious intentions out there. That in itself, becomes mind-boggling. In the end, when it all shakes out, I guess that it is about what is right and what is wrong. It is about justice. In the end, it is about truth."

Mrs. Christina Fuentes-Colombo nodded.

She wiped away the tears from her eyes and said, "Truth. So hard to find, yet so easy to lay bare. Yes. I understand. I really do."

She squeezed Lyle Odell's body in tighter to hers, and now that they stood next to the vehicle, they slipped into a full hug and held each other for a long time. As they continued to hug, Christina spoke in a voice just above the wind.

"But what about you, Odell? You deserve to know love and not to be lonely. This woman that you told me about that you are in love with. That apparently you are both in love. Still. If I might ask. Without causing you too much pain. What is her name?"

"Marlin. Marlin Santini. Ah, yes, romance. So precarious in its trepidations. Sometimes, rarely, but it does happen, in my sad life, I will switch out my Irish whiskey in exchange for gentle kisses. Marlin is forever embedded in gentle kisses interlaced with Irish whiskey and pizza and beer. Facts. Marlin is a police detective in Des Moines, Iowa. We worked on a case together a few years back. We fell in love. We proved our love. Constantly. Our love filled this entire world. It was so hot that summer. A few years or so ago. Awful. You might recall how hot that summer was for us. Here in upstate New York. Legendary. The hottest summer in forever and in many years. We fell in love in the hiss of summer. Things happen. Even love for old fools, such as I am. It was not only the heat that melted the damn paint off the walls of my house. She did, too. Gorgeous. A red, hot, flame."

"You should be with her."

Homicide Detective Lyle Odell broke the hug, and he turned and faced Chrsitina with wearisome eyes. Eyes that told the pain of love lost and love gained in his own way. He had an unusual softness to his demeanor. His emotions washed away his messiness. Odell was suddenly sober in his usually drunk world.

"I dunno. Maybe? Maybe not."

Odell deeply sighed, and he lifted his eyes to Heaven and then back again and he continued to speak.

"No. It is best this way. For us to be apart. I will be honest.

Shortly after we solved the Alan Hudson case, I sat in my chair one night and was enjoying some sips of the old Irish and some wonderful classical music. It was a Saturday evening concert and those concerts are always special and something that I greatly look forward to listening in on each week. They are a highlight for me. Ten O'clock at night until 'round midnight. Rather surprisingly, and very unusually, I fell asleep during the music. That was very strange. I never fall asleep during such concerts. Anyway, I dreamt that Marlin called me. That she was on the way to visit me. That we would share our love. To reunite. It was very vivid, Christina. Very strong and powerful. It is funny how love plays with your mind. But it is best if we both stay where we are in life. I am sure she will find a proper man to marry. Someone better than Homicide Detective, or Mr. Lyle Odell is. Someone that deserves her and is not a mess. When I wake up in the morning and go and look in the mirror. I only see me. I don't see beauty, or flowers, or the sunsets, or Marlin, and her loveliness. I do not see anything else. Just me. I see me stripped down and naked. Bare. I am a mess. Unworthy. A drunken, chain-smoking fool. Yet, I guess in this crazy world of chasing evil and phantoms, I do the best that I can do."

"Wrong, Odell. You are so, so, so, wrong, Odell."

Christina forcibly grabbed Odell and pulled him tight into her body and he could feel the warmth of her body and he could feel every curve of her generous body and the fullness of her large breasts on his chest. She motioned for him to lean over and she gently kissed him on his right cheek.

"Hear me. Loud and clear. There is no man better than you are. Believe it. Know it. Feel it. You are not a mess! You stand for honor. I love you. You are a very dear friend."

Odell's eyes welled up with tears and he said, "Thank you. I love you, too. Now, I have two dear friends. George and you."

"Sometime soon, Odell, you need to have more friends and realize your incredible value in this weary world. To you, to me, to George, to everyone. You are very, very special."

Odell broke the hug, and he was visibly affected and he

was touched at the outward display of affection and at the memories of Marlin and all they shared and at Christina's words. Odell fumbled around while mumbling and after some futile attempts, he finally found his cigarette lighter, and snapped off a flame and lit the cigarette.

Odell took a few long drags and he gazed out at the cemetery, and his eyes filled with tears. Christina also gazed around at the world around them and she allowed him the moment to pause, and reflect on his life, on Marlin and their love, and all he accomplished for so many other people.

After a few minutes, she turned and smiled at Homicide Detective Odell.

He smiled back at her.

Her beauty permeated the air, his soul, and the world around him, and everything else in the universe.

Odell took a long drag on his cigarette until it finally expired.

Once the smoke was done, Odell lifted and tipped his left boot up to his right hand, he snuffed the smoke out on the sole of the boot and then once convinced that the cigarette burned no longer, he stuffed the spent butt in his suit jacket pocket while mumbling, "Right side suit jacket pocket."

"I swear, Mrs. Fuentes-Colombo," Odell said while checking to make sure that he safely tucked the spent butt inside his suit jacket pocket, "you either added ten-years to my life, or you took ten-years off of it."

Christina Fuentes-Colombo was very smart, quick-witted, and extremely sharp of mind.

Without hesitation, Mrs. Fuentes-Colombo answered while puffing out her ample chest and lacing it with a seductive smile, "Well, now, Homicide Detective Lyle Odell, let's just wait and see what ten years will bring to us. Shall we?"

Odell smiled and said, "Deal."

"You should smile more often, Lyle Odell. You have a great smile. You are so ruggedly handsome. Now, I am frozen within my body and within my soul, and I am very hungry. Can we ring up Grundy and see if he is down to meet us at Gulliver's? You pay.

Of course. I do not have an extra dime to my name."

Odell playfully winked at her.

"Huh? Who must pay? The wind was howling."

"Ha! Odell, you could hear a damn single violin string strike a single note through static on that old radio of yours and tell me about the musical selection, the violin player, and the symphony orchestra and conductor, too. You will even know the conductor's shoe size and his dog's name. Who are you kidding?"

"Okay. Maybe. I sure as hell cannot kid you. Of course, you are hungry. Of course, Grundy will meet us. Of course, I will pay. Now I have two friends who are exactly the same. Always hungry, always broke, and always making me pay. I have a flask here with some Irish. Here, go ahead and take a nip. It will warm ya beautiful ass and other parts of ya up."

Christina gladly took a sip, and they smiled and they laughed.

Together.

Friends.

Joy.

A wonderful thing in a funny life.

As the vehicle drove away and left the cemetery, the wind blew hard and it suddenly blew extremely cold. It is always so cold in cemeteries. No matter the season.

It is always so cold.

A NOTE FROM THE AUTHOR

I dedicated this novel to my beloved Uncle Ed. He is my father's younger brother, and we were very close in life, and I loved him dearly. I hope we will be close forever. My Uncle Ed was always a tremendous supporter of mine; through my youth to my adulthood. He was a special man. Uncle Ed was very intellectual, and he taught me many wonderful things. He also was an avid reader; and he read most, if not all, of my books and encouraged me onward. I owe him much for his love and support.

Of all my many, many characters, Homicide Detective Lyle Odell was Uncle Ed's favorite character. He loved his cases and the fact that he was a, "Good guy, but he was so grimy. He is the best of your characters, Paulie. I love him!"

When I heard that Uncle Ed was not doing so well and was seriously ill, I was already working on the framework of this novel and I dug in hard to begin my work on it. PJH worked very hard to finish this novel before this world and our family lost him. Alas, despite my best efforts, it was not to be. We lost Uncle Ed many months before I could complete this latest case of Detective Lyle Odell. It will always be a great regret of mine; however, you cannot just dial up a novel. I did my best; sometimes, that is not good enough.

My prayers and wishes are that Uncle Ed is smiling at this work and that he enjoys Odell, his cases, and his "griminess."

Paul John Hausleben
November 2023

ABOUT THE AUTHOR

Way back in time, when the dinosaurs first died off, at the ripe old age of sixteen, Paul John Hausleben, wrote three stories for a creative writing class in high school. Enrolled in a vocational school, and immersed in trade courses and apprenticeship, left little time for writing ventures, but PJH wrote three exceptional and entertaining stories. Paul John Hausleben's stories caught the eye of two English teachers in the college-preparatory academic programs, and they pulled the author out of his basic courses and plopped him in advanced English and writing courses. One of the English teachers had immense faith in Paul's talents, and she took PJH's stories, helped him brush them up, and submitted them to a periodical for publication. To PJH's astonishment, the periodical published all three of the stories and sent him a royalty check for fifty dollars and . . . that was it. PJH did not write anymore because life got in his way. Fast forward to 2009 and while living on the road in Atlanta, Georgia (and struggling to communicate with the locals who did not speak New Jersey) for his full-time job, PJH took a part-time job writing music reviews for a progressive rock website, and that gig caused the writing bug to bite PJH once more. He recalled those old stories and found the old manuscripts hiding in a dusty box. After some doodling around with them, PJH decided to revisit them. Two stories became the nucleus for the anthology now known as, *The Time Bomb in The Cupboard and Other Adventures of Harry and Paul.* The other story became the anchor story for collection known as, *The Christmas Tree and Other Christmas Stories, Tales for a Christmas Evening.* Now, many years and over thirty-eight published works later, along with countless blogs and other work, PJH continues to write. Where and when it stops, only the author really knows.

On the other hand, does he really know?

If you ask Paul John Hausleben, he will tell you that he is not an author, he is just a storyteller. His mission is to continue to write and tell stories to warm your heart, make you laugh, and sometimes make you cry, just a little. Most of all, he deals in memories, and helps you to remember the good times of your own life, and the special people who touched you along the way. Paul was born and raised in Paterson, and then nearby Haledon, New Jersey, and began writing at an early age. He revisited a writing career later in his life, and he now is the author of a number of novels, compilations, short stories and audio and video works. Most of his work touches upon nostalgic remembrances of simpler times, and tells the stories of heartfelt, humorous, and special human relationships. Other than writing, among many careers both paid and unpaid, he is a former semi-professional hockey goaltender, a music fan and music reviewer, an avid sports fan, photographer, and amateur radio operator. He now resides in Somewhere, U.S.A., but his heart always remains along Belmont Avenue in good old Paterson, and Haledon, New Jersey.

Other Work by Mr. Paul John Hausleben

The Time Bomb in The Cupboard and Other Adventures of Harry and Paul

The Night Always Comes, Another story from the Adventures of Harry and Paul

Reunion, A sequel to the Night Always Comes and Another story from the Adventures of Harry and Paul

The Miracle Tree, Another story from the Adventures of Harry and Paul

The Chronicles of Henson

Crows on a Highwire

O'Malley

Heaven's Gain
The Final Adventure of Harry and Paul

Geyer Street Gardens
Beneath the Mask of a Hockey Goaltender
Another story from the Adventures of Harry and Paul

The Cases of Detective Lyle Odell
A Series of Novels featuring Homicide Detective Lyle Odell

And a few others too!

You may write to the author at ctte27@gmail.com

Published by God Bless the Keg Publishing LLC
Henrico, Virginia, U.S.A.
You may write to the publisher at
Godblessthekegpublishing@gmail.com

"Life's simple pleasures are so often the best ones!"

Follow Paul John Hausleben on Facebook and enjoy samples of his photography, receive updates on new releases, and enjoy his general meanderings

www.ingramcontent.com/pod-product-compliance
Lightning Source LLC
LaVergne TN
LVHW090601110826
845146LV00001B/217

* 9 7 9 8 9 8 9 4 4 9 0 0 2 *